Holiday
Leftovers

Also from B Cubed Press

Alternative Truths

More Alternative Truths: Tales from the Resistance

After the Orange: Ruin and Recovery

Alternative Theology

Firedancer,

by S.A. Bolich

Alternative Apocalypse

Oz is Burning

Stories for the Thoughtful Young

Poems for the Thoughtful Young

Space Force

Alternative War

Spawn of War and Deathiness

Alternative Holidays

The Protest Diaries

POST ROE Alternatives

Holiday Leftovers

Edited by
Alicia Hilton and Bob Brown

Cover Design
K.G. Anderson

Published by

B Cubed Press
Kiona, WA

Copyright

Foreword

Bob Brown

After the crowds have left.
After the noise is gone, the football games silent.
After grandmother's china is washed.
There is that special time for Leftovers.

Leftovers are truly the reason for the season. From the morning after the Last Supper where leftover lamb was placed between two slabs of bread and dipped in wine to the modern traditions of sticking leftover turkey between slabs of bread and washing it down with wine.

And oh the pies... but I digress, this is about the book. Wonderful stories by wonderful writers.

You can tell a lot about the book by reading the biographies of the writers. The talented work-a-day writers that turn out work at a rate that amazes me, winning awards I can only envy, and finding humor in the holidays.

So, I'm liking to think that on the day after, when the leftovers come out, you will curl up under a light with a big slice of pie and this book and laugh a little bit.

Holiday Leftovers

Table of Contents

Foreword   Vii
Bob Brown
Christmas Truce   1
Eric Lewis
12 Zombie Days Of Christmas   3
Gregg Chamberlain
Things That Chap My Ass About Christmas   7
Jim Wright
When Friends Come To Call   11
Zach Shephard
Booty   13
Michael H. Hanson
The Changing Table   17
Salinda Tyson
The Dragon And The Santa   27
Emily Martha Sorensen
Things Which Wash Up On Terran Shores   33
Jason P. Burnham
A Plague Of Santas   35
Emily Dorffer
Honey And Apples   39
A. P. Howell
Happy Christmas   41
Debora Godfrey
Last Mission   43
Alex J. Smith
Consoliday   45
Wayne Lee
Founders' Day   47
Kim Sheard
A Call From Beyond   57
K.G. Anderson
The Santas   65
David F. Shultz

Earth Day   71
  David Sklar
Dreaming War   75
  Marisca Pichette
Boughs Of Holly   81
  Jenna Hanchey
Dear S.   83
  Pat O'malley
Haunted   93
  Gerri Leen
Charles Edward Tuckett's Yuletide   97
Message
  Robert Bagnall
Tourists   103
  Gerri Leen
Red On White   105
  Darren Todd
Distaff Day Dues   117
  Brianna Malotke
Away In The Manger: A Christmas Tale   119
Of Horror
  Tim Kane
I Must Go   133
  Scott J. Couturier
Machines In Motion   135
  Benjamin C. Kinney
Barcelona Sandals   147
  Lynn White
Good Science   149
  Michael Wertenberg
Holiday Baggage   159
  Ann Gibson
A Cup Of Holiday Cheer   161
  KC Grifant
Tricksters   169
  Amanda Cecelia Lang
Don't Count Your Eggs   175
  Elle Hartford

Future Tourism Promo For Antarctica   187
   Kurt Newton
Xmas Letter   189
   Stephen Schwei
Heebie Jeebies   191
   John Wolf
Rest Stop For The Stars   209
   Maxwell I. Gold
The Tree Hunt   211
   Marissa James
The Perfumer In Purgatory   215
   Alicia Hilton
The Christmas Zombie   227
   Marissa James
A Daffy Holiday   229
   Irene Radford
About The Authors   241
About B-Cubed Press   251

Holiday Leftovers

Christmas Truce

Eric Lewis

Stille Nacht, heilige Nacht
Alles schläft, einsam wacht

Dawn had not yet broken as the melody rose into the air.

John looked out across the scarred field of trenches and remnants of artillery craters in the predawn gloom. It was all overgrown now, but they were still there.

"Here we are again, Heinrich," he said. "Another year passed. I've forgotten how many."

Next to him, his old enemy gave a *hrrumph*. "We never left it. Not really."

"No. The battlefield's almost unchanged, except for more grass and no bodies."

"It's no memorial, you know," Heinrich insisted, "quite the opposite! People want to leave it be, to forget entirely and get on with things as though it never happened. It is truly a no man's land."

Round yon virgin Mother and child
Holy infant so tender and mild

"I can't blame them," said John with a sigh, "I would forget, if I could... except for Christmas. You remember it, our little truce? We came out of our trenches. We played football, traded cigarettes."

Heinrich smiled. "I remember. I remember the officers were furious when they found out. The very next day, the artillery fell

1

again. They both looked a dried crust of a shoe sticking out of the mud."

John nodded. "Our last day."

"I'm glad it wasn't me that killed you." Heinrich mused.

"And I you," said John.

"Until next year then?"

"Until then."

As the sun rose, the two long-dead soldiers evaporated into the air for another year, though never to leave the place. Not really.

Across the meadow, the music slowly faded.

Sleep in heavenly peace
Schlaf in himmlischer Ruh!

12 Zombie Days of Christmas

Gregg Chamberlain

On the first Christmas zombie day
My partner gave to me
A promise to keep my brain free.

On the second Christmas zombie day
My partner gave to me
Two clips of bullets
And a promise to keep my brain free.

On the third Christmas zombie day
My partner gave to me
Three Molotovs
Two clips of bullets
And a promise to keep my brain free.

On the fourth Christmas zombie day
My partner gave to me
Four good used tires
Three Molotovs
Two clips of bullets
And a promise to keep my brain free.

On the fifth Christmas zombie day
My partner gave to me

Holiday Leftovers

Five loaded guns!
Four good used tires
Three Molotovs
Two clips of bullets
And a promise to keep my brain free.

On the sixth Christmas zombie day
My partner gave to me
Six tins of dog food
Five loaded guns!
Four good used tires
Three Molotovs
Two clips of bullets
And a promise to keep my brain free.

On the seventh Christmas zombie day
My partner gave to me
Seven jugs of water
Six tins of dog food
Five loaded guns!
Four good used tires
Three Molotovs
Two clips of bullets
And a promise to keep my brain free.

On the eighth Christmas zombie day
My partner gave to me
Eight shots of morphine
Seven jugs of water
Six tins of dog food
Five loaded guns!
Four good used tires
Three Molotovs
Two clips of bullets
And a promise to keep my brain free.

On the ninth Christmas zombie day
My partner gave to me

Nine packs of batteries
Eight shots of morphine
Seven jugs of water
Six tins of dog food
Five loaded guns!
Four good used tires
Three Molotovs
Two clips of bullets
And a promise to keep my brain free.

On the tenth Christmas zombie day
My partner gave to me
Ten cans of petrol
Nine packs of batteries
Eight shots of morphine
Seven jugs of water
Six tins of dog food
Five loaded guns!
Four good used tires
Three Molotovs
Two clips of bullets
And a promise to keep my brain free.

On the eleventh Christmas zombie day
My partner gave to me
Eleven books of matches
Ten cans of petrol
Nine packs of batteries
Eight shots of morphine
Seven jugs of water
Six tins of dog food
Five loaded guns!
Four good used tires
Three Molotovs
Two clips of bullets
And a promise to keep my brain free.

On the twelfth Christmas zombie day

Holiday Leftovers

My partner gave to me
Twelve rolls of T.P.
Eleven books of matches
Ten cans of petrol
Nine packs of batteries
Eight shots of morphine
Seven jugs of water
Six tins of dog food
Five loaded guns!
Four good used tires
Three Molotovs
Two clips of bullets
And a head shot to set my brain free.

Yes, a head shot to set my brain free!

Things that Chap My Ass About Christmas

Jim Wright

It's Socialist.

Really, think about it for a minute.

Christmas is just a big old pile of steaming liberalism.

Take this guy, Santa Claus.

Santa was never elected, he apparently just took over the whole process when nobody was looking.

He wears a *red* suit. Duh.

Claus sounds a lot like *Claws*. And a claw looks a lot like a sickle, which as everybody knows is the symbol of communism. He's got the population under continuous surveillance, and he keeps lists of people based on some arbitrary socialist measure of *good* and *bad*. People stand in line to see him, in fact there are queues *everywhere* during the Christmas season—and standing in line is one of the defining pillars of socialism.

Then there's the whole gift thing. He apparently sneaks into your house at night—without a warrant or probable cause or any kind of Constitutional controls, I mean you don't need to be sent to a reeducation camp to see this do you? And he leaves presents for the "good" kids based on some kind of arcane request system – which to me sounds a heck of a lot like "From each according to his ability, to each according to his need."

And the presents. Don't even get me started. It would seem they're made in some kind of *collective* factory run by an oppressed ethnic workforce. And the "bad" kids? They get a lump of coal—the very symbol of the lumpenproletariat— it's like he's just rubbing your face in it, isn't it?

Next there's the whole green vehicle thing. Santa's sleigh runs on hay and grain like something Ed Bagley Jr. would

7

drive to his weekly party meetings at the Al Gore I Hate America Sustainable Headquarters. And reindeer? Where do they come from? Right, exactly, *Russia!*

And this entire political apparatus is propped up on the backs of the workers, who are expected to support the power structure with the fruits of their labor—i.e. they are forced to give up a portion of their grain and dairy production in the form of cookies and milk—in support of the *entire* society. What's next, socialized healthcare? My God, before you know it, we'll be living in *Canada!*

You have only to look around, shake off the shackles of oppression, to see it:

And the music: Music has long been a tool of the power elite. Designed to lull the masses into a malleable state of submission through endless repetition. Two months of Joan Jett's *Little Drummer Boy* and *Dogs Barking Jingle Bells* will turn all but staunchest anarchist into a pudding-brained drone. People will band together in collectives and go door to door spreading the propaganda of socialism through the vehicle of "Christmas carols." The more easily influenced will actually leave their homes and join the mob of carolers like Bolshevik peasants joining the October Revolution.

And speaking of the Mob: Have you *been* in the stores during the holiday season? The shelves are stripped bare by crazed crowds driven to a frenzy by the sounds of *Carol of the Bells* blaring from every speaker in the nation. Let the rumor spread that Wal-Mart might have a new shipment in from the state factories and mile long lines form almost instantly. What is it? Zhu-Zhu Hamsters? Fisher-Price's Elmo Live Encore? Toilet Paper? Shoes? Cabbages? We don't care! Get in line! Wait, what's that? black market Twilight Barbies sold from the back of a nondescript truck? I'll take two, Comrade!

The Secret Police: If mind numbing music wasn't enough, while you're standing in line for hours on end you get to listen to the endless ringing of little bells. It's the Salvation *Army*, Santa's intelligence gathering arm. They're everywhere, on every corner, in every store, always watching like the pervasive surveillance system they are. Shaking you down, demanding a cut, all in order to "redistributing the wealth."

Socialist Art: The symbols of this Socialist Season are everywhere. Armies of giant inflatable Frosty The Snowmen and Santas dominate the landscape like those concrete statues of Marx and Lenin that once filled the squares of Moscow. Yesterday I saw a pickup truck that had its "Truck Nutz" replaced with two large red mirrored balls and a garland of tinsel—my friends, when the state comes for your testicles, you're living under the jackbooted heel of communism.

Propaganda: The socialists are piping their message directly into the minds of our children. The airwaves are filled with TV specials like that one with the Island of Misfit toys, a not so subtle reference to Gulags and the fate of those who don't fit in. Who can fail to see the subliminal message in the final climatic battle scene when the imperialists subvert The People's Heroic Heat Miser into a decadent display of dancing? Or how about when that communist Charlie Brown attempts to convince the gang that his miserable substandard shrub is really a beautiful Christmas tree? For the love of the Almighty Dollar, people, open your eyes!

Fruitcake. Yes, I know, you were wondering where the hammer in the "hammer and sickle" was. Look no further than this abomination. When the revolution comes, it will be fruitcake that smashes the windows and staves in the head of the free man, mark my words.

And finally:

Karl Marx   Saint Nick

Coincidence? Not bloody likely, folks, not bloody likely.

When Friends Come to Call

Zach Shephard

"This'll never work."

"Of course it will."

"Do you really think no one's tried before?"

O'Hara adjusted a knob on the machine in his living room. The scent of peppermint grew stronger in the air.

"Of course people have tried," he said. "Probably for centuries. But now we actually have the technology to make it happen."

Blackman squinted at O'Hara's machine. It was a boxy, dryer-sized contraption with a plate of cookies on top. He reached for one of the treats.

"Don't touch those," O'Hara said, slapping Blackman's hand. "Those are for him." He carefully nudged a lever on the machine's side. "There. You can practically taste the cookies on the air, can't you? He's sure to come any minute."

"Yes. And he'll probably have the Easter Bunny with him. Although I don't know who's going to feed the Loch Ness Monster while they're gone."

"Santa does *not* live in Scotland."

"Right," Blackman said, lowering himself into the recliner. "Because that would be silly."

O'Hara ignored the comment and returned his attention to the machine. He checked the monitor on its side.

"Cookie and peppermint aromas are high." He moved his hand to the machine's vent and felt the output that flowed into the fireplace. "Temperature is cozy and inviting. Perfect."

"Would you like to know why this won't work?"

"If you're going to tell me Santa isn't real, you can just go home."

"It's not that. It's that he'd never fall for something this obvious. He's some sort of wizard-illusionist-thing, coming in any form and leaving magic glitter in his wake. Do you think he can't tell the difference between love-baked cookies and this store-brand bait your machine is using? And that milk— it's soy, isn't it? I can tell from here."

"He might be lactose intolerant."

"He's not. Also, he isn't real."

"I told you not to—"

"You're fifty years old, man. Why do you still believe?"

O'Hara's gaze moved to the tree in the corner. Its lights twinkled in his eyes, fairy-sparkles of red and gold. "I believe," he said, "because when I was four, my parents told me not to."

He turned away, busying himself with the machine.

"All right," Blackman said. "I'm sorry. But I have to know—what'll you do if you catch him? What happens if he comes down that chimney and your laser-grid keeps him from going back up?"

"I—" O'Hara stopped. "I don't know. I suppose I just want to make sure he's real. Then I'll let him go."

"Hmphf." Blackman looked at his watch. "Well, I've got to go. I just came to drop this off." He handed O'Hara a glittery box from his pocket.

"But—I didn't get you anything. I was just so busy—"

"It's fine." Blackman stood. "I don't need anything else. Good luck with the project—and merry Christmas."

~ ~ ~

Ten minutes later, there was a knock at the door.

"Sorry I'm late," Blackman said, shedding his snowy coat. "Is that the machine?"

Booty

Michael H. Hanson

*"Nothing on Earth so beautiful as the final haul on
Halloween night"*
– Steve Almond

Rakal and Nachash, two powerful fearless beings, and
the first demonic scouts to physically manifest upon *terra
firma* in over 2,000 years, explode into existence with a burst
of flame and the stench of brimstone.

"Yo!" A stumbling malnourished demon-form shies away
from them. "Watch it with the stink bombs buttface!"

The two fallen angels just stand on the suburban
sidewalk, mute with shock. The sun is setting, the full moon
rises, and all around them hordes of diminutive monsters
and shamanically robed acolytes prowl the streets.

"This doesn't make any sense," Rakal spouts. "Where did
they all come from?"

"Shaddup," Nachash replies. "Just stick to the mission
profile. We need more information."

Close on the heels of a skipping werewolf and a giggling
dark princess, the two scouts approach the front door of a
yellow aluminum-sided ranch style house.

The werewolf pushes a small button and the front door
swings open to reveal two smiling adult humans, a man and
a woman.

The dark princess barks out the traditional All Hallow's alternatives.

And then, to Rakal's utter amazement the cowering humans surrender fistfuls of confectionery appeasement.

The human male then looks up at the two hellspawn.

"Aren't you boys a little old for this?"

"Well, you see..." Rakal mumbles nervously. "We, uh..."

"We demand the dark offering," Nachash yells. "Lest your skin be flayed from your sniveling form and your very soul damned to the deepest pits of Hades!"

"Yah yah." The man chuckles. "Whatever. Here." And the two demon scouts find themselves walking down the street devouring the most delicious and tasty meals of their immortal lives, candy-coated apples.

"I'm so confused," Rakal whines while licking sweet residue off his fangs with his foot-long tongue. "What of the Great Accord? The fear of retaliation from The High Ones? What brazen devils these are to travel so openly on this night. Surely they will all be struck down upon the hour."

"Perhaps," Nachash replies contemplatively.

"We should report back, now," Rakal says.

"No," Nachash spouts. Then noticing Rakal's look of surprise adds "I, uh, think we should study this phenomenon of, uh, demon appeasement a little more closely. Yes, uh, that dwelling over there, the red abode. The humans there appear to be handing out larger than normal amounts of edible offerings to the dark horde."

"Yes," Rakal replies, already drooling, "Of course, you're right."

~~~

"Hazzuuuhh! Hazzuuuhh!" The gathering demon horde shouts in approval.

Rakal and Nachash stand upon the highest peak overlooking and addressing the massive fire-plain in the eastern reaches of Hell. Each scout clutches an overly stuffed bag in an upheld clawed hand.

"And finally," Rakal says. "Upon facing our wrath, the cowardly humans begged our mercy and gave unto us these offerings. Delicious victuals far more enthralling and gastronomically resplendent than any flesh feast!"

"Hazzuuuhh!" The horde shouts again in even greater fervor.

"Somehow," Nachash yells in glee. "Some way, a sister hell-dimension has broken The Great Pack and created a new one. A new agreement whereby this one night, every single year, we may roam free upon the human cities, gathering this wonderful tribute upon the pronouncement of a most unholy and evil ritual chant!"

"Tell us!" One demon screams.

"Let us learn it now!" Another howls. "Lest we be unprepared one year hence!"

"Hazzuuuhh!" The ravenous half-insane horde scream as one. "Give us the magic words!"

And so Rakal raises both his clawed hands, silencing the undulating mob with but a look. And then he speaks the ancient enchantment, the dual query which will reduce any human adult to a cowering fearful underling groveling at the entrance of their abodes, enthusiastically offering sweet appeasement. And the words pound through the air, burning into the minds and demon souls of all present, echoing back and forth, and building into a lusty formidable chant which shakes the very foundations of Hell itself.

"Trick or Treat!"

Holiday Leftovers

16

The Changing Table

Salinda Tyson

Tiffany rushed into the café restroom, pushed the lock button with her elbow, pulled down the changing table with her chin, set Marti down on it, and fastened the safety strap. She fumbled her pants down, plopped onto the toilet seat and peed a bucket full. What relief. Eyes never leaving Marti, who was cooing, hands and feet in the air, tiny fingers grabbing her pink booties, exploring the shape of her feet and toes, tugging, tugging.

"Marti, honey, don't pull your booties off. Not again."

Of course, there went bootie number one, arcing off Marti's tiny right foot. Marti cooed, wiggling her bare toes in ecstasy, her eyes barely following the trajectory of the pink knitted footwear. With both her hands she worked at her left foot.

"No, Marti, no."

Tiffany finished and turned to flush the toilet. The lever stuck so she turned her back on Marti—just a second—and lifted her knee to her chest to use her foot to flush. Toilet aerobics, yeah. Dang. She had forgotten again that this was the bad stall with the flushing lever that stuck. Of course, it had been the only one open. Marti was gurgling and cooing, a sure sign that she had wrestled off the other bootie.

Tiffany whipped around to peek at her baby girl. As she turned, a streak flashed by in her peripheral vision. The left bootie? She shook her head. Floaters? Too much late-night online reading? She blinked, then soaped and rinsed her hands, careful to keep an eye on Marti in the mirror.

The mirror had fogged over. Everything was blurry. Tiff frowned at her reflection. Darn. She hadn't run that much hot water. Could heat from the giant coffee makers next to the adjoining wall cause that?

"Oh, Marti," Tiffany almost cried and almost laughed. What's a mom to do? Marti had wiggled out of the left arm of her shirt and was grabbing at her undershirt. Tiff rescued the booties from the tiled floor, pulled them back on her daughter's feet.

Someone pounded on the door, "Hey, you gonna take all day?"

"Just a minute," Tiff yelled at the door, "I've got a baby."

Muttering from outside the door, "Sure, sure. A likely story."

Tiff ditched the soiled diaper, got Marti's shirt back in order, swept up her baby, closed the changing table, collected all her things, purse over her shoulder, diaper bag over her purse, and balancing baby and bag on her right hip, opened the door by bumping it with her left hip.

"Oh, you really do have a baby," said a goth girl outside. Her silver nose ring gleamed.

Tiff remained calm and walked by. Once past she did a private eyeroll and used her left hip to bump open the front door, which was decorated with black cat cutouts, witch on broomstick silhouettes, and cardboard skeletons in top hats and tails. The smell of spicy pumpkin lattes, specialty of the season, followed her out the door.

Such a beautiful day, all Technicolor blue skies, Indian summer in Salem, Massachusetts, with the air turning crisp, and the smell of leaves and their crunch underfoot. She had managed to avoid the tourists who flocked to the witch museum, but wouldn't you know it—Marti fussed the whole way home.

Needs a nap, Tiff thought.

~~~

A stray cat sat on the doorstep as if it belonged there. Tiff shooed it away. It stared at her, blinked, and stalked slowly off. Marti cried. Tiff had grown used to fussy spells and getting by on hardly any regular sleep. First, she took Marti's fussing in stride, figuring it would end, but it grew worse. Marti drummed her feet on the surface of the cot so fiercely that her booties slipped off. Then she kicked them through the slats of the crib into the far corner of the nursery. She ripped off her clothes in record time.

"You little quick-change artist, you," Tiff said, kissing her forehead and nose.

Marti slapped her, the tiny hand open. It stung. Tiff felt a scratch across her right cheek. She grabbed Marti's hand. Ran her finger across the palm, soothing her, and pressing the small fingers open. The nails had grown amazingly fast. Hadn't she just trimmed them? She ran for the baby nail clippers. How could she have missed that?

Marti kicked and howled when her pearly nails were cut. The howls turned into cries.

Tiff abandoned the nail clipping, scooped baby girl up, and bounced Marti on her knee. The cries turned to shrieks.

Crying is the way a baby communicates. What are you trying to tell me, baby girl? Tiff wondered. Another few hours, and she made an urgent appointment.

As Tiff laid her on the examining table, Marti peed right on the front of the doctor's jacket. A dark stream that smelled odd.

Tiff was embarrassed. "Is she sick?"

Dr. Earnshaw took a sample of urine, thinking she knew that smell but could not put a name to it.

"What are you feeding her?"

"Just regular things, strained baby food, milk. Nothing different. Do you think it's allergies?"

"We can run some tests."

~~~

That night Tiff noticed that Marti's nails had grown again, thicker and darker. They curved. Marti was not cooing, but gurgling constantly, her eyes closed, but moving rapidly beneath the eyelids. REM phase, Tiff assumed. Dreams. What was Baby Girl dreaming? Tiff leaned over the crib, watching her sleeping daughter. She bent closer.

Marti's eyes opened suddenly.

Tiff jumped. No sleepiness, no confusion. It was as if the baby was staring into Tiff's eyes as an equal, measuring her, almost mocking her. As if she knew I was watching her and she wanted to catch me at it, Tiff thought.

Her skin crawled. She checked the baby monitor and left the room.

Baby girl was definitely different. Constantly fussy. Throwing tantrums. Biting. Licking. Smacking her lips—its lips—in an un-baby like way.

~~~

That night Tiff stood listening to the baby monitor. A sound like ripping and wet munching. She waited inside the nursery door, hidden in shadow, willing her heartbeat to silence, watching the crib. A cat, the feral cat Tiff had sometimes fed but had chased away after Marti's birth, and which had appeared on the doorstep, climbed into the crib, a mouse in its mouth. It dropped the tribute onto the baby's chest. The cat straddled Baby Girl, feasting on the back end of the mouse, while Baby Girl ripped into the front end, head and all, growling.

Help, Tiff thought. She swallowed, trying not to vomit. Is it the postpartum blues, my anti-anxiety meds? Am I going bonkers? She slipped from the room, hoping, praying, that she was not losing it. Was Baby Girl possessed?

Lines of ants invaded the kitchen, marched across the floor and up the wall, forming sharp right angles to the honey jar on the shelf, and at last crawling under the lid. Tiff put the honey in the fridge. The ants kept coming, carrying bits of leaf across the floor. Tiff opened the sink doors and found a nest of leaves and noodles full of lizards with yellow eyes, a big one, the mother, and three babies emerging from green eggs the size of fingernails. The big lizard stared at her and hissed. Outside the kitchen door at night a chorus of bass croaks sounded until midnight. Frogs? Toads? Strange insects with opalescent wings appeared on the windows, as if they were looking into the house. They clustered especially at the nursery window.

The doctor's office left a message that the tests showed nothing—all perfectly normal. Tiffany called her mother to watch Marti—grandma and grandpa just adored the little girl. Tiff hated herself for leaving Marti, but wondered—if Mom and Dad saw nothing wrong, then was she nuts?

At last, she called Anna. "We've got to meet. I need to talk with you." Anna, unlike a shrink, would listen calmly and not dismiss her as a nut case.

Anna, an old friend who could see ghosts, who read tarot cards, who conducted séances. Anna whom she had mocked for her... beliefs, which had ended the friendship. Anna was likely the only one who would not laugh at her, wave a dismissive hand, and mutter about postpartum depression.

Anna did listen carefully. Offered tea and scones in her kitchen. She looked straight at Tiffany. They had known each other for ten years, the last two of that in estrangement, but Anna never said, "I told you so."

Anna set down her teacup, pressed her hands to the table. "There are old stories... I'd have to see her. She seemed fine last time I sat with her. Perfectly normal."

Tiffany shook her head. "Not now. Things... changed. I feel like I'm going crazy, but I've seen things that no baby, no human baby, would do."

Anna raised an eyebrow.

"Ripping a raw mouse apart. Smacking her lips. Maybe my mom and dad will report some weirdness, but somehow I doubt it."

Anna frowned and swallowed. "Like the car not doing the weird thing when you take it to the mechanic?"

"Exactly." Tiff nodded.

"I have to see for myself."

So Anna did. She watched solemnly through the whole gruesome scene late that night. She beckoned Tiff into the kitchen, shut the door, and stood with her back against it. "Friend: I'd say she's a changeling."

"Like the fairies' nasty trick of switching babies?"

Anna cradled a teacup in her hands. "When did this start? When exactly did normal stop and weird begin?"

Tiffany shook her head in despair. "I don't know."

Anna put a warm hand over hers. "Just think about it. When and where things stopped being OK." She made her friend a wreath of rosemary, had her sniff it, and bundled several small sprigs in an amulet bag with an agate and a pyrite crystal. "For memory and protection," Anna said, "Wear it."

They retraced Tiff's steps, everything she could remember, every place she'd gone the last few days. Crossed and re-crossed neighborhoods, strode by the Puritan statue in front of the witch museum, crossed the Commons, the Howard Street cemetery, visited the Peabody-Essex Museum, checked every bathroom and café and baby clothes store, every park and library and jogging path. Nothing rang a bell.

"A glamour may contain a spell for memory loss," Anna said. "We are close to Halloween. This is Salem. The fey have a strange sense of humor, so this place might provoke them." She touched Tiff's hand. "There was something odd about Marti's dad."

Tiff's mouth tightened. That was as close as Anna would come to an I told you so. He had disappeared: Mister Seductive one day, Mister Into Thin Air the next. Tiff was unsure if his name was Ulrik Green. He had muttered something that sounded like that once. As for his birthplace, his parents' names, who knew? The hospital staff had looked at her as if she were to be pitied, or to be questioned about harboring a criminal.

Hours later, they stopped in the Witches Cauldron Café on Derby Street for a pick-me-up. Tiff stared about her and suddenly paled. "Damn. This is the same café."

"Make certain," Anna said. "Name certainly fits."

They visited the toilet and read the warning on the changing table.

"Do not leave infant unattended," Anna read, running her fingers over the lettering. "They all say that, of course." She looked grim. "Did you turn your back for a second, take your eyes off her?"

Tiff felt sick with guilt, "A nanosecond."

Anna paced. "Might be enough time for magical beings to make mischief. Notice anything weird at the time?"

"I thought I had a floater in my eye. I watched her the whole time in the mirror, but it steamed up. Something flitted in my peripheral vision."

Anna sighed. "What if...it's a portal to the other side? This time of year, near Halloween, All Hallows Eve, Samhain, the boundaries between this world and other worlds, between living and dead, mortal and fey, grow thin. Fragile enough to let things pass through.

"And if we're lucky, things can travel back."

"I'll try anything." Tiff was near tears. "So somewhere past that line, beyond that wall, in some other place, some other creature, has my Marti?"

"I think so."

"How do we get her back?"

"We trade for her. We catch one of them and make a deal to get her back," Anna said.

"Like a POW swap," Tiff murmured. Tears rolled down her cheeks.

Anna embraced her.

~ ~ ~

Marti was a model baby for Tiff's parents. Tiff and Anna rigged a ceiling video cam focused on the crib to verify the nighttime visitations. The resulting film horrified them, showing the cat bringing the mouse, and the hideous shared feast. The video reassured Tiff that what she had seen was not due to the postpartum anxiety medications. "A comfort knowing I'm not nuts" She groaned. "Not a story we can tell any doctor."

"We've got to trap that cat, hold it for ransom," Anna said. "It's fey in the worst sense of the word."

The plan backfired. The cat and Marti clawed them. Marti grabbed the cat's fur and it leaped from the window, baby aboard, and disappeared into the neighborhood.

By morning, Marti was in her crib, sleeping fitfully, her eyes shifting beneath her eyelids. There was a smear of blood on her mouth with a tuft of gray fur stuck in it.

~ ~ ~

They closed the windows, but the magic opened them wide. The changeling was inviting the cat in.

"Should we use garlic?"

Anna snorted. "That's for vampires."

Just after full moon would be the best time, Anna said, because a banishing spell works best when the moon is waning. Next night they lay in wait for the goblin cat. It came through the window, Marti riding it, her fists clutching the black fur of its neck. It leaped into the crib and Marti rolled off. She crawled about the crib, growling. Anna leaped, stretching a huge linen sack over the top and bars of the crib, trapping the cat, which hissed and screamed and jumped to escape the bag. Tiff spread a circle of salt around the crib, the pale lines joining the iron objects—old keys and antique clothing irons and pyrites—which Anna had placed on the floor earlier. Together the women wrestled the creature down against the sheets, ignoring the claws and teeth that ripped and snapped through the cloth.

"I bind you, goblin," Anna said. They struggled to hold the sack closed. It was like holding Proteus. The goblin writhed and screamed. Flames and steam shot through the weave of the sack, but its claws and teeth drew blood and human blood contains iron. As Tiff's blood dripped down her arm, the horrible cat settled at last, yowling. Marti gave a cry that sounded almost human again.

They loaded the cat inside a carrier and four more bags for good measure and tied it tightly. Anna stowed the writhing package in her large tote bag, along with a pint of cream, salt, and her ritual objects. They headed to the café, where they had to wait in line for the bathroom, of course. Marti clawed and scratched Tiff, who had put mittens on her hands. At last they were next in line. They got some strange looks because of the yowling that came from Anna's tote.

At last they were inside. "It's a unisex bathroom," Tiff said.

Anna nodded. "I'll be as fast as I can." She disabled the smoke alarm, purified the space with sage and candle flame. "They'll think we're smoking in the toilet, but it can't be helped. Make sure the door's locked."

"Pray they don't have a master key."

"Stay by the door, Tiff, in case they try to force it."

The ritual was halfway complete when someone thumped the door.

"Hey," a male voice yelled, "What are you doing in there? You're taking forever!"

Anna locked eyes with Tiff and went on murmuring, chanting a binding and banishment spell.

Anna kept a tight grip on the twisting, howling goblin cat. It got its head free of the bag, but Anna held it tight. The fur of its throat steamed as Anna pressed her iron-bladed knife close. The goblin hissed, snarled, and clawed. The creature began to shrink. The bathroom filled with a rain of red and gold and brown and skeleton leaves, rustling and swirling as if to form a shape. Forest litter covered the tiles and the smell of wet, rotting leaves and mushrooms filled the air. Acorns rolled across the floor. Spiders scurried everywhere, but the black cat hissed, showing fangs like locust thorns. It bit Anna's hand so that she almost dropped the knife. The beast leaped onto the changing table and disappeared into the shimmering wall.

"Door's open," Anna whispered, cradling her hand.

People were pounding the door. Someone landed an open-handed strike that made the wood shudder, but the angry male voice retreated. Next came a business-like clatter of solidly heeled shoes, "This is the manager. Is everything all right in there?"

"My baby's sick," Tiff said, "Please understand."

The heels clicked away down the hallway.

The baby changing table dropped open. Tiffany gasped. The changeling in her arms hissed furiously, scurried onto the table, and vanished into the wall. A shower of forest floor litter, brilliant red sumac and gold maple and oak leaves, dried berries, pebbles, and a tangle of thin branches spewed from the wall and fell onto the floor. There was a snarl and a whistle. A rumble followed, and a cry—a human baby's cry. Tiff was blinking away tears. Marti slid through with another rain of acorn caps and pine needles, dried mushrooms, and some spiders that swiftly climbed the walls. Tiff caught Baby Girl as she came through the portal. Marti was okay. Crying, but okay. Her diaper was soaked. Her clothes were filthy and her left bootie was gone, but she was back. Tiff cradled her. Blew away the cobwebs twined in her hair and snagged on her jacket. Picked the burrs from her hat. Kissed her all over, tugging off socks and mittens, examining her fingers and toes.

She changed the diaper, scooped up Baby Girl, stood back to close the changing table. A streak flashed out, a scrawny wild-eyed tuxedo cat whose ribs showed. It yowled and raced around the bathroom, batting the air as if pursued by and fighting imps.

Anna pulled a pint carton and saucer from her tote and poured the cat a saucer of cream, which it approached warily. It let her fasten a collar around its neck, a collar with nine iron studs to protect it from future mischief.

"Everything's OK," Anna yelled at the door. "The baby was fussy and sick, okay, people?" She was stowing what remained of the forest litter in the garbage can and a garbage bag she'd brought along. She put the cat in her tote bag and the quartet made a somewhat dignified exit from the café.

"Where did all those leaves come from?" the guy next in line asked.

"Fall colors. They're everywhere this time of year," Tiffany said. She cradled Marti close.

The Dragon and the Santa

Emily Martha Sorensen

Irri's stomach growled as he flew. He hadn't eaten in three days, and he was extremely hungry. The elders *warned* him against flying too close to the worldgate, but had he listened? Of course not, because he was the great Irri.

Irritably, Irri scanned the sky for birds. He'd seen precious few since he'd come to this wasteland, and all had escaped him. What kind of place was this, all snow and ice? How could any reptilian person live in such a place?

A jingle made his ears prick up.

The slightest red glow, danced through a distant cloudbank. He dove, roaring fire in his wake.

He seized his prey, a big woolly horned thing, and prepared to gulp it down.

"RELINQUISH RUDOLPH!" a voice roared.

Irri paused, looking down at the prey in his talons. It bucked and reared, showing the whites of its eyes. Defiantly, he moved it back to his jaws.

A blast of energy blew him back. With a shriek of terror, the woolly thing wriggled free. Eight more woolly things writhed from the cloud, and all nine stampeded away.

The cloud was silent for a moment. Then it said, "Blast."

Irri growled in frustration.

A round, red-and-white head popped through the cloudbank. From the lack of fear in its eyes, Irri surmised that this was not a prey species.

"Thank you very much!" the creature snapped. "Do you have any idea how long it takes to breed a reindeer with a glowing nose? Not to mention one that can fly! And they'll have scattered miles away! How am I supposed to deliver my presents *now?*"

"Need food," Irri growled. "Or I'll eat you."

"Dragons," the newcomer muttered. "Wait there."

The head disappeared for a moment. There was a rustling sound. Then a huge chunk of raw meat dropped from the cloud.

Irri shrieked in triumph. He seized it in his talons, tore his teeth into it, and gulped strip after strip of flesh. As the meat sizzled in his stomach, he began to feel a trifle better.

"You really shouldn't be in this world at all," the creature said, poking its head back up through the fog. "The last time I saw dragons was—oh—back when they still called me Odin."

"Came through by accident," Irri snarled, snarfing through his meat. "Flew too close to a gate. Turns out it was open. Closed behind me again."

"Ahh." The creature rubbed his eyes with two fat fists. "Of course. I could have told the humans that concentrating their world's magic on top of a pole, right around a solstice, was asking for trouble. But does anyone ever listen to me? Noooo. All they let me do these days is give their children presents. It almost makes me wish I was still Odin, even without the depth perception."

Irri bolted his last scrap of meat. He reared backwards, flapping his wings, and snuffed loudly for more. Sensing nothing, he narrowed his eyes in the direction of the escaped prey.

"Oh, no you don't!" the creature said from behind him. "You scared away my reindeer—*you're* going to pull my sleigh."

Sudden weight fell onto Irri's wings. He hissed and bucked in fury. But the creature behind him paid him no heed. More and more restraints fell around him, across his nose and face, until even his flame-centers were extinguished.

"Horrible creature," Irri gasped. "Release me!"

"No, I don't think so." There was a jingling behind him, and a string of little bells was heaved over his back. Irri bucked and shivered as the freezing metal itched him. The red-and-white creature paid this no heed. "I have few enough believers these days. I refuse to let you jeopardize the few I have left. Besides, there's nothing you can do about it. My magic's at its peak today."

Irri tried to spit fire, but nothing came. He writhed in fury.

"My current name is Sinterklaas, by the way," the round creature said, tying the last tether of its sleigh in place. "Or Weihnachtsmann. Or Santa Claus, if you insist."

"Hate you," Irri hissed.

"I'll send you home when we're finished. Unless you'd rather wait until the gate opens in another year?"

"*Hate* you!"

"If you must, but we've no time to waste on that silliness. Now... which one is closer from here, Greenland or Norway?"

~ ~ ~

Irri's opinion of the Santa did not improve as they continued on their journey.

The creature kept an enormous list that it flipped through incessantly. "Joseph... Emma... Johnny," it would murmur, making notes with either a thick feather or a black stick it called a pen. "I wish they'd let me upgrade to a smartphone, but not enough folks envision me that way."

"Why do you let them determine your life?" Irri growled. "It is stupid."

"Magic works best with the rules people believe in. I like magic. So I use the role they give me."

"It is stupid!"

"I've been worse," the Santa murmured, squinting at its long list. "Naughty... nice... I wish they'd give me a third option. Most children are both, and many things in between. Ah well, I never leave coal anyway."

Irri licked his teeth. Coal sounded tasty.

"There!" the Santa shouted, pointing at a cluster of lights. "Hold still while I freeze time so we can get down there safely."

~ ~ ~

The creature also had an irrational prejudice against hunting.

"No cats," the Santa told him firmly, as they hovered right over a rooftop with some tasty looking fuzzballs on it. "No dogs, either. And if I catch you eating a horse, I will trap you until the next solstice comes, so help me."

Irri sulked as the round creature squeezed down a too-small chimney.

And then there was the food that the Santa *did* bring him.

"My reindeer are supposed to eat these," the creature said, dumping a pile of plants by Irri's mouth while they stopped to rest. "That means they're yours tonight."

Irri stared at the orange roots incredulously. "Do I look like a prey species?"

"Try eating like an omnivore for one night. It won't kill you."

Irri picked up the offending roots in his talons and flung them away.

The most annoying thing, however, was the way the creature kept *humming.* Sometimes it even added words, and the words were always inane.

"Up on the housetop reindeer pause... out jumps good old Santa Claus..."

"Do you *mind?*" Irri roared. "I'm trying to concentrate on flying!"

"Good for you. I'm trying to enjoy my one day out. I enjoy singing."

"You are tone-deaf," Irri growled.

"No, I'm not. Dragons just compose differently."

"You sound like half-dead rodents," Irri snarled.

"If you say so. But it's my sleigh. And there's nothing you can do to stop me. On the first day of Christmas, my true love gave to me..."

Irri wondered if the Santa was *officially* on a list of non-prey species.

~~~

"That's it," the Santa said finally, pulling off Irri's restraints after a night that felt like it had lasted for weeks.

"We've finished the last house. We're back at the pole. Ready to go home now?"

"Past ready," Irri growled. "Never want to see you again."

The Santa laughed. It sounded like a drum bouncing on a rock. "You know, you're the first six-limbed steed I've had since Sleipnir. It's been fun, hasn't it?"

"No," Irri retorted.

"You actually might stay," the Santa said shrewdly, unstrapping the harness. "Dragons are getting more popular every year. I'm sure you could cash in on quite a bit of magic."

"Not interested," Irri growled.

"In fact, given the hoards humans believe dragons have, you could even do what I can't, and accumulate a lot of money." The Santa brightened. "Money that could fund Hollywood movies to shift public opinion about me..."

"Not listening!"

The creature put its arm around Irri's snoot. "We should talk about this further."

"You should *open the gate!*"

"One year. I'm sure you could stand that."

"I'm sure I could find a way to eat you."

The Santa paused. "Ah. Perhaps I shouldn't teach you magic to rival mine."

Irri showed off his teeth.

The Santa sighed and waved its hand. The portal opened.

Irri flapped his wings, rose in the air, and darted through it.

"Tell your friends the offer's open!" the Santa called as the portal sealed again. "Any dragon who wants to come next year could cut a great deal!"

Irri snorted fire in derision. He backwinged up into the red sky. As if he would send any of his friends into such a fate.

His *enemies,* however... now, that might be worth considering.

Things Which Wash up on Terran Shores

Jason P. Burnham

A two-headed dolphin
A Portuguese man o' war
An undetonated explosive
From the time before

You walk the sands
Picking your way
A misplaced footfall
Will be your doomsday

For the dolphin still lives
Twice the brain power
Watching closely
In your final hour

The purple siphonophore
Casts out it its net
Venomous nematocysts
A touch you'll regret

The missile sits
Least threateningly of all
Its creators now gone
They'll have no curtain call

Holiday Leftovers

You back away slowly
Filled with aquatic dread
Get back on your ship
Or soon you'll be…

A Plague of Santas

Emily Dorffer

It starts innocently enough in November. A shortage of cookies and milk at the grocery store, a faint jingling at night, the lingering scent of peppermint. To the children, this means a flood of presents is right around the corner, but the adults know there's much more to it than that.

Soon, people start spotting obese men dressed in red and white, their snow-white beards permanently speckled with crumbs. They know everyone's names from the most reclusive shut-ins to newborns. With little more than a glance, they know exactly how naughty or nice you've been. If you so much as jaywalk, they will know, and everyone will know they know.

Even your deepest desires can't hide from the jolly men. They see you when you're sleeping, and they know when you're awake. When a Santa glances at you as he blares Christmas carols from his sleigh on the I-10, you know he knows exactly what you want for Christmas, perhaps before you do yourself.

Of course, things only get worse as more and more of them appear.

Airports shut down as reindeer clog the sky. Collisions faster than the speed of light wouldn't end well for anyone, so travelers must seek other means of travel. Unfortunately, the roads are little better as more than a few Santas prefer to keep their reindeer's hooves on the ground until

Christmas Eve. Nothing says true misery like a traffic jam that reeks of lichen and reindeer dung.

So much for heading home for the holidays. You're lucky if you can make it by January.

The best you can do is send cards or maybe a present, assuming you can get your hands on some wrapping paper. That's never easy when dozens of gloved hands are grappling for the last roll. The shortest employees in every department store are stuck hiding in the break room or trembling behind shelves as Santa after Santa attempts to jostle so-called lazy elves into their sleigh for a speedy trip to the workshop. He may see you at all times, but Santa doesn't always have the best eyesight.

Meanwhile, the bakers, those poor, brave souls, are stuck slaving away at their ovens twenty-four seven. The overpowering smell of freshly baked cookies will cling to their very soul weeks after December, yet they keep trying to satisfy the seemingly endless, sugar starved swarms. They don't have the time or resources to bake anything else, not even a single cupcake. And they wouldn't dare try to turn a Santa away, oh no. Getting between a Santa and his cookies is as dangerous as getting between a grizzly and salmon, especially if he's got a loaded sack with him.

As Christmas draws near, parents exchange emergency preparation strategies in hushed whispers. Tips for who can reinforce roofs so they can withstand countless hooves, how to safely extract a stuck Santa from a chimney, and how to deal with excessive presents blockading them in their own homes are exchanged over mugs of eggnog. Parents warn their children to stick to requesting small gifts. It's far easier to deal with a thousand candy canes than a thousand German Shepherds.

But the children don't understand.

How could someone who brings gifts be bad? To them, the horde of Santas is little more than an army of doting grandpas who just want to make them happy. So they write their letters to him in secret and tiptoe to the mailbox in the dead of night.

On Christmas Eve, the world sounds as if it's covered by a thunderstorm as hooves thud against roofs around the globe. With no cookies or milk left thanks to their month-long binging at bakeries and grocery stores, the Santas take what they can get. While they gorge themselves on sugarplums and other goodies, their reindeer devour entire gardens. In the morning, not a single crumb or weed remains. Despite the Santas shoving themselves down chimneys and shoveling junk food down their throats, not a single person awakens before they've all left their presents. Why that is no one knows.

Perhaps it's better that way.

At last, morning arrives. For the lucky families with nice, wise children, cleaning up is a mere inconvenience at worst. Candies are easily stashed away in pantries; stuffed animals infest attics while staying out of everyone's way. The cleverest children's families are delighted to find pounds of jewelry they can sell so they can afford all the presents they really want and then some.

Not everyone is so lucky. Emergency rooms are packed with parents who broke bones tripping on the toy cars scattered across the stairs. Animal shelters open to find thousands of kittens and puppies abandoned at their doors. Even with the Santas gone until next year, the chaos is far from over. And they will return.

As long as people still believe in them, they will return.

Holiday Leftovers

Honey and Apples

A. P. Howell

The knife scrapes the rim of the glass jar, coming away with a thin strand of gold. Like cheap jewelry covered with a gold wash, creating an illusion of great value.

There used to be bottles shaped like bears: whimsical, disposable, plastic. Now glass jars are reused. They seem bigger every year as bees grow ever more rare.

The apple is small and soft, the skin bruised and broken even before the knife touches it.

There used to be better apples: healthy, varied, colorful, juicy. Delicious. But this is all that remains to mark the beginning of a new year.

Happy Christmas

Debora Godfrey

"Happy Christmas!"

"'Merry Christmas'."

"What?"

"It's 'Merry Christmas,' not 'Happy Christmas.'"

"They say 'Happy Christmas' in England."

"Are we in England? No. Say it the right way."

"If you say 'Merry Christmas' just like everyone else, no one even listens anymore. They just tune it out. If you say 'Happy Christmas,' though, everybody notices, because it's different. Then they think about it."

"Then they'll think that you're a weirdo."

"They know I'm a weirdo. I'm okay with that. As I said, Happy Christmas."

"It's still wrong. I'm sure it's in the Bible where Jesus said 'Merry Christmas,' not 'Happy Christmas.'"

"It is not in the Bible where He says 'Merry Christmas.' Christmas is a celebration of when Jesus was born. He wouldn't have said anything."

"Well, Mary would have said 'Merry Christmas.'"

"Actually, no, Mary was in labor, so I doubt she would have been saying anything like that. Probably screaming or whimpering, not 'merry' anything."

"So, Joseph would have said 'Merry Christmas' then."

"I don't think so. Joseph was stuck in a stable on tax day helping his wife deliver a child fathered by someone else. Not the most joyous occasion. I don't think 'merry' would have been foremost in his mind."

"Well, the angels, then. They wouldn't have been involved in the whole birth thing, do you think? They would have been saying 'Merry Christmas!'"

"I don't know what language the angels spoke, but English won't be invented for another 1500 years or so. Probably not 'Merry Christmas.'"

"I hate you."

"Merry Easter."

Last Mission

Alex J. Smith

The first sign of trouble was the book. The *Naughty or Nice* book.

The book had always had a nice heft to it. It seemed... less substantial today.

Santa shrugged. After all, he'd been spending some time in the gym. You had to do something about the cookies. For heaven's sake, when had three home cooked gingersnaps of years past turned into triple stacked cream filled monstrosities?

But, so be it. He opened the tome to the slender red ribbon that told him where he'd left off.

Ah yes, the "G" section. He started at the top. Gaarwain Williams, such a nice boy. Helped in the garden, took out the rubbish, nice to animals. There was that one incident when he lied about who ate the last piece of kidney pie, but... It was kidney pie. Forgivable. Six years old, lived in Lancashire.

Santa picked up his pen, and as he went to make his mark, the name faded under the poised pen. Santa hung his head. He knew what that meant. A soul had left the mortal plane. It happened too often. Too many died young. Not so bad as during the plague, but bad. He flipped the pages. Gaarwain had a sister, she would get a little something extra. Her name too was gone. The parents as well.

Santa felt a cold chill crawl down his spine.

Name after name was gone, some vanishing before his eyes. Even as he sat the book shrank visibly. He knew time

43

passed differently on the other planes, but this spoke of disaster.

He closed the book and carried it back to its shelf. He sighed heavily and opened another door. Seldom used, the hinges squeaked. The opening revealed the mirror, a simple thing in a pewter frame. He picked it up and carried it to the table.

He rubbed a hand over the glass until it glowed. "Mother," he said and waited.

She looked terrible.

"You've heard?" she said.

"No, I just know that humanity is dying."

She turned her head and spat.

"No," she said. "They are un-dying."

"I don't understand," Santa said.

He looked over at the book. No longer a tome, but a slender volume.

"Zombies," she said.

"Everywhere?"

She nodded.

After a moment of silence he asked hesitantly, "And England? Has it fallen?" Memories of the sweet smell of hay being gathered on the last days of summer. A mental glimpse of his mother's red cheeks. Of times long ago, before...

"One village survives," she said, interrupting his memories. "Plockton, it is called. But the hoards do approach."

Santa sighed. Names and faces. He knew them all. It came with the job. "Thank you," was all he said as he turned away from the mirror to another door.

He shouted for the sleigh to be made ready and he opened the door and stepped within. Minutes later, he looked again in the mirror. His armor gleamed in the lamplight. His great axe almost glowed.

He stepped into the darkness and went to where the sleigh waited.

The world needed a Santa Claus.

Consoliday

Wayne Lee

A Memo from the Department of Observances
Re: Consoliday

Due to budgetary constraints, we are hereby consolidating all federal observances and celebrations, effective immediately.

On January first at 12 a.m. Eastern Standard Time, a turkey, wearing a leprechaun outfit and carrying an ice-chest full of Valentines, Easter eggs, popcorn balls and Hanukkah gelt, will hop down the Bunny Trail to Plymouth Rock, then climb into a pumpkin coach pulled by eight tiny unionized reindeer.

While competing in the ensuing high-speed, 500-mile Indie race, the craft will land on the rooftop of every mother and father in the country, whereupon the turkey will slide down each chimney, snack on barbecued ribs, lite beer and halvah, then distribute gift-wrapped firecrackers, fruitcake and flower baskets.

Festivities will conclude in our nation's capital, where a white-bearded groundhog wearing diapers and an American flag will chop down a cherry tree and light a menorah, thus igniting the National Christmas Tree, triggering a massive fireworks display and causing a giant ball to drop on the Washington Monument.

Holiday Leftovers

We sincerely hope you enjoy your new Consoliday, after which all able-bodied Americans will report immediately for work.

Founders' Day

Kim Sheard

The summons came very early in the morning and woke me from jumbled dreams where I searched desperately for a French-Valis dictionary while two angry Valisians kept the barrels of their blast guns trained on me. Looking back, I should have been happy to be spared further moments in that scenario. At the time, though, I only felt confused, and more apprehensive than was normally appropriate for just a call to the comms.

I shuffled from the bedroom in the dark, feeling my way carefully past the edge of the bed, the dresser, and the door frame. When I reached the adjoining office, I rubbed my eyes and called for lights at one-quarter their normal intensity, which was just about right to allow me to see without shocking my dilated pupils.

I was unaccustomed to waking quickly. Most visitors were courteous enough to comply with our duty hours when the sentries told them that our officers were currently on the dark side of the planet. Not this visitor, though. This one insisted on immediate attention. So the sentries had called me, apologetic.

It was one of the few times I cursed the fact that we had kept our government small and bureaucracy to the bare minimum. I would have liked for a middle manager to handle calls like this.

At least the foreign spacecraft was too far away for a visual call, as I doubt its captain would have been impressed by my dented hair and rumpled nightgown. Still, I had to clear my throat and take great gulps of water from the office cooler before my voice would work well enough for the audio-only communication through our deep space radio network.

Finally I stood, barefoot and blinking, before the transmitter terminal next to my desk and politely introduced myself as Jeannette LaMer, Governor of the human planet Gastonia. After a few seconds' delay, a gravelly voice returned syllables not unlike my own, but with a high squeal punctuating the end of each phrase. It was incongruous, like the gruff speech of a cantankerous old man melting into the giggles of a little girl. His was a strange language (I assumed, hopefully correctly, that the voice belonged to a male of his species), but apparently one of our satellites had encountered it before, as the computer was able to scroll a translation across my otherwise dark view screen.

"We are coming to trade," he said.

"That can be arranged," I replied. "To whom am I speaking? Where are you from?"

"I am Golitsin of the fifth planet of Star 145."

That was no help at all, considering I had no idea how his planet numbering system worked. I didn't press the issue, though. If he did indeed bring his ship to Gastonia, the Trade Commission would certainly learn all the details.

"It is nice to meet you, Golitsin. How long will it take you to arrive? We will arrange a meeting in person."

The subtitle indicated almost exactly two of our planetary days. I nodded at that and said, "Let's set your meeting with our trade commission for four days from now."

Golitsin didn't answer. The silence lengthened between us, causing me to fidget, fluffing my hair more or less into its proper position with the left side long and draped over my shoulder and the right side just covering my ear. I finally said, "The government officers are currently on the dark side of the planet and will be again when you get here. Your meeting will be not the night you arrive, and not the day after, but the second day you are here."

Golitsin growled a response, and I was not surprised when the translation came through as, "That is not acceptable."

I forced a smile. He wouldn't see it, but maybe the expression would help improve my tone, as I was quickly losing patience. "It will have to be acceptable, sir, as it is the first appointment I have to offer you. As I said, you are arriving during night for our Trade Council members, and we do not conduct business during the night. Then, the day after you arrive is Gastonia's Founders' Day, our biggest holiday of the year. We cannot meet with you then." Not that I owed him an explanation.

"Holiday!" he spat. "You are still so backward that you worship invisible gods and celebrate worthless religious days?"

His raised voice apparently alarmed Jacques, my husband, and he came trotting unsteadily from the bedroom, trying to fasten a robe, not even noticing that it was *my* robe. Seeing that I was using an audio-only transmission, he came to my left side and wrapped his arm around me, resting his large, warm hand on my abdomen. His comforting touch allowed me to relax the muscles there I hadn't even realized I was clenching. Within an instant, though, my unborn daughter kicked hard beneath his fingers, causing me to tighten up again.

After a deep breath I responded to Golitsin in a faux patient tone I usually reserved for the children. "It is not a religious holiday, sir, though some here still have practicing beliefs, which we take care to respect. Founders' Day is a celebration of the discovery of our planet and the establishment of a successful colony here. Now, one hundred and fifty years later, we are independent and strong in numbers and technology." I added that last bit as a warning of sorts that we would not be taken advantage of.

"We care nothing for your celebration. We care only about trading, and trading as soon as we arrive," Golitsin said.

I drew back from Jacques' embrace and looked at him. His suspicious expression mirrored my own. What was Golitsin's hurry? Did he need aid in some way? If that was the case, couldn't he just say so? I sighed. I was up now, so I might as well get things settled. I leaned back against the desk, pulling Jacques with me.

"Golitsin, what is it that you need? Perhaps we can gather it while you approach, so when we do meet, we will be able to move more quickly."

"We will negotiate when I can see your face. I will contact you." The red Receiving light blinked off. Golitsin was gone. Jacques and I went back to bed without speaking, but I didn't sleep. Neither did my baby. She kicked me until I finally arose, ragged, at daybreak.

Publicly, I went through all the right steps, assuming Golitsin's race was friendly and that they would meet with us on the designated day. I had the Trade Commission clerks send the standard instructions on when and where to meet us and our rules for commerce. They also requested a written language key so our computers could supply translations for the contracts and asked about any special nutritional, medical, or atmospheric requirements. The ship never replied, but I was not surprised.

Privately, I couldn't decide what I expected Golitsin to do. One minute I feared he would arrive hostile, firing on our cities and taking whatever natural resources and technology he could. A similar tragedy had befallen another human colony during the time of our grandparents and was still commemorated during days of remembrance on Earth. The next moment I backed down and assured myself he would arrive and meet with us the day after Founders', grumpy but harmless. Then I would picture him kicking up a fuss, demanding that I see him in the middle of a Founders' Day parade or at the restaurant where my family ate its holiday meal.

My first scenario was, fortunately, unlikely, though not completely ridiculous. We had orbital defenses capable of easily subduing one ship, at least one at the technological level we were used to seeing. So unless Golitsin's ship was much more advanced than anything we'd ever encountered before—which I doubted based on the compatibility of our communications--we could handle it if we had to. Besides, all Golitsin's communiqué had done was warn us of the potential threat. He wouldn't have contacted us if all he planned to do was attack.

On the other hand, our defenses were designed for just that, defense, and Golitsin might get off a damaging shot or two before they kicked in. If he chose to fire on a highly populated area, even a single shot could be devastating. But he *was* coming, so the only thing I could do to prepare for these possibilities was alert my staff of the few facts I knew and have them activate our special watchdog security procedures.

I vacillated between slight concern and alarm. Would he wait and meet with us as requested or insist on ruining my holiday? I had been polite and welcoming, but firm, with Golitsin, I thought, and he had no obvious reason not to abide by my wishes. On the other hand, I knew next to nothing about him and his people, and he didn't seem very concerned about social graces. If he interrupted partying Gastonians on the ground, things could still get ugly.

Okay, yes, the Head Honcho of the great planet Gastonia worried. It was part of the job description.

At the same time, I tried desperately to enjoy my Founders' Day activities. Normally it is my favorite time of year. Presenting opening speeches for the various festivities, singing along with the holiday songs, and bringing gifts and food to the less fortunate were duties of my position, but ones I relished each time. I enjoyed them this year, too, but suspected my brow creased with worry, even as I smiled as warmly as I could. I kept my eyes and ears open for any signs of disruption and held my portable communications fob open to any signals.

I reserved Founders' Day afternoon and evening for my family, and we packed in as many activities as we could. To my relief, Golitsin appeared at none of them.

First, the children opened their gifts. Delphe had begged several months for his own air skiff so he could visit his friends without taking public transport. Jacques and I had finally broken down and complied. The boy spent two hours soaring and dipping around the backyard, dark blond braid flying, until we dragged him away for dinner. Kristelle had much simpler tastes. A new doll with several little outfits in the latest style earned us hugs and big smiles. We had even purchased something for the baby, a mobile of stuffed red, green, and blue stars that each played a different children's song when touched.

As we hung the mobile over the baby's crib, Jacques gave me a soft kiss and reminded me of the promise we had made to each other in lieu of Founders' gifts. In a month when the baby was born, we would spend an uninterrupted week at home, just the two of us and our new daughter. My sister would care for Delphe and Kristelle, and the Lieutenant Governor would take over all official duties. "No matter what," I assured him. Jacques knew me well enough to know that, as with the holiday not being completely ours this time, I might break that promise, but he tolerated it.

That evening we dined at Fantaisie, our favorite restaurant. Jacques and I ate traditional Founders' Day fare, roasted *oiseau de la nouvelle planète*, bird of the new planet, the first game hunted by humans on Gastonia. We allowed the children to make their own choices from the menu, an unusual occurrence of which they took full advantage, filling up on sweet bread and Brie. We even allowed them to taste our wine. They both made disgusted faces and rinsed down the tang with milk while their father and I laughed.

Jacques, bless him, noticed when the smile suddenly disappeared from my face. He sent the children to the entertainment room to check on the evening's weather forecast, and then asked what I was thinking.

I wondered, not for the first time, how I warranted the solitary title of Planetary Governor, for my husband certainly deserved half the credit for sharing my burdens. But aloud I said, "I just had the horrible thought that our baby girl may never have her first taste of wine. She may never enjoy Founders' Day or open gifts. I grieve for what may happen to Delphe and Kristelle, of course, and everyone on Gastonia...."

"But?"

"But what about those who would be denied living at all? Our baby doesn't even have a name, Jacques."

He covered my hand with his. "We'll name her tonight, then. What better time to be named than during a Founders' Day celebration?"

I nodded. My gaze traveled involuntarily upward to the glass ceiling, as though I expected to see Golitson's ship in the night sky beyond. Before long, the children were bustling back, reporting that the evening would be warm and dry, and that we should go to the beach.

"Jean-Pierre will be there, *Maman*," Delphe said, and that clinched it. The beach it was.

Not surprisingly, Delphe left us as soon as he came upon his friends, but little Kristelle stayed with Jacques and me happily. She clutched one of each of our hands as we strolled the coast, winding around the other families who had obviously come up with the same idea. When we paused to view the stars twinkling red, yellow, and white in the blue-black sky, she said, barely loud enough to be heard over the waves, "It looks like a Christmas tree."

Jacques and I both turned and looked at her. "A what?" he asked.

"A Christmas tree with twinkly lights," she said firmly.

My husband and I were both familiar with the concept, of course, but hadn't realized our six-year-old daughter was, too. "Where did you learn about Christmas trees, Kristelle?" I asked.

"Madonna-Marie had one," she said.

Ah, yes, our elderly neighbor and one of Kristelle's special friends. I had seen her with a beaded necklace once. Perhaps it had actually been a rosary.

I couldn't do the calculations in my head quickly enough. "When did she have the tree?"

Kristelle shrugged. "A while ago. Before I lost my tooth." She pointed to the place where her first adult tooth had grown halfway in. "It was really pretty."

"I bet it was," Jacques said. "Maybe we should start having Founders' Day trees."

Kristelle laughed, causing her yellow curls to bounce. "Daddy!"

He pretended to be hurt. "What? You didn't want the special bird for dinner, so what else is there to make the day exciting?"

"Presents!" she cried, then remembering, added, "Madonna-Marie had presents underneath her Christmas tree. And a little doll house."

"I think that's called a *crèche*," I said.

Kristelle cocked her head. "Yes, that sounds right."

There was a shout from one of the boys down the beach where we'd already passed. It might have even been one of Delphe's friends. Jacques and I both turned from our daughter toward the noise and then immediately looked back to the sky to where the boy and his cohorts were pointing. A spot of jade green, a color never seen naturally in our sky, shone there. And it was growing.

I pushed Kristelle into Jacques' arms and, holding my swollen stomach, began to run. My feet slipped on the smoke-colored pebbles of the beach, but I didn't fall down. "Delphe! Delphe!" I called for my son. I had to find him. We all needed to run, to get away. And if we couldn't escape, at least we could be together in the end.

Jacques caught up with me, Kristelle under his arm, as I fumbled with the communications fob I kept on a chain around my neck. He plopped Kristelle down next to me and motioned for me to stay where I was. "You check in with the sentries," he said. "I'll find Delphe." Then he was off, jogging down the beach.

Kristelle huddled against my side as I called the sentry station. I skipped the usual greetings. "What's going on?"

The voice on the other end was female and calm, though I could hear other, more frantic, voices in the background. "We're not sure, Ma'am," the woman said. "We can see energy traveling toward Océan Noir to a point five clicks from shore, but the satellites can't identify what it is."

One of the other voices got louder, but I couldn't understand the words. "It's *not* a weapon," my contact said firmly, as if to the speaker in the background.

"How do you know?" I asked. The green dot was now as big as my thumbnail if I held my arm fully extended.

"The others don't agree with me," she said. "But I studied astrophysics before I became a sentry. That thing in the sky just doesn't have enough energy to *do* anything. As far as I can tell, it's nothing more than a ... a light bulb reflecting off the atmosphere."

I frowned. "Is it coming from the ship up there?"

"Yes, Ma'am. It originated three minutes ago and bypassed the defense sats without even a low-level alarm."

And it was getting here quickly. It was now the size of my fist. Kristelle was staring at it, mouth open, eyes unblinking.

"No answer to calls to the ship?"

"No, Ma'am."

Of course not.

Jacques came trotting back with Delphe on his heels. I breathed a sigh of relief and reached out to hug my son. For once, he didn't make a face. "Is there anything we can do other than wait for it to hit?"

"I don't believe so, Ma'am. It would be dangerous to fire on it, as low in the atmosphere as it is now. Besides, it will hit the ocean, not land."

"Any danger from water displacement?"

"Not enough mass. I strongly believe it is not a threat, Ma'am."

Jacques and I made eye contact, trying to reach a silent agreement. Should we run or stand our ground? Would it even make a difference? Finally, still looking at me, Jacques clasped Delphe on the shoulder with one hand. He wrapped the other arm behind my back and ruffled Kristelle's hair on my other side, linking us together as a family in good situations and bad.

And unknown.

I held my breath and watched the green light come closer and closer. Finally I could see its trajectory turn down toward the ocean. It fell toward the water like a *tacheté* hawk descending on its prey.

I braced myself for the splash, but it didn't come. From the perspective of our distance, the light seemed to stop and hover mere meters from the water's surface. I was vaguely aware that everyone on the beach had, like us, frozen, and we shared the sight—and whatever would follow it—together in silence.

Then the shell of the light burst and more brightness gushed out of it, flinging purple, gold, and red across the black velvet of the sky and into the shimmering silk of the ocean. I was reminded of a volcano spewing ash and lava. A beautiful sight, but deadly.

Kristelle had other ideas, though. "*Joyeux Noël!*" she called in a clear voice, obviously delighted.

The reactions from those around us were mixed. Most gasped, taken aback by the joyous outburst in such uncertainty. Teenagers laughed at the silly little girl not so much younger than they were now. My gaze not leaving the spectacle, I lifted my comms fob and whispered, "How does it look now? Any radiation or other danger?"

I could hear the smile in the young woman's voice. "No danger at all, Ma'am. Just enjoy the show."

So I did. I closed the link, leaned back against my husband's strong arm, and watched until the streams of color became trickles, then soft glows, then, finally, after fifteen minutes, disappeared completely. There was applause across the beach as I kneeled to whisper back to my daughter, "*Joyeux Noël.*"

The next day I met Golitsin face to face and thanked him for his patience and his gift. His response was as gruff as ever, and he muttered something about one of his offspring begging for him to share the light show, but I could tell he was pleased. Our trade negotiations went smoothly.

Oh, and our baby did get a name on Founders' Day. We call her Noël.

A Call from Beyond

K.G. Anderson

The boy who appeared at the end of the evening quickened Gina Mondauf's broken heart. He'd thrown together a Halloween costume from a man's threadbare raincoat and a battered brown fedora. He looked to be about 13—her brother Ethan's age.

"Trick or Treat!" Wonder Woman, Batman, and Thor ran up the steps, held out their bags for Gina's candy, then raced off into the night. The odd boy stayed motionless at the foot of the stairs, holding out his battered plastic bag.

"Kind of late, isn't it?" Gina said softly. Her voice trembled.

The boy stared. Grasping the rickety banister, Gina limped down one step at a time. On the last step, she held out the basket of candy. Her hand shook. Would he choose the peanut-butter bars her brother had loved?

The boy snatched up a fistful of the caramels. Gina sighed. But then he palmed two of the peanut-butter bars. And ran.

"Ethan?" Gina called after him. She held tight to the railing to keep from falling. "Hey! Ethan? Is that you? Stop! Ethan!"

He'd vanished. It was as if the damp autumn night had swallowed the boy. Or the ghost. Whichever he was.

Gina's shoulders sagged as she limped up the stairs and into the house. She slammed the front door and sank down on the dusty couch. Her family's deserted house was cold and empty. The heat had been turned off. She lived with her late mother's brother now. She was supposed to be helping Uncle Mike get this place ready to sell.

But what she'd really done was get it ready for Halloween. She'd swept the porch. Replaced the burnt-out bulb in the front light. Bought a pumpkin, carefully carved it, and set it out at the stop of the stairs. Handed out caramels to small superheroes, pirates, and princesses. Watched as they snatched up her candies and scampered into the night.

A few of the kids she'd recognized from her brother's middle school. But most were strangers, kids in expensive costumes whose parents had driven them up to Whitcomb to see a real, old-fashioned New England Halloween. A Halloween in a town where, legend said, ghosts appeared. Ghosts like the ones Gina was waiting for.

The ring of her smartphone startled her. It was an unfamiliar ringtone, mimicking the sound of a vintage rotary phone. She brushed tears from her cheek and fished the phone from her pocket. "Hello?"

The call dropped, but an odd name had appeared on the screen. *Beyo?* A minute later, a voicemail appeared. Gina tapped Play.

"Gina! It's Dad. You know I can't hear you, but I hope you can hear me." Her father's ghost! A voicemail from her father's ghost. "I love you, Gina," her father's voice went on.

Her eyes filled with tears. She hadn't heard her father's voice since the night their car had crashed on the snowy mountain road. Pinned in the wreckage, he'd called out for her mom, for her, and for her brother Ethan.

"It's OK here," her dad's ghost was saying. She could tell from his tone that it really wasn't OK, but that he could put up with it. That was so like Dad. "But I'm worried. About your mom and Ethan. I'm hoping they're back there with you. I'm hoping they survived."

"No! They... they died!" Gina whispered. "I am so sorry."

The voicemail went on. "I'm trying to visit tonight, Gina. Ghosts really can visit Winthrop—just like the legends say. But for some reason ghosts can't appear at our house. There's a woman here who used to be in IT and she figured out a way for me to leave this message and tell you another place to meet. Your mom's phone doesn't answer, but I got you! So how about we all meet up at Wolf Hill, where we used to go hiking? It's easy to—"

The call dropped. Gina stared at the phone, then pawed the screen frantically until she found the list of Recent Calls. She had to call her dad back. But his call had no number. Just the name: *Beyond.*

She quickly tapped Call Back. Her heart leapt as a phone rang, thin and reedy and far away. The number rang and rang, but no one answered. Was Dad expecting her to meet him at Wolf Hill?

Gina pulled on her parka and grabbed her cane. Leaving the basket of candies on the porch and the candle flickering in the pumpkin, she started for Wolf Hill. To avoid the trick-or-treaters crowding Main Street, and any chance she'd run into her uncle, she took the cobblestone road that wound through the town's historic mill district. The sounds of parties and people faded and the temperature dropped as she approached the slow-moving river and the old covered bridge. On the other side of the bridge Wolf Hill towered above the graveyard.

Gina took one step onto the rough wood planks of the bridge. Then she stopped. What if the boy who looked so much like Ethan came back to the house while she was gone? She hadn't been able to tell Dad that she, too, was searching for her mother and brother. Or, at least, for their ghosts. Maybe she should go back.

Then the sound of voices from the other side of the bridge caught her attention. A man. Maybe a woman. Were Dad and Mom waiting for her? She took a deep breath and hurried across. When she stepped out onto the moonlit roadway, the iron gates of the graveyard stood ajar. Thin granite headstones dating back to colonial times bent together, in twos and threes, as if in conversation. Elongated figures wafted among the stones like wisps of smoke from a dying fire. And, yes, there was a low murmur of conversation.

"Go home, Gina!" a man called out.

She peered into the darkness. She'd recognized the voice—it was her music teacher, Mr. Linn. He'd died from cancer three years ago.

"Go—" The cry cut off, just as a bank of clouds passed overhead, erasing the half-moon and throwing the roadway into darkness.

Gina panicked. *This was crazy.* In the dark, she could not begin to find the hiking trail. Could not even see Wolf Hill. She checked her phone: no signal here. What if Dad had called back?

Gina turned. The interior of the covered bridge was now blackness itself. She willed herself through, stumbling on the uneven planks and barely catching herself with her cane. She emerged, blinking, relieved to see the cobblestones lit by streetlights. Her heart rose at the sound of a dissonant tune—music drifting down from a party on Main Street.

She followed the wavering duet of violin and piano up the hill and into the center of town. It was nearly midnight, and the Halloween festivities were reaching their peak. Scents of sugar, chocolate, and singed pumpkin filled the air. Gina checked her phone again: She had a strong signal now, but there'd been no second call from her father.

In one of the candlelit mansions, shadows of whirling dancers flickered on the walls. Costumed revelers clustered on the porch, laughing. Gina recognized the house where her parents had gone dancing last Halloween. *How much had changed in a year.* She glanced down at the ugly orthopedic boots she wore now and swore, tasting salt tears on her dry lips.

"Gina?" A burly man in a pirate costume called from the porch of the mansion. "Gina? Is that you?"

Mike! Gina cursed as her uncle, in silver-buckled boots and an eye patch, hustled down the walkway.

"Just out for a walk," she said. Mike would be worried if he found out Gina had spent the evening at her family's old house, waiting for ghosts. Mike didn't believe in "all that ghost stuff."

"A *walk*?" Mike frowned. "By yourself? You told me you'd gone to the dance at the high school with friends." Her uncle looked around, as if Gina's friends were nearby.

Friends? Gina thought. Not anymore. Not since the accident. "Listen, Mike," she said. "I... I think got a phone call from my father's ghost."

"OK." Mike spoke slowly, the way you did when someone was ill.

"The voicemail was from 'Beyond.' He said he's trying to visit me but can't get here."

"Oh, Gina." Mike threw a glance back at the party, then pulled Gina into a hug. "I feel pretty bad about this. I should have known that Halloween would be tough for you kid. Look, I've had enough of this party. We'll go home. I'll make us some hot cider."

"No!" Gina pulled away. "I have to find Dad's ghost tonight. Because of the accident. Because," she took a deep, ragged breath and spoke the secret she'd kept for nearly a year. "Because—the night of the accident—*I* was the one who was driving. It was *my* fault that Mom and Dad and Ethan died."

"But your father was driving. It was in the papers. Gina, you're confused."

Gina backed away from her uncle. Closing her eyes, she saw the crumpled car, heard her father's voice. Her mother's screams. Remembered pulling her brother's lanky body from the back seat, then blacking out in the snow.

"They never asked me," she whispered. "I was unconscious in the hospital, and they just assumed Dad had been driving and when I was better...they never asked."

Mike caught her by the shoulders. "Gina, it was *not* your fault! The road was sheer ice! Three other cars went off that road that night!"

"I wasn't paying attention." Gina choked on a sob. "Because Mom and I were...we were fighting!"

"Gina, maybe it's better if those, ah, ghosts don't come. Not yet, at least. Maybe some other year..." Mike's voice faded.

Gina saw her uncle glancing back at the party, at his friends chatting on the porch. *Friends. Parties. Uncle Mike lived in another world.*

"Let me say good night to a few people," Mike said. "Stay right here. Wait for me. It will just take a minute." Mike ran up the steps and into the house.

As soon as he was inside, Gina hurried around the corner and headed for her family's old house. She'd wondered for months if telling someone the truth about the accident, about what really happened, would make her feel better. Or different. But now she'd told Uncle Mike, and nothing had changed. Nothing at all. Nothing would change until she saw Mom and Dad and Ethan again.

Gina arrived at the house to find the candle guttering in the pumpkin and the trick-or-treaters long gone. A few peanut-butter bars were all that remained in the basket. She was fumbling with her keys when a man in a Colonial militia costume, a bandage wrapped around his head, shouted at her from the street. Another drunk partier, she supposed. It was getting late. She jiggled the key in the lock, relieved when it finally turned and the door swung in and she could slip inside.

"Your house stands warded against spirits and revenants, mistress," the man called. "We cannot enter there."

She turned and saw the soldier's ghost fading away. And just down the street, on the bench beneath the streetlight, she spotted the boy in the brown fedora. *Ethan!*

Gina limped back down the steps. The boy stood up, but this time, instead of running away, he waved to her. She crossed the street to him. He wore a smile this time—but it was sad and twisted. He looked older than Ethan—did ghosts age? "Ethan?"

The boy nodded. "Yeah," he said. "It's me. Mom misses you, Gina. She's really sorry about the fight. And... we can't find Dad. Is he still here, with you? The house...it looks kind of empty. And for some reason, I can't walk up the steps."

"Dad called tonight," she said. "His ghost, I mean. He's over there, with you guys, but he says he can't find *you*."

Ethan's ghost looked up at her with huge, dark eyes. She hadn't realized ghosts could cry. She pulled him, cold and bony, into her arms.

"Watch out, Gina," he whispered. "If you leave with me tonight, you won't be able to come back."

"I don't want to," she said. "I just want to see Mom. And find Dad."

As the bells of Winthrop tolled midnight, she felt a small, cold hand slip into hers. The ghost led her around the corner, through the park, and into another world.

Holiday Leftovers

The Santas

David F. Shultz

Jacob stood in the pale glow of the tinseled tree. Christmas Eve. A time when the loneliest among us, in the quiet solitude of their homes, can reflect on their emptiness.

A blizzard outside. Cold as death. It was like this when the officers came to Jacob's door. Their words were a blur. Something about a transport truck, and a slippery highway, and how the paramedics did everything they could. Either Jacob asked about it, or they offered, but he didn't need to identify the bodies. Or he wouldn't want to. Then he thought of the strawberry-rhubarb jam his grandma used to make at Christmas.

He gripped the wooden rail of his stairway. Coloured lights wound along its length. They glowed like nothing had changed, mockingly oblivious. Stockings hung lifeless over an empty fireplace, quiet and somber. And Jacob realised how meaningless the holiday really was.

He found himself in the bathroom. The bathtub was full, ready. There was his straight razor on the counter, ready, only ever used once. He'd bled everywhere. "Not yet," he said. "Advil first".

One Advil, two Advil, three Advil, four. Five Advil, six Advil, seven Advil, more. And the caps and bottles floated like little boats on the bathwater. Then the lights went out in the bathroom, and the background hum of the house went dead.

"God damnit," Jacob said. A powerout in the middle of a fucking blizzard, he thought. I'll freeze to death! "Christ

65

almighty," he muttered, then fumbled through the dark house.

Jacob put on pajamas. He lit the fireplace, grabbed a blanket, and bundled on the couch next to the fire. Then he went to sleep.

Jacob awoke to a creaking floorboard. A gangly silhouette stood in front of the fireplace. The figure turned its head slowly towards him. In the flicker of the dying fire, Jacob saw a sickly-green face with a strange rash.

"I know when you're awake," the man said in a raspy voice, then snickered.

Jacob screamed, and the man scrambled away. Wet footsteps slapped the floor towards the stairs. Emboldened by the stranger's retreat, Jacob leapt from the couch, grabbed a fire poker, and pursued.

"Come here, ya bastard," Jacob yelled. Jacob nearly slipped on the slick floorboards. Then he heard a loud thud, and a groan. There was the man, no longer fleeing, but curled in the darkness at the base of the stairs. Tripped on the cord of the Christmas lights.

Jacob approached slowly. "Who the hell are you?"

"I'm Santa—"

"Don't fucking tell me you're Santa Claus."

"Santa Claus?" said the man. "That fat asshole? No, I'm Santa Murggis."

And just then, the power came back on. The skinny stranger was lit by the glow of a hundred coloured lights. He wore something like a Santa Claus costume, but blue and green instead of the usual red and white. His face had green scales, like a fish, two holes in place of a nose, and enormous yellow eyes.

"Are you just gonna stand there," the creature said, "or are you going to help me with these lights?" It fumbled with the cord caught around its leg.

"What are you?" Jacob said.

"I just told you. I'm Santa-fucking-Murggis." Then he stood, drops falling from his sopping costume. "You weren't expecting Claus, or you wouldn't have lit the fire, am I right?"

"I wasn't expecting anyone."

"Well, here I am. Now are we gonna do this, or what?"

"Do what?"

"What do you think? You're the one who summoned me."

"What in God's name are you talking about?"

Santa Murggis sighed. "Santa Claus comes to give presents to good kids, right?"

"Right."

"And Santa Piotr comes to give coal to bad kids, right?"

"I thought that was Santa Claus."

"You don't even know about Piotr? What are they teaching in schools these days?"

Jacob shrugged, still wielding the fire poker like a baseball bat.

"You mind putting that thing away?" Murggis said.

"Not until you tell me what you're doing in my house."

"Why don't I just show you?" Then Murggis started slowly up the stairs. "Come on."

Jacob followed with fire poker raised. "Where the hell do you think you're going?"

"Everyone knows about Claus," Murggis said. "Stockings by the fireplace, milk and cookies, all that shit. But they never teach you about the other Santas."

"Other Santas?"

"Like Santa Piotr. And Santa Tobias. And me."

"Santa Murggis."

"You remembered," Murggis said with a grin, and made his way into the bathroom. He motioned to the bathtub, full of water. "Claus uses chimneys. I use the bath. So of course you understand, when we saw the chimney was lit and the tub was full, we thought it was my turn."

"I don't know what to tell you. I don't believe in Santa Claus, and I've never even heard of you. I wasn't trying to invite you in."

"Well, I'm here now." Murggis dipped his hand into the water. "So you want your gift or not?"

Jacob shuddered at the thought of what sort of gift this freakshow might have in mind. "I'll pass."

Murggis squinted his big yellow eyes. "We Santas have a sort of power-sharing agreement, you know. Division of responsibilities and such. Claus gets the good kids. Piotr gets the bad kids." Murggis waited awkwardly for his prompt.

"And you?"

"Single adults with suicidal ideation."

"You get a lot of work?"

"Not as much as Claus. But it's still busy this time of year. Anyway, Claus has his bag of gifts. Stupid toys and bullshit, because he's got to deal with kids. But me, I give the gift of clairaudience."

Jacob stared blankly.

"It means," Murggis said, "that I can let you hear things from the spirit world. Like, for instance, your family. You want to hear from them, don't you?"

Jacob lowered his poker.

Murggis swirled the water. It bubbled. Then Jacob thought he heard, from somewhere in the gurgling water, the faintest trace of a voice. No words, just a distorted murmuring.

"Sorry," said Murggis. "That doesn't sound quite right."

"It's them," Jacob said. It was unmistakable now, even without words. His wife and daughter. Their voices bubbled up from the tub.

"But no words," Murggis said. "No, no. This isn't right. You deserve better, don't you? You should get to talk to them. Come. Come with me and we'll fix this."

"Come with you where?"

"To my workshop," Murggis said. "Through the tub." Then he grabbed Jacob by the wrist with a cold and wet clamp of reptilian fingers.

Jacob yanked his arm away and lifted the poker. "Don't touch me, you creepy shit."

"I'm creepy? What about Claus? He's the one who 'sees you when you're sleeping'. Why would he watch you while you're sleeping? Can't be to figure out if you're good or bad, now could it? That's creepy if you ask me."

"You really have it in for Claus, don't you?"

"He gets all the credit," Murggis said. "Sorry I got so upset about it. I just want to do my part, you know? And then the water didn't work, and you didn't get to talk to your family. I just want to make it right. So what do you say? Will you go with me?"

"Into the tub?"

"It's like a magic sleigh. Just a little more wet. And no reindeer."

"You first."

"Of course," Murggis said, and splashed into the tub. "Room for one more. Then we can get you in touch with your family."

Jacob thought about his family, how he would do anything for just one more minute with them. Maybe even get in a bathtub with Murggis. And besides, what did he have to lose? So he joined Murggis in the tub, cold water soaking into his pajamas, with the two of them facing each other, and Murggis grinning widely.

"Here we go," Murggis said, and the walls of the house melted away like waterfalls. A blur of coloured lights raced by faster and faster, and suddenly stopped.

They were in the middle of a cave with smooth polished walls, brightly lit with coloured lanterns. A large wooden table spanned the room, surrounded by strange people. Jacob recognized only Santa Claus, the white-bearded fat man in the red suit. But there were many others there. In a green suit, a purple skinned newt-faced man. In a yellow suit, an apparent burn-victim. And all the other Santas, staring at Jacob in the tub.

"You brought him here?" roared an enormous yeti Santa in an orange suit.

"My gift wasn't working," Murggis said.

"Murggis, Murggis, Murggis," said the newt Santa, "when will you pull it together?"

"Ho, ho, ho," said Claus.

"Now's not the time," Murggis said. "Are you going to help me or not?"

The Santas looked at each other.

"Alright then." An impish Santa in brown hopped from his seat. "Let's figure this out." He walked over to the tub and put his ear to the water. It bubbled and gurgled, and hummed. The imp nodded at the sound. "So your family's all dead, right?"

The bluntness caught Jacob by surprise.

"Yeah," Murggis answered for Jacob. "On the way home from Christmas shopping."

"Ho, ho, ho," said Claus. "Merry Christmas." And the other Santas laughed.

"Yes, yes," said the imp, "but how?"

"Car accident," Jacob said.

"I see, I see," said the imp. "And how long did it take them to die?"

"Instantaneous," Jacob said. That's what the officers had told him.

"No, no, I don't think so," said the imp. "That's not how water-talking works. They get to use their voice from before their death. They must have been alive for at least a few minutes."

Then Jacob heard the murmuring again. The distorted, tortured gurgling of the bubbles in the water. And he felt a stabbing pain, like his intestines were being eaten from the inside.

"Jacob," Murggis said, and hopped out of the tub. "Are you okay?"

Jacob sat alone in the tub. The water was filling with brown and red, leaking from Jacob's body.

"You're shitting blood, man," Murggis said. "How much Advil did you take?"

"Eight or nine," Jacob said. And he clutched his gut.

"Eight or nine pills won't do it," Murggis said. Then he turned to the other Santas. "He's still mine."

"Bottles," Jacob said. "Eight or nine bottles."

The Santas murmured to each other. Then a white-robed Santa stood. He had translucent flesh, giving a clear view to organs and bones.

"This one is mine," the translucent Santa said.

Murggis looked at Jacob. "Sorry, buddy. He's right. I only deal with people who fuck up their suicide attempts. Santa Sephtis will take over from here."

Jacob could only groan as the pain intensified. Sephtis loomed over him.

"Are you ready for your gift?" Santa Sephtis said.

"No," Jacob said.

Sephtis placed slimy hands on Jacob's head. "I will send you now to see your family." Jacob thought of the strawberry-rhubard jam his grandma used to make at Christmas. Then Sephtis pushed his head below the water.

Earth Day

David Sklar

from the collected works of Kaia MareImbrium

Everyone's wearing green today, or blue,
and some have long-haired wigs; I'm not sure why.
A paper dragon winds through the parade
with plastic face and fifty human legs,
and bells and whistles sound throughout the crowd,
and once or twice a personal alarm.

I do not share their mood, or understand;
it feels more like a battle, like a war,
and I make my escape the best I can,
past the Starbucks booth—as if you couldn't find
their stores on every corner of the street.
"All water synthesized on premises"
their signs say, even when, as in this booth,
it's patently untrue. I buy a cup
and struggle like a salmon through the crowd
(I've never seen a salmon, and, you know,
most people haven't—but the phrase remains),
and when the press of bodies is too much
the aroma of my coffee gives me strength,
the rippled cardboard holder in my hand
restores my balance through my fingertips,
and I escape. The crowd is now behind.

Holiday Leftovers

I hear their cheers, their clatter, and their sirens,
but like a distant thunder. I can breathe.

I make my way. The skylights will be packed
with tourists on the observation decks;
I do not even bother going there
but take the long walk to the outer rim.
The taxis stop for me; I wave them on,
the rickshaw bikers too; I let them pass,
a drunken stranger coming from a bar
says "Hey baby." I fix him with my eye.
He stumbles, hesitates, then steps aside.

I walk until I reach the Eastern Gate
and there I rent a suit and go outside
(my own's in storage back at the hotel).
It's quiet now—for the first time today.
I'm not the only one; there's people here
in scattered tiny groups, and some alone,
their glass-domed faces gazing at the sky.
I follow where they look and pick her out,
with naked eye for the first time this year,
the reason for the fireworks inside,
that blue-green pinprick, mother of us all,
the place where water falls out of the sky,
and you could even drink it, long ago.
Where ancients wondered, once upon a time,
if there was water here, because they saw
the long canals carved out by Martian winds.

I wish I could go back in time and say,
"Stay home, protect the water that you have;
there's nothing here but tourist traps and noise."

I breathe a heavy sigh, not even worried
about the cost of air. I wander out
and walk the planet's surface by myself
past honeymooners walking hand in hand,

past glass-roofed buses with their lights all out,
past a circle of neo-Druids in heavy cloaks
over their suits, dark green against red ground.

I walk until I cannot see the crowd,
a mound conceals the lighting from the dome,
I see a woman sitting there, alone.
I find her channel and I say hello.
She crackles back across my intercom.
"It's strange," she says. "I'm red-green color blind,
so all this Martian rock you see around
to me looks just like photographs of Earth,
but I can feel the difference in my bones.

"I wonder—long ago—what it was like
to walk in open sky and breathe the air
in forests that had grown there on their own."

"I know," I say, and gaze up at the Earth.
"I wonder what it's like to have a home."

And we sat there and watched the Earth together
all night, until my oxygen ran low
(cheap, rented suit) and we went back inside
and found ourselves an all-night coffee house
with hydroponic wood on all the walls
and shared a plate of fries, and talked about
our pasts, our plans, our hopes, our obligations,
and as the early customers filed in
we paid our check and went out on the street,
climbed up the metal stairs to the nearest skylight,
stepped over people camped out on the platform,
and watched the sun rise as the sleepers stirred.

And that was Earth Day. She went to her job
and I back to my room in the hotel
and lay in bed and stared up at the ceiling,
engrossed in thought, and crazy with fatigue:

Holiday Leftovers

When all we have is crafted by machines,
to find a friend's the closest thing to home.

Dreaming War

Marisca Pichette

We were wolves, once.

I walk across the fields that abut the mountains' feet, feeling the hardness of the ground where my ancestors once hunted with claws and teeth. A winter separates that age from ours, the time of fur and packs as distant as the Shornbacks' territory far to the south. My harvest from the day is strapped to my back, a basket of potatoes coated in coal-black soil, smelling still strongly of the earth.

Tonight the moon is like a cat's pupil, its slivered black gaze watching from above, iris pocked and white. As I near our village I drop onto all fours, quickening my pace, heading for the light of the fires.

Our village grows from the mountains at its back, rocks tumbling down into caves and pillars carved with stories that glow when the moon finds them. In the light of the night wolves dance, wolves hunt.

We do not dance anymore. We do not hunt. Looking at the pillars reaching up into the night, I wonder—not for the first time—what it was like to live before the winter that spanned a millennium. A winter that changed us from what we once were into something more, and less.

I trot past our village's gate and into the fire's warmth. In the soft blue light emanating from the pillars I see Grandmother sitting with my brothers near the center of the village. I drop my basket onto the hard-packed soil and it leans, coming to a rest against the base of one of the pillars.

Black soil colors the grey-blue ground like storm clouds over a twilight sky.

Grandmother looks up as I approach. She is balding, the hair that was once thick retreating from her limbs in shreds of grey and white. I enter the ring of light that holds her along with my two brothers, Mais and Horj. Grandmother pauses in the story she was telling before I arrived and waits until I am crouching beside them. Smoke in my nose smothering all other scents, Grandmother tells us of our ancestors.

"We grew from pups. Our teeth were longer, sharper, honed each time we tracked a prey to its end." Grandmother spreads her arms, skin hanging diaphanous from her thin frame. Her eyes glitter yellow in the firelight. "Our ancestors knew every track in the dust," she says, "every pebble on the lake's shore."

Grandmother pauses, and I think about how we have changed. I can smell better than a Shornback, and run faster, too. But the purity of what we once were has been lost to time.

There is no longer a lake between our civilization and the Shornbacks' territory in the south. Where our ancestors prowled around black waters there is now a trench of barren soil. Not even potatoes can grow there. And on the other side—Shornbacks.

My gaze wanders to the pillars shining around us. Along with the once-hunt they depict the war that came before the winter. Wolves not chasing, but being chased across stone, pursued by Shornbacks bearing axes, wearing wolfskins.

The outcome of the war was never decided. Instead the world shook, cracked open and filled the sky with smoke as black as soil. And the winter came. We fled to the mountains and learned to live on fungus instead of meat. Over the centuries, our bodies changed.

"Siku," Grandmother says, her voice the sound of wind in grass. I pull my gaze from the pillar and look into her wrinkled face. "You are thinking about the winter's end," she murmurs.

I nod and look down at my feet, not so different from a Shornback's. When the winter ended and our people emerged, they thought the Shornbacks would not have survived the long winter. But they did.

Grandmother nods. She tilts her snout to the moon. "And so the war continues."

Grandmother stands, her body moving smoothly despite her age. She lopes away, leaving us circled around the dying fire, exchanging looks that say nothing. I turn my eyes to the moon.

Ama is the name Mother gave to the moon. It has always captured me, the slit that grows and grows but never fills. Ama swings between brightness, a black disc the center of its pendulum path. On one end, it fills until it is a hair away from total revelation. On the other, it is a sliver of light pushed to the edge of a shadow world.

I have never seen it fill all the way. We sleep when the moon completes itself, when the spirits rise. When the wolves come back to hunt.

Tonight is the apex, the night before Ama completes its cycle. I rub my arms, flattening the hairs that stand on-end in the cold.

A restlessness chews at me as I stand and follow my brothers to our cave. For the first time, I feel a strong urge to run—away from the village, away from the mountains. I want to run all the way across the miles of open land that separate our civilization from the Shornbacks'. And at the end of that journey—what will I find?

I pause at the cave mouth and turn back to the night. Tomorrow, the ancestors continue the war that no winter, no death can stop.

"Siku," Mais calls from inside our cave. "Come inside. The blessing will not come if you are out here all night."

The blessing. My stomach flutters. It has been a month since we last tasted meat. Tomorrow's feast brings me back from the edge, and I turn away from the fires and retreat into darkness, to sleep.

~~~

But I do not sleep for long. After what feels like only a minute, my eyes open. While my brothers are resting, I roll onto all fours, and run.

Down the mountain's foot, skirting the edge of the village cloaked in the smoke of dying fires, the pillars gleaming blue beacons in the dark. I run past them, my shadow leading me south. I run faster than I've ever run, ignoring the scrapes of rocks on my hands, the scrabbling of my toes each time I slip.

As the village fades behind me, I hear them.

Howls fill the night and suddenly I am singing with the ancestors, singing a song of war. I run, the mountains shrinking behind me, the night cast in the glow of the near-full body of the moon.

But no. When I look up, Ama is a perfect sphere, a face bone-white and deadly. A mask of war.

When I look ahead, my shadow is no longer visible. Wolves made of moonlight run ahead of me, a pack of beauty and determination lighting my way.

I do not know how long or how far we ran together before the horizon flares with fire. The ancestors howl and I howl with them, my own voice unfamiliar in this altered world. The fire on the horizon brightens as we enter a territory as different from us as Ama is from the sun.

A crack splits across the night. The Shornbacks have seen us coming.

~~~

Morning. I twitch, the echo of a scream cut off as sleep leaves me. Someone is moving nearby, speaking with my brother's voice. I stir and open my eyes to find myself on my mat in my cave. Was it a dream?

"Siku, get up," Mais calls. "It is starting."

I roll onto my side, the images from last night flying away from me. I gasp as I try to stand, my legs quivering. I struggle upright, flexing my shoulders and wincing at the way they pull under my skin. If what I experienced was a dream, it afforded me no rest.

I walk shakily behind my brothers down to the village. A large fire blazes in the blessing pit and Grandmother is singing, her chin raised, her teeth blunt and bared. I look at her, and then my eyes wander to the struts suspended over the fire, their burdens shining in the sun. At the sight of them, I am not exhilarated as I usually am, when this monthly blessing comes. Instead all I hear is dream howling, and my muscles ache.

The Shornbacks hang from skinny ankles, their hairless arms limp and stiff above their heads. The ancestors have gifted us ten of the creatures, their throats emptied of blood, their entrails piled by the fire. Grandmother circles the offering, her claws unsheathed and translucent in the sunrise.

"The war continues," she chants, her voice dipping in and out of a growl, "and our ancestors are victorious. Siku!"

I jump at my name. Grandmother turns to me, her lips still peeled back. She raises her arms and I mimic her, my shoulders aching with the action. When I look up at my hands, my claws are not translucent, but stained red.

"Siku," Grandmother calls, her declaration buoyed by the wind. "You are now Siku Kali. You have joined the ancestors in dream-war, and you have triumphed at their side.

"The wolves live on inside you."

The ancestors run across moonlit grass. Their phantasmal howls echo in my mind.

We remember the wolves, and they remember us.

Holiday Leftovers

Boughs of Holly

Jenna Hanchey

She hovered over the deep green leaves before deftly pricking her finger on a spiked edge. Turning it over, she found only emptiness where blood once welled. Sighing, she lifted the heavy sack and continued her ordeal. She had known, before, why the leaves were so important, what the lack of blood meant. But the repetitions of menial labor—lifting, carrying, climbing, driving, lifting again—had worn her mind smooth, and the memories, unable to catch on anything, slipped away into the darkness.

She knew it had something to do with this body, this cursed, round, hairy body. Male, obscenely. White with years she didn't remember. Heavy with food she never tasted. Others ate the cookies, of course. They weren't part of her punishment. She knew the body was, vaguely. Something about her vanity, her rapacity. She felt flickers of her old self in the deep green of the holly: reverberations of the color in fabrics, echoes of the word through extravagant halls. She could only ever catch the first, tantalizing, syllable: "Ho-," she sometimes said aloud, as the remainder of her name caught on her lips.

The more she grasped at the memories, the more quickly they fled. It was her penance. She could no longer feel the soft caress of luxuries, only their weight as she carried them for others. Never-ending toil, hauling gifts to house after house after house, year after year after year. She trudged back to the sleigh slowly, shivering in the cold of hell.

Dear S.

Pat O'Malley

It was beginning to look a lot like Christmas at Pitts Creek trailer park. In a mobile home, further down the weed-ridden fence of the park, an assorted arrangement of grime-covered decorations hung lazily around on the oval frame of Trailer 37E. They had been there since the previous Christmas. The wreath on the trailer door was an ugly decaying brown and the plastic snowmen and Santa Claus, were filthy from a year's worth of rain damage.

Inside Trailer 37E, in front of a three-foot Christmas tree of fading health, Dylan, a nine-year-old chubby boy with curly red hair held a sheet of loose-leaf paper with a bright smile on his face.

"I finished my letter to Santa!" the boy said happily.

"Shut the fuck up." The crushed empty beer can narrowly missed the boy's head, crashing into the wall with a metal clang.

Travis, a thirty-five-year-old gas station attendant, was the latest in a long line of suitors for Dylan's mother Sabrina. Balding with long hair on the sides with a beard and potbelly, he sat in the stained EZ-Boy chair in the center of the trailer. A half-spent cigarette sat smoking in one hand while another hand rested on his growing paunch.

"What'd you say, Dylan?" his mother, Sabrina asked groggily as she emerged from the bathroom.

Her eyes were dazed. She was a small, curvy woman with disheveled auburn colored hair. A blue sweatshirt with

WEST VIRGINIA UNIVERSITY printed on the front hugged her torso tightly.

"I wrote a letter to Santa. Now he'll know what I want for Christmas."

"Oh, um, that's nice I guess?"

"How the hell did you write something? You can't read for shit," Travis growled.

Sabrina sighed. She learned a while ago that it was pointless to ask any of her boyfriends to be nice to Dylan. Whether it was the ginger hair, the baby fat, or maybe they all just hated being around their girlfriend's kid, none of them ever cottoned to her kid.

Still, Travis had a point: her awkward lump of a son wasn't doing well at school at all. His teachers at the public elementary school told her whenever she answered their calls that Dylan was in danger of repeating the third grade. The teachers kept repeating this word "dyslexia", or something like that, Sabrina hadn't been paying much attention. It meant that her son saw letters upside down or in the wrong order or something.

Just what the hell was she supposed to do, anyway? Weren't there pills for this kind of thing? Shit, she knew how to get pills. Anything to get this kid passed to the fourth grade.

It wasn't hard for her to see why her boyfriends or other kids at school disliked her son. A smelly, husky ginger kid who still believed in Santa made him the perfect bullying target for all the kids his age at school who outgrew Santa years ago.

She knew damn well that her son was a weirdo who slept with at least five stuffed animals in his bed. Even she was slowly beginning to resent him for being boyfriend repellent. More and more as the days went on, she swore to herself that she'd dump him on his father... as soon as she could figure out who he was.

"What's it say?" Travis asked with an evil smirk.

Happy to read his letter, Dylan's pudgy hands lifted the sheet to his face.

"Dear Santa, how are you? I am fine, school is still hard but I've been extra good with chores, being nice and everything else this year! If it's not too much trouble could you please bring me a puppy for Christmas? I'd give anything for one. Merry Christmas! Love, Dylan Farina. The End!"

Travis farted loudly. Even groggy, Sabrina couldn't keep from laughing.

Dylan frowned, his head sank.

"Sorry honey, but you know we can't afford to keep a dog."

"Christ, what a dumb ass," Travis snickered, cracking open another brew.

An hour later, Sabrina had taken her son with her to the local Community Center to get her Unemployment Benefits. She usually managed to get a slight raise in her unemployment check whenever she brought her son around to the Center. Who wouldn't feel bad about the strung-out looking woman dragging along her clueless-looking fat kid with her?

Alone in the trailer, Travis sat reclined in the EZ-Boy watching Family Feud. He went up to go take a piss and had made it halfway to the can before he spotted that little asshole's letter on the floor. Curious, he bent down and picked it up. It was obvious the tubby birth-defect had a serious reading and writing problem, always writing out letters backwards. Simple words like "CAT" come out looking like Chinese.

This time, however, from the jumbled-up letters on the dumb kid's letter to Santa came a bizarre surprise.

"Holy shit! Well God damn me how do you like that?" Travis laughed as he read the letter.

Well at least the brat had managed to spell the word "PUPPY" right but for fuck's sake, that stupid shit had spelled "dear" like "dera". Still, that's not what made Travis laugh the hardest. Let's just say the little water-head didn't spell Santa as "S-A-N-T-A." Oh no. From an outsider's perspective, it looked like a creepy crudely written child's letter invoking the powers of *another* man in red.

Travis could dig it. In his younger days, when he had more hair and less gut, he had gone through his own death metal/underworld phase to the eternal shame of his parents.

The tattoo of the Avenged Sevenfold skull with bat-wings logo on his arm could attest to that.

"This is way too perfect not to share." He took out his smartphone and snapped a picture of the letter.

An even better idea occurred to him. He pulled out and flicked open his Zippo. A lick of fire caught the corner of the letter as orange flames slowly crept up the paper. Travis laughed, dropping the paper to the floor. He took a few more photos as the corners of the sheet curled up in flames. Even amongst the blackening, charring paper, he could still make out the gist of the letter and the amusing misspelling.

"Now that is metal." Travis stepped on the smoldering ashes, mushing it into the carpet.

Maybe he'd post it on Reddit or show it to his buddies at the Hess Station. At least something finally cool came out of having a girlfriend with a kid, even if it was a freak accident. He was still chucking over the kid's learning disability when he finally made it to the bathroom and unzipped his pants.

A week later, it was Christmas morning. This year it was a white Christmas as over a foot of fresh snow stacked up outside in the trailer park. The merry sounds of holiday songs and Christmas movies drifted from the various mobile homes throughout the park.

Inside Dylan's trailer, his mother and her boyfriend were three sheets to the wind, laughing and snorting lines of Xanax on the surface of their phones. Their depravity was drowned out by Alvin and the Chipmunks "Christmas Don't Be Late" chirping from the small television.

Even with glowing rainbow lights, the sullen Christmas tree in the corner of the trailer had no luck in raising the holly jolly spirit in this sinkhole of a home.

In the center of it all, on the dirty, ashen floor sat Dylan. Plopped there in his red pajamas with white snowflakes and reindeer, made the boy resemble a sad Christmas stocking full of meatloaf. It was hard to believe that he had been so excited to wake up that morning. This wasn't the Christmas he had been expecting. All night he had dreamt of the moment he would see the yipping, happy puppy that Santa had left him.

To his heart-shattering disappointment, all he found that morning was an empty plate and glass where he had left extra milk and cookies for Santa. He looked down sadly at the only presents he had received: a couple of Hershey bars and three pairs of socks with Star Wars characters on them. Dylan had never seen any of those movies, but at least the socks were comfy.

The boy was confused, even more so than usual. This didn't make any sense. Wasn't Santa Claus supposed to bring you presents if you were nice? Didn't he get his letter? Travis said he dropped it off. Dylan wasn't mean and for the past year he made sure to help out with extra chores for his neighbors around the trailer park. Shouldn't that have made him worthy of being on the Nice List? How could this be? Unless...

"Sorry honey, but you know we can't afford to keep a dog."

No. He wouldn't even consider it. The problem must have been him. He had failed to prove his worthiness to Santa, so now he didn't get the puppy, that's all there was to it. All he could do now was spend the next year being extra, super-duper nice. Then, maybe next Christmas he would finally get the puppy he wanted and he would finally have his best friend. Trying to find comfort in the presents he had received, the boy began peeling away the wrapper to one of the candy bars, pulling the chocolate to his pudgy freckled face.

"Merry Christmas babe, Merry fucking Christmas," Travis sniffed, rubbing his nose.

He unwrapped one of the candy bars by Dylan and took a big bite.

"Hey, that's mine!" the boy whined.

"What's the matter, Scrooge McDuck? Haven't you ever heard that it's better to give than to receive? Plus it ain't like you're starving over there, fat boy." He smiled with chocolate smudged on his teeth.

"Mom!" Dylan turned a pleading look towards his Mother.

Her head was in her arms which rested on top of a stack of magazines and broken candy canes piled on the small kitchen counter. Raising her head groggily, she looked at Dylan, then Travis and just shrugged.

"Dylan, honey, why don't you fix Travis and me another drink?"

Resigned to a disappointing Christmas, the boy wobbled over to the liquor cabinet. He couldn't read the labels on the colorful amber and green bottles so he just started mixing whatever he could find. Neither adult noticed the tears rolling down his chubby red cheeks.

"Jesus wept, will you turn the heat down, Sabrina? I know it's snowing outside but it's starting to feel like a god damn furnace in here." The gas station attendant held a cold beer to his head.

"I know but I already turned off the heater," Sabrina said anxiously as sweat began to form on her pale brow.

Indeed, the temperature inside the trailer was beginning to rise. Dylan wobbled over to the trailer's window and couldn't believe his eyes. Only moments ago, there had been at least a foot of snow blanketing the trailer park. Now, that was all gone. While it was still snowing, the mounds of snow were rapidly melting, revealing the damp grass underneath. The sun wasn't anywhere to be found in the white blizzard sky.

"What the hell?" Travis stared dumbfounded, fanning himself with his hand.

Y-you see that too, right?" Sabrina grasped on to him, her pupils dilated.

"How is this possible? Even if someone's having a huge bonfire, it shouldn't cause this."

"Look!" Sabrina pointed out towards the window.

Outside in the melting snow, it looked like at least half a dozen of their neighbors were running away, fleeing from the park, hollering incoherently. Dylan turned his view towards the center of the park towards what everyone was running from and saw what looked like...was that a crater? While they had been "celebrating" Christmas, some kind of large crater had erupted in the center of the trailer park as though something had dug out from it. Now ungodly ripples of heat coming from it were overpowering the blizzard.

"What's happening? What are they running from?" Sabrina was growing increasingly hysterical; the pills hadn't been helping.

"Shut up. Just shut up for a second. I think a gas pipe must have burst or something, that's gotta be it."

Just then, there came a loud, insistent scratching sound at the door.

"Aw fuck me, what now?" Travis groaned.

"It's Santa! He came back because he forgot my puppy!" Dylan perked up immediately.

"Oh for the love of, Santa Claus isn't real you clod. It's obviously the Park Supervisor telling us to evacuate. Cheap bastard ruining our Christmas. Well, I'm going to rip him a new asshole. Ho Ho Ho." He turned towards the trailer door.

He had only taken a few steps towards the trailer's door when a vicious force blasted the door off its hinges. The flying claw-marked door narrowly missed the bearded pot-bellied man as everyone screamed and ducked for cover. The heat that had steadily been rising shot up to sweltering, furnace-like degrees while the rotten smell of brimstone filled the trailer. When Travis uncovered his eyes he saw what had been scratching on the door.

It was the last thing he would ever see.

"Holy-" but Travis couldn't even finish.

There was nothing holy here.

It wasn't a dog, not exactly. To human comprehension, it certainly *resembled* a dog, the way a wolf might. The visitor was the size of a motorcycle, a black snarling beast-shaped cloud. What passed for its lips shriveled back in the front revealing a row of sharp white fangs. It was a dark phantasm that stood on four legs but didn't touch the ground. Instead of paws, the legs of the creature seemed to fade away when they reached the ground, instead fluttering as wisps of some kind of horrifying charcoal mist.

Two glowing red eyes on the nightmare's face made eye contact with Travis. All he could do was listen helplessly as a haunting, ungodly howl filled his mind. In the span of a few seconds, Travis experienced every last drop of pain he had inflicted on others in the thirty-five years he had lived. He felt the pain and misery of every beating he gave his siblings growing up, every woman he had slapped and the torment he gave to others just because he could. So much cruelty and pain, Travis never would have cared but unfortunately for him, his heart grew three sizes that day.

"No," he begged.

Then his eyes burst into flame.

Travis started screaming. He turned to face Sabrina and Dylan as twin rockets of fire ignited from his eye sockets. Melted jelly of what used to be his eyes dribbled down his bearded face. It wasn't long before the screams stopped sounding human and turned into a high-pitched wail.

As he fell to the floor convulsing, the four-legged terror lunged at him. It made an awful roaring sound as it barked, like a thousand agitated pit-bulls eyeing a juicy steak.

In a ferocious chomping motion, razor-sharp teeth sank into Travis' jugular. The hound's snout pulled back and tore ribbons of gore from the blinded man. Travis' limbs flailed about as his screams turned into watery gurgles. A geyser of crimson blood splattered the wall of the trailer, some drops even getting on the small Christmas tree. The wolfish shadow tore and bit while Sabrina screamed, covering her eyes, while her son jumped and cheered.

"Awesome!" Dylan pumped his fist.

By now Travis was reduced to a vaguely human-shaped pile of carnage on the carpet. The hound pulled its snout from the pile of intestines and howled. It was an incomprehensible sound normally found in hurricanes and moments of uncompromising forces of nature. This was the sound you heard as you were being dragged screaming off into hell.

Mad with terror, Dylan's mother got up and ran screaming from the trailer, almost tripping over Travis' entrails as she did so. She flew past the carnivorous shadow dog, out through the hole it had created in her trailer. The beast's silver eyes darted in the fleeing woman's direction briefly before turning away as if due to lack of interest.

In a blind and drug-addled panic, Sabrina ran in a beeline straight through the warm grass. Her downfall came when she craned her inebriated head around to see if the monster was chasing after her. It wasn't, but she had been so concerned with getting as far away from the monster as possible that she didn't realize she was heading directly towards the crater. That brief moment of distraction was all it took for her to step over the edge of the dark pit and fall screaming all the way down.

Trying to ignore the fading echo of his mother's screams, Dylan walked over and turned up the volume on the blood sprayed television. Mariah Carey's "All I Want For Christmas Is You" filled the slaughterhouse known as Trailer 37E. He stared in fascinated awe as the hound fed amongst the cheap Christmas decorations. Without realizing it, he gulped anxiously.

The hound raised its intangible head and turned its gaze to Dylan. This time the red eyes weren't threatening, instead, they made the boy think of everything red that came with Christmas: candy canes, stockings and most of all, Santa's big red suit. It craned its head to one side then the other before it started making what sounded like a curious whining noise. Dylan's jaw dropped open as he saw what looked like a short tail wagging at the back of the wolf shaped shadow.

"It's okay I won't hurt you. C'mere boy or... girl?" The chubby kid smiled patting his large thighs.

The large, four-legged shadow slowly crept forward, appearing to sniff cautiously at the boy with what could have been a cold wet nose until it stood in front of him. Its tail continued wagged as Dylan began petting the waves of flowing black shadows along its side. He knew he was petting shadow but to the boy, it felt like he was touching warm black fur. The hound's jaw extended as a large pink forked tongue lolled out and began licking his face.

Dylan laughed happily as the dog licked him. He didn't even notice when he wiped bits of slobber away from his face that they burned and sizzled like hydrochloric acid once they hit the ground.

"I knew it! I knew Santa got my letter!"

Tail wagging, the hound phantasm barked as if it agreed.

"I never had a dog before, what should we do?" the boy pondered.

The hound made another whining sound as it pointed its snout towards the pile of gore in the corner.

"What's the matter, girl? Ohhh, I know!"

The ecstatic boy trotted over in his red pajamas and picked up a bloody severed forearm on the floor. The limb was hairy and had a faded tattoo of a large black skull with bat wings sticking out on the sides. Smiling, the young boy waved the arm in the air.

"You wanna fetch? Huh, do you?"

Another deep, bellowing yip came from the hound as ear-shaped points on the shadow's head perked up and it crept back to the boy. The hound's fangs carefully pulled Dylan up from the back of his pajama shirt and placed him on its back. Despite its wriggling, mist-like appearance, the boy had no problem sitting on what felt like a solid, furry back. Heavy snowflakes fell around them as the boy and his dog headed outside into the melted, trashed wonderland of the trailer park.

Out past the park's fence, where the snow hadn't quite melted yet, there came the faint but growing sound of police sirens.

"This is the best Christmas ever!" Dylan patted the hound as the long viper tail wagged back and forth behind him like hell's metronome.

A dozen flashing police cruisers and a large black S.W.A.T. van were parked haphazardly on the street. Officers ran towards the trailer with their weapons drawn but froze when they saw what they were up against. It was already bad enough that they had been dragged away from their families on Christmas, now the unrelenting force of hell itself stood before them, and it looked hungry.

Dylan heard them yell something at him but he was too excited about his new puppy to notice. Turning in the direction of the officers and their lights, the hound growled. It sounding like a motorcycle revving its engine as its back arched and prepared to lunge, fangs bared in anticipation.

There's nothing quite as pure as the excitement of a child on Christmas morning. In that very moment, with his family dead and his home in ruins, Dylan couldn't have been happier. He had gotten what he wanted for Christmas and it was even better than he could have hoped. Now it was time to have some fun. With all his strength, the boy threw the bloody arm as far as he could, straight into the air towards the red and blue lights.

"Go, long girl, fetch!"

Haunted

Gerri Leen

The ghost manifests in front of her
As she stands in the cemetery in Pomuch
His body sheds water, phantasmagorical sweat
The drops melting away to nothing
Where spectral meets tangible
He carries an obsidian knife, a compass
And the tools of his trade: spades and brushes
To sweep dirt off the ruins he spent his life unearthing
Brushes not terribly different than those
Used by the descendants of the Maya
In this cemetery, on this Dia de Los Muertos
To clean the bones of their familial dead

He roars at her but there's no sound
He reaches for her but can't grip
She killed him and he can do nothing
Except follow her around

An old woman eases bones from a box
Removing dusty cloth, layering in a new white one
Embroidered with reds and greens, yellows and pinks
She picks a bone, inspecting it, her face
A study in reverence, her brush strokes smooth
This task doesn't unnerve her
She'll do it every year, for this

Holiday Leftovers

Celebration of *Hanal Pixan*
The Maya day of the dead because those
Who aren't tended may walk, may...haunt
The way her father does her

He wanted to be obeyed, so she did what he told her
He wanted to keep the cache of codices *they* found a secret
Doling out the six dozen so *his* fame never died, but at what cost
To science, to those who studied the Maya—and to her?

So she pushed him into a cenote
She'll never forget his yelp of surprise
His doormat of a daughter
Daring to put an end to his reign of terror?
He died slowly, loudly: drowning isn't pretty
The guilt fresh even though it was five years ago
Because he won't leave her alone
Although his rage seems to ease with each visit
To the codices—all of them, in the hands of epigraphers
Who daily add to the store of knowledge
Even dead, he cares about that

Does he haunt her or does she hold him to her?
She let him disappear without a trace
She got away with it because she was known
For her devotion—foul play was never in question

It didn't hurt that she said he drank to excess
His bombastic temper was already known
Surly *and* drunkenly clumsy—such a tragedy
The jungle swallowed any trace of him just as it had
The Maya cities—she re-discovered the codices once enough time
passed
The ghost stabs at her, in one hand an obsidian dagger
His lucky stingray barb in the other: neither connect, of course
Does she wish they would? He never drank anything stronger than
the local
Cacao, thick and bitter, much like him—but what's one more lie?

Holiday Leftovers

Now she wanders the cemetery, where some graves sit untended
With room for him—she can dive the cenote, drag him up, hide his
bones here

The residents of Pomuch wait three years before bringing
Bones out to be cleaned and she's waited even longer
He could rest easy here among the Maya dead and
Maybe she'll let them both finally find some peace

Holiday Leftovers

Charles Edward Tuckett's Yuletide Message

Robert Bagnall

It was the second glass of wine that was making Charles Edward Tuckett reminisce. However, it was that self-same second glass that also meant he couldn't remember whether he had left a day later than planned, or whether the kit had arrived a day earlier than scheduled.

In his twilight years at the company, he'd felt quite proud to be one of the silver surfers, those with seniority who had taken, against type, to the new technology. He liked dropping his reading glasses onto his nose, squinting at the screen. The machines then had been comfortingly boxy, beige like the walls of his dentist. They whirred when they were first turned on, then beeped, and finally a flowing screen of runic code gave way to columns of icons on a reassuring blue background. Like the Wizard of Oz unwittingly revealing himself for a moment before pulling the curtain back around.

But what was on his desk that last day, his retirement day, was different. Like the waiting jaws of some creature, all contacts and connections laid bare. A 'docking station', he'd been told. For laptops. Detachable. For machines that came with you to meetings. He remembered looking at the 'docking station', like a horse eyeing a traction engine. It was at that moment he realized that he only liked the new technology as far as it could be tethered. After that he was no longer sure who was master and who was servant.

His mind flitted further back. When he'd joined the company it had been all paper forms typed in triplicate, carbon paper in between, filing cards in mahogany trays. He had thickened, slowed, grayed. There were now flaps of skin below the eyes of the face that stared back at him from the shaving mirror. He didn't know if he liked what he saw.

"I think I'll stop looking in mirrors," he said to his son-in-law across the table, over a candle shaped like a snowman, a natural continuation of his inner monologue but outwardly a propos of nothing.

"Is that why old men grow beards?" Jeffrey responded playfully. He'd had at least four glasses of shiraz.

Charles Edward Tuckett grunted as his daughter bustled in with the Christmas pudding, brandy-soaked flames flitting and flickering blue.

"Still doesn't explain why you all wear hats in cars," Jeffrey joked, himself wearing a ridiculous paper crown.

"Everything goes south." And, as the room lights came back on, Charles Edward Tuckett remembered again those bags under his eyes. Perhaps he should get surgery. He'd never thought he'd contemplate going under the knife. You think it's just narcissism, until you see the stranger staring back at you.

"You really shouldn't," Charles Edward Tuckett said, surprising even himself. "All this," and he waved a hand across the table.

"Why not, Dad? It's Christmas. Christmas is for family."

"You have Jeffrey's family. And work. That's more family than family."

Wendy paused, a spoonful of gluttonous pudding between dish and plate. "What do you mean?"

"You must have already had more Christmas dinners than you can stomach. And then you have to accommodate me."

Wendy poured cream. "But what you said about work being more like family than family?"

"Well, isn't it? I spent more time there than with you and your mother. Quality time. Daylight hours. You have a sense of purpose, a sense of achievement. Family doesn't give you that."

Wendy shrugged, exchanged a glance with Jeffrey. Two glasses of wine had made him melancholic. He hadn't meant to dampen the mood. "Forget it," he said, raising his glass.

"No, no," Jeffrey responded. "Charles has a point. Work makes you feel like you're alive for something. It's true that I don't mind how much time I spend there. I get things done. Things happen because of me. I like coming home to family, but because of what it's a contrast to. I'm still thinking about work at home. I'm not sure I'm thinking so much of home when I'm at work."

"We have good jobs," Wendy said. "It's not true for everybody."

"Even so."

"But what about when it's over?" Wendy wondered. "You come home to family. How often does work remember you? Family remembers you."

"Percival remembers," Charles Edward Tuckett said with gravity. "Wallace Percival. He was my manager, briefly. He became a vice president later, I understand. He remembers and calls me up every Christmas."

"That's nice," said Wendy breezily.

"You must have got on well," Jeffrey said.

"Reasonably, I suppose."

They chewed their pudding. Wendy related a story about their nieces, Jeffrey's nieces, strictly speaking. Jeffery was quiet, pondering. "You worked with him, you say, briefly?"

Charles Edward Tuckett dredged his mind. "A month, maybe three. He arrived to look after all of the south-east just before they restructured on product lines rather than by region."

"And he became a vice president?"

"He retired three, four years ago. Good twelve after me."

"And he phones you up?" Jeffrey was intrigued.

"Yes."

"Why?"

"To wish me Happy Christmas." Charles Edward Tuckett was conscious that he'd just spat pudding in his surprise.

"No. I mean, why you? You worked together for a few months out of a career of decades. There must be hundreds of people that he knew just as well or better."

"I suppose he rings lots of people over Christmas. My point was that I'm not forgotten." He waved his spoon for emphasis.

"I bet he rings at exactly the same time," Jeffrey said.

"Yes, he does. Bang on. Five past three, December the twenty-third. Every year."

"Do you find he can't quite recall past events? Or relate back to what you've talked about previously in the same conversation? Or to the previous conversation?"

What an odd line of questioning for the Christmas dinner-table. Charles Edward Tuckett considered. His son-in-law had a point. But what was he suggesting? That Percival had the beginnings of dementia?

"You don't think," "Forget it," Wendy and Jeffrey said over each other, exchanging looks. Charles Edward Tuckett looked from one to the other, his eyebrows knotting. There was a meaning here he wasn't quite grasping.

"It's just," Jeffrey began, sounding as if he was regretting the conversation's direction of travel. "It sounds very much like your Wallace Percival is a me-jah."

"A what?"

"A me-jah. A bot. A program that this Wallace Percival uses to make calls and put things online. It does his social media, so he doesn't have to."

Wendy put her hand across her father's. "It's not that big a deal. Lots of people use me-jahs. I do. Mainly to respond to people who tweet pictures of their dinner. But then, it's probably their me-jahs that put them up there to start with. We all do it." But the old man's shoulders had slumped.

"Look," Jeffrey said placatingly, "me-jahs work on the basis that they reproduce what you would do; they imitate you. If you're inclined to call up old acquaintances at Christmas, then your me-jah will do that. So, Wallace Percival's me-jah calls you up because that's what he'd do. More wine?"

Charles Edward Tuckett through he ought not but held his glass out anyway.

~~~

For ten years or so Charles Edward Tuckett had enjoyed his calls from Percival. At first, he'd been surprised, caught off guard, suspicious that Percival was meandering towards asking him for money, or inveigling him into some scheme. But that was not the case. It was just an old-fashioned Season's greeting; a throwback to when people cared.

But recently, come to think of it, it tended to be Charles Edward Tuckett downloading his review of the year. He had even become to enjoy looking forward to composing his monologues and ad-libs in advance. But he'd heard very little of Percival's year. Was that just because he, Tuckett, liked to talk, or was it because Percival's me-jah had at some point taken over?

He brooded on the subject, turning it over and over in his mind until New Year's Day. And then he phoned Percival.

"Wallace. Charles Tuckett. I enjoyed our chat the other day; thought I'd call and wish you Happy New Year."

The voice at the other end of the line gave away a degree of bemusement combined with pleasure at being the recipient of a call, even if wheels were clearly turning in placing the name. "Charles. Happy New Year to you."

"Wallace. I thought that I'd just correct something I said the last time we spoke."

"Charles, no need, social chit-chat."

"No. You remember what we spoke about last time?"

Wallace Percival paused, letting Charles Edward Tuckett fill in. "Wendy. My daughter. About her children." And he went on with an elaborate but ultimately banal story about his grandchildren, about their schools and their subjects, about their impending skiing holiday but the boy had twisted an ankle doing a paperchase—"Did you know they still did those, Wallace? I didn't. Thought they were Victorian"—and that the girl was worried whether the dog would be alright whilst they were away. "Do you recall all that, Wallace?"

"Well, I," Wallace Percival hedged. "Yes. Wendy. Jimmy and, what was it? Tabatha."

"I don't have grandchildren," Charles Edward Tuckett said coldly, common courtesy not being an issue when talking to machinery. "Wendy can't. Medical condition. She's barren. There is no Jimmy or Tabatha."

Silence.

"Charles?" asked Wallace Percival, confused.

"Happy New Year, Percival," Charles Edward Tuckett signed off brusquely.

~~~

Wallace Percival put the phone down slowly, carefully, like it may jump up and bite him if riled. He wasn't sure what to make of Tuckett's call. Although they had worked together for only a short time, he had always held him in high regard, made sure he had a contact number when Tuckett retired.

Perhaps he'd been drinking? No, Tuckett wasn't a drinker. But there was a haughtiness there, a disconnect Percival didn't get. Should he call him back? His hand hovered near the handset. He felt he should, but the path of least resistance got the better of him.

His children had suggested that he hand his calls over to a me-jah, but he'd never wanted that. Christmas was about connecting personally. In retirement Percival had built up an extensive network for nothing but the pleasure of human interaction. A good old traditional chinwag. That, and a background fear that his ever-increasing 'senior moments' presaged oncoming dementia, and that keeping mentally active was as good a medicine as anything else on offer.

But with each passing year Percival's Christmas call list began to look more and more demanding. He'd considered just sending cards, a round robin letter. His children had even suggested using something called a 'me-jah'. But that just wasn't the same and he was determined to hang on to what had become a tradition.

Still, with Tuckett off his list, that would be one less call to make, his burden lifted, albeit only marginally. Silver linings, and all that.

Tourists

Gerri Leen

The welcome center is light, bright
And round with no sharp edges to
Harm our newest angle-free visitors
But also it's to appeal to them: they and
Their ships are spherical; the tablets they use
Are round, so clearly they dig the shape
And yeah, we sucked up and built things
In their image, hoping they'd share
Important things like a cure for cancer and
How to reverse ecological devastation
But so far they've been taking what they want
From shops and eating for free, and they swim in
Any pool or fountain they can find, sinking
To the bottom like it's the first water they've
Seen in a while, sitting blissfully while a weird hum
Emanates and the water changes color—and smell
They leave their trash everywhere and their temporary
Settlements are starting to look way less temporary
They sure are having a good time with our stuff
And what the hell are we getting out of it?
People are growing restless; the government says to
Adjust expectations—but really, we're all getting
The feeling that other than being round
These visitors are acting pretty much like we would
If we'd found them first
Karma's a bitch

Red on White

Darren Todd

The snowflakes fattened, coming steady now. Farmer paced the dayroom, staring out the row of windows. Tinsel adorned the upper panes, fluttering in the air from the heater vents. The facility manager had decorated the drab walls with a cardboard Santa, snowmen, and elves. Classic Christmas music poured over the loudspeaker. *It's a Wonderful Life* played on the television.

All of these things failed to uplift Farmer's mood. He thought only of the pending dull ring of the missileer comm line inside the dispatcher's office. The snowfall all but guaranteed an alarm. His first Christmas away from home, and he'd spend it plodding around a missile site in the snow, looking for bogeymen. Even expecting the call, he jumped when the muted sound interrupted his thoughts five minutes later.

Like a Pavlovian dog, the sound sent chills through him despite the warmth of the dayroom. Not only would he miss the commander and the first sergeant coming around to serve Christmas dinner, he'd be freezing his ass off for nothing.

The dispatcher's voice came muffled from behind the steel door to his office. Conley bounded out of the computer room at a jog. He approached the dispatcher's door and peered in through the tiny window. Farmer joined him.

The dispatcher had stripped off his camouflage top, now wearing only a paper-thin cotton t-shirt. A cheap Santa cap sat askew on his head, worn seemingly with neither shame nor levity. He leaned back in his chair, phone held in place by a shoulder. Eventually, he looked at them, giving a thumbs-up and a quick nod of his head.

"Suit up, Farmer," Conley said and dove into a drab green duffel bag by the door.

Farmer's stomach sank. "We got an alarm?"

"Well, yeah, it seems that way."

They hustled, though everyone knew the culprit was the soft flakes collecting on top of an already substantial foundation of snow.

After Conley and Farmer donned their thermals, shirts, jackets, and headgear, they paused in the foyer between the station's lounge and the outside. The facility manager had plowed the day before, leaving huge piles of snow surrounding the buildings. Still, fresh powder already covered the blacktop. Conley hopped from foot to foot, staring at Farmer from underneath the hood of his Gore-Tex parka.

"We're gonna miss the dinner," Farmer said.

"Yep. Why don't you bring the truck around?" Conley said.

"I'm not supposed to drive."

Conley rolled his eyes. "I'll still drive, ya fool. Just bring it around."

Farmer sighed. "To warm it up, you mean."

"Well. You *are* the trainee, and I *am* the leader."

Farmer took the Bronco keys, zipped his parka to the top, and pulled the rim of the hood over his eyes, leaving only a couple of inches exposed.

Outside, the air felt dry and frigid. No wind yet, for which Farmer felt immeasurably grateful. The Montana climate proved challenging enough, but frequent high winds made adapting harder still. Even in the momentary calm, he was shivering by the time he reached the truck and threw his gear into the back. Already, numbness sank into his exposed flesh. His lungs replaced the hot, recycled air of the station with air so cold it burned.

Farmer unplugged the truck from the engine block heater, hopped in, and turned the ignition. He engaged the heat and defrost at their highest settings, which sent tiny ice particles into the cab, up the windshield, and over his head. They hit the roof and fell in imitation of the flakes outside.

The radio crackled, startling him. He lowered the volume, then keyed the mic to check the level.

"Get to movin'," came the dispatcher's voice over the radio. Farmer looked out the windshield to find him watching through a giant window.

Farmer pulled alongside the building. Conley had propped open the door with his gear and was puffing a cigarette inside the foyer, exhaling through the crack.

Farmer exited and circled around to the passenger side. Conley opened the back and loaded his duffel. He shouted around his cigarette. "You got your weapon?"

For a moment, Farmer thought he'd forgotten it, and panic seized him. But when he looked down into the plastic, U-shaped storage racks on the bed of the truck, he saw his M-16 resting there. "Yeah, I got it."

Conley deposited his butt into the fire engine red can outside the station and then pulled himself up into the driver's seat. The cab immediately filled with the smell of musty tobacco smoke.

Conley placed his own rifle into the rack, and they headed through the gate.

The sky shone a pale off-white. As they drove, flakes rushed at the windshield, reflecting the headlights and obscuring visibility. The ubiquitous triple-stranded barbed wire fences on both sides of the gravel roads acted as guideposts. Each road they took to the site lay covered with virgin snow.

When they neared the site, Farmer put on his flak vest, gas mask, and helmet, expecting he would be the one to perform the sector checks. They pulled up to the gate, and Farmer jumped out of the vehicle and moved around to the driver's side.

Conley threw him the handheld radio through the window, but Farmer missed it. The radio disappeared into the snow, leaving behind a light gray ghost in the snowbank. "Jesus, Farmer," Conley said.

"Nice throw."

Once he found the radio and keyed the mic to check that it still worked, Farmer approached the site. A high fence topped with razor wire surrounded the area. The only entrance was through a gate secured by thick chains and a Schlage lock.

Inside, Farmer called in his sectors, running from one part of the site to another in a tightening spiral pattern, checking the fresh powder for tracks. The wind kicked up as he cleared the last sector. The falling snow became less a nuisance than the loose powder already on the ground, which flew in Farmer's face.

Nearing the gate, he threw one more glance over his shoulder—nothing but miles of pale plains beyond the westward fence. Then he spotted something in the stark white. He blinked back the stinging wind, even kept his eyes shut for a few seconds, and looked again. For a while, nothing. Then it came once more—a red glow, like a tiny ball of crimson hovering somewhere in the alabaster. Bolstered by certainty now, he lifted the radio and engaged the button, the tonal beep overriding the whistle of the wind.

The glow disappeared. He saw movement, maybe, but could report nothing more specific. He released the button and the radio chirped. Jogging back to the entrance, he imagined the glow pursuing him, and kept turning to look. He circled the heavy chain around the gate and engaged the lock. He peered back toward the west but saw only the snow now. He shook his head. With the wind kicking up gusts of snow, the motion sensors would never reset, and he wanted away from there.

Farmer approached the vehicle and slung his rifle, winded and freezing. He locked eyes with Conley but said nothing. Customarily, whoever didn't sweep the sectors performed the required perimeter check along the outside of the fence. The site's north side faced a steep grade, which would make the walk-around bearish. Then there was that glow.

"Yeah, I'll do it," Conley said, soured. "Consider it your Christmas present." He shouldered his weapon, barrel down, and held out his gloved hand for the portable radio.

Ten minutes later, Conley returned.

"Anything?" Farmer asked.

Conley stared back him, shrugging finally. "Like what?"

They took turns hauling their gear to the back of the truck and stowing it in their duffels. Conley turned the truck around to face the access road, leaving whatever Farmer had seen at his back. He dropped his visor and checked the mirror, but the wind-whipped flakes obscured even the site gate twenty feet away.

While they waited for the sensors to reset, they listened to holiday tunes on the radio. Conley brought out a Ziploc of some dried meat and gnawed on it. Farmer flipped through a magazine but grew restless. He turned around to look behind them every few minutes.

"Staring at it ain't gonna make it reset, Farmer."

"Sorry."

Conley sighed. "You got family 'round here? This part of the country, I mean."

Farmer shook his head. "They're all back East. How about you?"

"Same. God knows why. My daddy's a hunter and a fisher, like me, like my brothers. I don't know how they can be satisfied with those little whitetail deer back home when they got mulies twice that size out here."

Farmer swallowed, turning toward the frigid glass of his window. "Seen anything else out here?"

Conley humphed. "What do you mean? Any action?"

Farmer shrugged. "Anything weird. In the snow. I mean, we're a hundred miles from civilization, so who knows?"

"You trying to scare me with some missile field ghost story? A newbie who hasn't even seen a whole year of this shit?"

Farmer shook his head. "Only wondering. You didn't come across anything on the walk-around? Nothing odd?"

Conley pulled out a pack of cigarettes from his sleeve pocket and put one of the sticks between his teeth. "Better luck next time, Farmer." He stepped out into the winter wind and smoked.

As night fell, the snowfall ceased. All hope of leaving darkened with the sky. Farmer worried less and less about the light in the snow. Just his imagination. Instead, his thoughts returned to how meaningless the holiday had become for him. He'd requested leave time to return home, but not only was he low man on the totem pole, his sergeant found it in bad form.

"A lot of these guys got wives at home. Kids, too. You'd rather they spend Christmas Day in the field so you can go back home to Mommy?"

Conley killed the site floodlights then turned off the Bronco headlights, putting the access road into total darkness. Then—as if the tiniest glow would disturb him—he dimmed the dash lights and even took off his watch-cap and stuffed it into the recess that housed the illuminated dash clock. He put his seat back a few inches and pulled down the hood of his parka.

He turned to Farmer. "Keep watch. I'll let you sleep later."

Farmer's stewing anxiety and disappointment had already exhausted him. There was no chance in hell anyone would come out to check on them, not tonight. They should both sleep, if he could. He shrugged at Conley. "We expecting trouble?"

"Don't get wise, Farmer. Leadership knows we're out here, Christmas or not. You start to nod off, spend a minute or two outside and you'll stay wide awake. Just try not to let all the heat out."

After twenty minutes, Farmer's head grew heavy and began to bob. He peered over at Conley, who either slept or lay so still that not a shadow moved. The only sound was the occasional gust and the subtle creaking of the truck's shocks thereafter.

Farmer opened the door slowly, slid out, and eased it shut. The air sought the tender flesh of his lungs like a parasite seeking a host. He coughed lightly, but grew used to it faster without the wind. He looked up to the stars, usually a canopy so packed with faraway gems that it illuminated the night with their collective glow. Tonight, the cloud cover kept all but a few bright shiners hidden.

Returning his gaze to Earth, he caught sight of a gleam in the distance. At least it seemed distant. He did a double take, then focused his full gaze upon it.

The same soft red glow he'd seen through the snow hours before now pierced the night air. It shone clearly one moment, hazy the next, without discernible edges or texture. All he knew for sure was that it did not come from a taillight or flashlight. It seemed natural, in fact. The undulating glow swelled to bright red—almost pink—before fading to nonexistence, only to start again a moment later. The waxing and waning was too smooth to be artificial, less turn signal than firefly.

Farmer was unable to reconcile the image, though something about it suggested life. Out of habit, he reached behind him for his weapon, but it was still nestled in the truck's rack. Getting it would mean rousing Conley.

Despite his fear, Farmer began to ease toward the anomaly. Every few feet, he stopped and stared, trying to figure out if the light moved. Perhaps it only seemed to move because the warmth of that glow clung to the back of his eyelids when he blinked.

As he neared, he thought he detected the sound of breathing. It seemed out of time with his own respiration. He stood still for a moment, eyes fixed on the glow, and held his breath.

For a few seconds, nothing. Then his body filled with adrenaline when he heard the distinct sound of an exhale. The glow bobbed up and down in time with the breaths. They grew louder, and the glow expanded.

A shape came into view when the glow peaked every few seconds. Farmer's heart increased its already frantic pace. His breathing came quick and erratic. Fear demanded that he run, but curiosity fixed his feet to the cold earth.

In the glow shone eyes like pools of dark water, reflecting the soft red light. Then a sound like someone walking through the snow, but heavier and yet more surefooted. It was animal. He fought back the fear of being attacked and the urge to scare it away, if he even could.

It was nearly upon him by the time he made any sense of it. The glow continued to throw him. It didn't belong in any logical sense, though it seemed fitting, even if he couldn't say why. The thing had horns of a sort, and a long head ending in nostrils that blew white plumes of vapor in steady rhythm.

Brown fur covered the animal from top of head to top of hooves, pocked with clumps of snow. It appeared thick and comfortable, like a favorite blanket.

Farmer knew little of wildlife. Enough to suggest that "deer" didn't quite work. "Elk" felt wrong as well, though both lived in Montana, denser than humans in some parts.

The light swelled and contracted over its face, but not until it took another step did subtler features emerge. Something on its flank glinted in the periodic light—a buckle. An ornate and ancient harness hugged the animal's chest and back, a slightly lighter brown against the fur. Redolent of an Old West gunslinger's belt, the rig held volumes more character than his own tack of plastic and nylon. It spoke of care and time, of precision and purpose. Someone long ago had spent countless hours working intricate detail into the leather, so that now it told a story, even if Farmer could only guess its meaning. It covered the animal's body like a second hide, moving with the rhythm of its breathing as if no more artificial than its broad antlers.

In those mirrored eyes—all but invisible when the glow faded, but bright and beckoning when the light peaked— Farmer found the same veneration. The animal aspect loomed, certainly, but behind that he felt something wiser and knowing. He stared long into those eyes, trying to decide how to feel, wondering if the night and the weather had addled his mind.

But then he began to form a connection. How had it remained subdued for so long? When this fantastical explanation surfaced, his initial reaction was to smile so broadly that his teeth soon grew cold from exposure. His eyes widened like a child's and his jaw slacked.

A name took center in his mind. A title that called up imagination and wonder. He wanted to speak it. The animal seemed to lean in, as if anticipating it.

And yet, Farmer considered the absurdity of it all. There he stood, seeing the incarnation of childhood fantasy not an arm's length away, but the logic and reason of his life intruded and continued to hedge out his wonderment.

The glow, the eyes, the breathing of the animal was communication of a sort, despite Farmer's inability to interpret it. He owed more in return than a listless simper.

He spoke, as much to ground the spectacle in reality as to communicate. "But if I believe in you," he said, his voice weak and dry, "then anything is possible."

The weight of this sank in, and he imagined the implications. Every story he'd ever heard as a child now feasible. Each tall tale now viable enough to have a place in a world working so hard to explain itself and make all things safe. Maybe there *were* fairies and giants and elves, if there was a....

"Rudolph," he said, finally.

The animal huffed and pawed at the snow. He moved his head down and up, as if satisfied that a formal introduction had been made.

"I'm Farmer," he said. "Well, Patrick, I guess. To you."

The reindeer inched closer, turning sideways, revealing himself to Farmer in full. He picked up the subtle smell of the animal, of earth and musk. The nose let out a soft hum as it went from a wet black to a blazing red.

The reindeer pushed his head closer still, so that Farmer's eyes were dazzled by the light, and he knew he was meant to touch him. Meant to receive this connection as a gift, one more important than any worldly object, or even any human bond he had made since stationed there.

He eased his hand out, though the reindeer showed no signs of distrust, and he gingerly put the pad of his middle finger to the nose when it waned. As it glowed again, Farmer tensed at the prospect of being burned, though he knew it created no heat. He stood so close, he would have felt it.

He ran his hand down the muzzle of the beast, feeling the fur both soft and unyielding. Being so close to the animal made Farmer warm and comfortable. Not like the artificial heat from the cab of the truck, but a truer, deeper warmth. He grew content with the cold, instead of simply existing within it.

In that moment, Farmer didn't want to leave the site at all. If not for their replacement crew coming to relieve them

113

sometime in the wee hours, he would stand there in the cold until daybreak.

And then his eyes slammed shut instinctively. Before the impulse could even register, a crack ripped through the night air. His training and rote muscle memory dropped him to one knee as he pulled a non-existent weapon to port arms. He opened his eyes to a hot spray across his face—slung over his eyes and nose and mouth as if choreographed, followed by a second crack. He blinked frantically, eyes stinging, then they refused to reopen.

He had time to form a single, horrid image: the reindeer's eyes wide and scared. His body, faltering in the snow, kicking up powder, looking for purchase to keep his knees from bucking. Mouth agape, white teeth and pink tongue spewing hot breath, emptying his lungs in a fume of rising vapor.

This image stayed in front of him while he wiped at his eyes with gloved hands cold and damp. The image became the still-frame for the terrible noises permeating the air. The reindeer bellowed over and over, a sound somewhere between a foghorn and a screaming child. In this, Farmer heard pain and fear above all. But there was something else—accusation, even anathema, as if the animal blamed Farmer for what was happening.

Through the pain, Farmer forced his eyes open and looked around.

"Out-fucking-standing!" Conley said. He marched over, rifle resting on his shoulder, the bright white glow of a flashlight coming off his harness.

Without another word, Conley slung his rifle, removed a long folding knife from his gear, and straddled the dying animal.

The reindeer now lay in the snow, gyrating up and down, clinging to life, but slipping nonetheless. Head slightly turned, he kept his eyes on Farmer—wide and sharp, knowing. His nose lit once more, but it was subtle and weak, only enough to seem a trick of the brain.

"Wait," Farmer shouted. "What are you—"

Ignoring him, Conley pulled the blade across the reindeer's throat, rending the flesh and spraying the snow with crimson, where it steamed. The animal made a final gasping rattle, and his nose retreated to a dark, fleshy color. His eyes rolled skyward, only now void of judgment and disdain.

"Man, this hoss is gonna make fine eatin'," Conley said, preparing the carcass further in practiced motions. The sound was that of plunging a toilet. "What the hell?" Conley barked, his hands on the harness. "Jeez-us. This is a goddamn petting zoo animal or somethin'."

"You don't know what you've done," Farmer told him. He vomited into the snow, the hot liquid melted the pristine white and exposed the frozen ground beneath.

"Christ, Farmer. Get a hold of yourself. It's just a reindeer." He cut away the great harness with some effort, his hacking motion causing the carcass to buck and loll. He inspected the leather in the beam of his flashlight for a moment, then tossed it into the snow. "He was about to attack you, right? I probably saved your life. Some asshole makes a stink about a missing reindeer, you remember that."

Farmer spat and spat, trying to catch his breath. "You don't understand."

"Oh, yeah. Right. Don't worry about the ammo. I keep some rounds in my backpack in case I gotta replace a few. I ain't sayin' I've shot at anything out here before, but I ain't denyin' it either."

"You killed him," Farmer mumbled.

Conley quit cutting and looked up at Farmer. "Your light's on," he said, pointing with the bloodied and dripping knife, which steamed as if alive.

Farmer reached to his harness, where his angle flashlight shined subtly red through a translucent lens. The beam went on and off in undulating projections of milky light.

"No," Farmer said. "This wasn't on. That's not what happened."

Conley grunted, still looking down. "How do you think I could see to take the shot, Farmer?" He looked up for an answer, received none, and just shook his head, returning to his work.

Holiday Leftovers

116

Distaff Day Dues

Brianna Malotke

The weeks leading up to Christmas
are filled with excitement, and such
joy and happiness, all of the little kids
eager for new clothing, new toys, and
any little gift from Old Saint Nick will
do when the holiday season is nearing.

The long winter days means extra work
for me – and all the other women in
town – and more energy focused on the
spinning of threads and yarns, sewing
the garments together, all of our daylight
hours are spent on these intricate pieces.

As soon as the clock strikes midnight,
the bell loudly ringing through town,
on Christmas Eve, ushering in the new
day for all to celebrate Christmas, it's
music to our ears, for all those who spin
wool have those next twelve days to rest.

While we rest our overworked and needle
pricked hands; we savor every moment
of silence, where the spindle remains
in the corner—lonely and collecting the
lightest covering of dust—until the seventh
day in the new year, when we must return.

And everyone avoids the spinsters, the
women who weave tall tales and whisper
about the fates of others, because while
the town may celebrate the Christian
holidays, we don't tempt Fate—and her
sisters—who hold the power, the scissors.

Travelers go missing, lost to the storms,
the truth, buried in their souls, the women
know that to keep their good fortune going,
they must make sacrifices during these
twelve long, wintery days, and blood is
shed in secret, away from the cozy homes.

Women—the powerful trio—spin threads,
weave yarns, and they decide when our
days are ultimately over, and for those twelve
days after Christmas, all the women in the
town rest, and secretly pay our dues, our
respects, to our dear Fates on Distaff Day.

Away In The Manger: A Christmas Tale of Horror

Tim Kane

"It's not even snowing," Marissa said, tapping on the car window. "Isn't that the point of living all the way up on bum-fuck mountain?"

Bill kept his gaze riveted to the road. The sleet poured down in wet globs, adding a sheen to the ribbon of asphalt.

"We deserve some snow for trekking out here," she added. "Instead, we get this sleety slush."

"It's Christmas," Bill said.

"Nope, tomorrow's Christmas."

Bill hunched his shoulders and concentrated on the curve up ahead.

"I could be at the Pearl Oyster enjoying a chocolate martini." She twirled a lock of black hair with one finger. "Maybe find a lonesome guy missing his family." She sighed and leaned her head against the glass but then jerked away. "Crap, that's cold."

As the Audi banked around the curve, the tires slid on the glossy road and kissed the rocky embankment. Bill cranked the wheel, veering away from the steep drop-off.

"Easy Tex. I'm still making payments," she said.

"Then you should have driven." He drew himself up over the steering wheel.

"Why? You're doing such a bang-up job."

"Gives you more time to bitch and moan," he murmured under his breath.

"Come again?"

The road leveled off, and he pried his gaze away. "Come on, Sis. It's Mom and Dad. We do this every year."

"I know. You'd think they'd give us at least one year off."

"It's Christmas."

She shook her head. "Not yet."

The sun sank behind the mountains fifteen minutes before the Audi turned onto the access road. The tires sloshed through the gravel ruts, now a soup of mud and ice. Bill pulled up behind the Lincoln Navigator parked in the drive and killed the headlights. The forest loomed like a black wall. The closest neighbor lived a mile down the road.

He peered through the windshield at the darkened house. "Well, the car's here."

"Maybe they're conserving electricity. Who knows." Marissa shoved open the passenger door. "Let's get this show moving. You grab the gifts."

She zipped up her parka and flipped up the hood.

"You could help me, you know," he said, eyeing the sleet still filtering through the tree branches.

"I love you, too." She winked and dashed out of the car.

She made a beeline for the courtyard. Even with the coat, she instinctively wrapped her arms around her shoulders. Once under the eave by the front door, she rang the bell, stomping her feet to remove the slush from her Kate Spades.

"Come on, Mom. Break away from the cookie baking for five seconds." She jabbed the doorbell three more times.

Bill popped the trunk and stepped out of the car. Even though the trees blocked most of the sleet, fat gobbets of half-frozen rain still dribbled onto his head. He tossed a scarf around his neck and trudged to the rear of the Audi. Marissa's three presents sat neatly arranged in an oversized Christmas bag, all looking far too festive to be her own shopping taste. His six presents fit like jigsaw pieces into a cardboard banker's box. Bill grabbed the lid and tried to cover his gifts, but the bottle of wine for Dad jutted up. He canted the cardboard lid sideways and propped the whole thing under one arm. With one finger, he hooked his sister's bag and then elbowed the trunk closed. He hustled past the courtyard wall and onto the stoop next to Marissa's bundled-up form.

"Quick, open the door," he said.

She raised her hands. "Houdini I am not." She grabbed the knob and shook it. The door rattled in its frame but stayed shut. "Did you remember your key?"

"No." He unloaded the bag and the box onto the stoop. The eave kept most of the sleet off the packages. "Don't they keep a spare somewhere?"

She smiled, opening her hands in gesture meant to say, "Be my guest."

"Some help you are."

"I didn't want to come, remember?"

He rolled his eyes and scanned the courtyard. Perhaps forty potted plants cluttered every conceivable nook. He ran his hands over his face. The key could be anywhere.

"Let me check the other doors."

"Knock yourself out," she said, leaning against the wall. "I'll wait here."

He flipped up the collar on his coat and disappeared around the side of the house. She began humming "Jingle Bells" and peered through the darkened window. Something crashed inside. It sounded like a plate shattering.

"Bill! Is that you?" she called through the window. "Hurry up, will you? It's freezing out here."

She stomped her feet once more, though the gesture didn't bring her any relief.

"Bill?"

"What?" The voice came from the courtyard. She spun around and saw her brother round the corner of the low wall.

"I went around the whole place," he said.

"Something broke inside. I thought it was you."

"Nope. All the doors are locked. Even the windows. I checked."

"Well, something fell over."

"It must be them." He rushed to the door, pounding. "Mom! Dad! Can you hear me?"

"Why not turn on a light?" she wondered.

"Maybe the power's out." He hammered on the door again. "Mom! Dad! It's Bill. Open the door!"

She flipped her hands up. "I say we call it a loss and head back."

"No, Mom and Dad could be hurt in there."

"Or they could be at a friend's house."

He glanced at the car. "The phone." He dashed toward the parked Audi.

Marissa watched as he sat in the driver's seat and dialed his cheap Samsung. No way was she diving back through the sleet for her iPhone.

She heard something scuttle across the wood floor just on the other side of the window. She wrinkled her forehead and leaned closer. As far as she knew, her parents didn't have any pets.

Then the phone rang inside, blotting out the sound. When the first ring abated, she leaned in again but heard nothing. After eight rings, the phone stopped as the call went to the machine. A glance toward Bill showed that he was leaving a suitably concerned message.

Marissa kissed two fingers, and touched them to the door. "Merry Christmas, Mom and Dad." She jogged back to the car and slid onto the passenger seat just as Bill ended the call.

"What are you doing?" he asked.

"They're not home," she said.

He stared at her, and she shrugged.

"What? I left the gifts. Let's go."

"We can't just leave."

"It's freezing, and I am not staying out here all night."

"But..." He glanced across the courtyard. "The gifts will get soaked."

"No, they'll be fine."

He stepped out of the car and plodded toward the front door.

She cracked open her door. "Just throw something over them."

He shouted back, "The door's open."

"Oh, for Chrissakes." She summoned up her courage and scurried through the sleet.

"Are you sure you checked the door?" he asked.

"Yes, I checked." She stomped her feet again. "Do you think I wanted to stand out in this muck?"

He twisted the doorknob, and the door creaked open. A gust of wind blew the rain in, spattering the wood floor.

"I swear it was locked."

Bill hefted up his box of presents. She stepped over her bag of gifts and entered the house. He frowned and curled a finger under the handle of her bag.

She flipped the light switch, and a scene of true Christmas splendor greeted her. The tree stood in the corner of the living room, festooned with ornaments and subdued lights.

"Wow," Marissa said. "Every year they get more of these things." She tapped the top of a crocheted Wise Man. "I swear they're breeding on their own."

Scenes of the nativity infested nearly every surface of the room. An embroidered pillow showed Joseph and Mary around the baby Jesus. Collages of Christmas cards depicting the nativity were framed and hung about the room. On every available flat surface sat a carved or cast version of that famous manger scene. There were versions of Joseph and Mary in ceramic, straw, and even crystallized salt.

Bill struggled through the door. "You want to help me?"

She plucked her bag from his outstretched hand.

"Hello?" she called as they walked down the hall to the dining room. "Mom? Dad?"

He elbowed the lights on and slid the box onto the table. She set her presents next to his and draped her parka over the back of a chair.

"Is that all you got them?" he asked.

She shrugged, scanning this room's nativity decorations. Some of the scenes looked like full villages of miniature people.

"Did you re-gift?"

She gave him a look, and the corner of her mouth hitched up. "Maybe."

He rolled his eyes and stepped into the kitchen.

"Listen, I'm not into all that Christiany stuff. Mom and Dad are. So why put them to waste?"

Propping the refrigerator door open, he reached behind the carton of eggnog for a can of V8.

"Unbelievable."

"Yeah, like you go to so much trouble." She flicked the bows on one of his packages. "I bet Sara bought those for you."

He popped the can and downed the contents. When he turned back, a frown crossed his lips.

"Ha!" She pointed an accusing finger. "Told you."

"Scrooge," he said.

"Grinch," she fired back.

He dumped the empty can in the trash and looked around. "Where are Mom and Dad?"

"Maybe they're really not here."

"I'm going to check upstairs."

He took the stairs two at a time. She could hear the floor creaking as he walked around up there.

She wandered toward the game room, but something crunched on the floor.

"Shit." She lifted her foot and glanced down. Too dark to see anything.

Marissa fumbled for the light, finally finding it and flicking it on. What was once a pool table sat drowned in half-finished baskets, strands of raffia, various thrown pots, and several painted nutcrackers shaped like soldiers.

She looked down and spotted the culprit — a tiny ceramic Wise Man, now shattered.

"Dammit."

She leaned down to retrieve the figure. The pieces around the arm flaked away to reveal a wire framework with miniature hinges. The rest of the porcelain looked cracked but managed to hold together.

A scan of the table revealed a new nativity scene next to a wooden box. All the figures looked like ceramic but had movable joints. A thin brass lever jutted out of the bottom of the manger. She pulled it, and the scene sprang to life. Baby Jesus sat up in his crib. Joseph and Mary bent forward under the roof of the manger. A pair of shepherds wiggled their crooks. The angel flapped its wings, and the two remaining Wise Men swiveled to face her.

"Cool."

After a moment, the scene wound down, and the figures sputtered into statues again. She inspected the crushed figurine. It seemed to fit next to the other Wise Men. She clicked it back into place.

"There."

Bill tromped down the steps. "They're not upstairs."

"You should check this out. Mom and Dad really outdid themselves this time."

He stepped into the game room. "Maybe they're not home."

"Yeah. What I said." She pulled the lever back, but nothing happened. A jiggle on the handle produced no movement. "There's got to be some way to... Aha!" She found a winding key on the side. Cranking it caused gears inside to click as the spring tightened.

"Maybe we should look in the bedrooms."

"Check this out."

"Since when have you been interested in nativity scenes?"

"This is cool. Just watch." She pulled the lever. At first, nothing happened; the figures remained still. Then Joseph and Mary quivered, as though some mechanisms were stuck. Suddenly the whole scene came to life. All the figures went through their motions. The cows rotated their necks, and the camels fluttered their eyes.

There came a snapping sound, and the third Wise Man tumbled to the ground. The fall shattered the remnants of its porcelain façade.

"Great, Marissa. You explain that to Mom and Dad."

"But I found him that way. He must have dropped before." She picked up the remains of the figure, now only a skeleton of wire. "He fell off and cracked."

"Great. Let's see if it holds water with Mom."

She stuck out her tongue.

"I'm going to check the bedrooms." He trotted to the hall that led away from the dining room.

"Knock first," she said.

He shook his head and proceeded down the hall.

Marissa knelt and collected all the ceramic bits of robe. Her head now level with the mechanical nativity scene, something caught her eye.

"Huh." She peered at the figure of Joseph. "Looks a little like Dad."

She went back to cleaning the floor. The remaining figures of the Wise Men clicked their heads, their tiny eyes trained on Marissa. When she stood, the heads rotated back to their original position.

She held the shattered Wise Man in one hand. "What am I going to tell Mom and Dad?" She placed the pieces inside the wooden box. The label on the side said: PRODUCT OF ARKHAM.

~~~

Bill checked the two guest rooms and the storage room. All empty. Finally, he came to the master bedroom. He hesitated, glancing over his shoulder, and knocked on the door.

"Mom? Dad?"

No answer.

He turned the knob and entered the darkened room. He felt along the wall but then remembered that he had to walk over to the nightstand lamps if he wanted light. Instead, he maneuvered around the bed and flicked the switch in the master bath. The light reflected against one wall and seemed to intensify the shadows in the room.

He sighed. "Where are you guys?"

A momentary shudder passed through him as terrible scenarios played out in his mind. He shook his head. "Marissa's right. They're not home." He reached to flip off the light, and his shoe knocked into something.

He bent down and picked up a small, hard object. At first, he couldn't tell what it was. There were little bits of metal and wire. When he turned it over, he noticed the ceramic face. The figure Marissa had broken from the nativity. *But how did it get in here?* he wondered.

Something scurried up his arm. Reflex action took over. He flicked at his sleeve with his free hand and knocked something loose. Whatever it was flew across the room. It bounced off the mattress and *thumped* on the carpet.

He moved over to examine the remains. Another of those Wise Men from the nativity scene in the game room. He furrowed his brow. The little figure jerked its arms and legs and stood. It swiveled its head toward Bill and charged. Several more figures emerged from under the bed and scurried up his pant legs.

Bill dropped the shattered figure of the first Wise Man and began sweeping at his body, trying to dislodge the tiny people.

Two had reached his arms. *Damn, they were fast.* He shook them loose, but the third Wise Man and one of the shepherds had climbed up his back and reached the nape of his neck. The Wise Man removed his crown and, together with the shepherd's crook, they repeatedly jabbed at the skin.

Bill swatted at his neck but failed to dislodge the tiny figures. The Wise Man used the jagged pieces of his broken jar of myrrh to slash at Bill's neck. By now the other discarded figurines, another Wise Man and a shepherd, had recovered and scrabbled up his pant legs.

Bill plucked the first shepherd off his neck and saw the end of the crook stained crimson with his blood. He tossed this one away and grabbed the Wise Man from his shoulder, holding this figurine aloft. Thin cracks zigzagged through the ceramic robes. He closed his fingers around the figure, crushing the Wise Man in his fist.

The other figures had skittered up his shirt and reached his head. The second shepherd hooked the corner of his mouth with one end of the crook. The Wise Man seized the other corner, and together they yanked the mouth open. Bill threw the squashed Wise Man aside and grasped the two figures with his hands. Both kept their grip on his mouth, pulling his lips open.

Now he spied the angel, hovering above him.

It clasped the shattered remains of the first Wise Man in its arms. The angel dive-bombed his open mouth. His scream was cut short as the angel shoved the metal and wire skeleton down his throat.

```
```

127

Marissa stooped under the Christmas tree, arranging the gifts. She cocked her head.

"Bill?" She stretched out the word.

It had been a while since he went to check the bedrooms. He would have come back if he'd found Mom and Dad. Even if he hadn't, he should have been back by now.

She set down the wrapped snow globe and stood. Hundreds of tiny ceramic and wooden eyes stared placidly out of their mangers. She walked back into the dining room.

"Bill, is that you?"

She peered down the hallway leading to the bedrooms. There was only one light, muffled under plexiglass in the ceiling, which created a gloomy glow. Marissa hated this hall. As a girl, she would charge down it to the safety of her bedroom, but now she proceeded slowly.

The door to the master bedroom lay open, and light shone out from the bathroom light. She stepped inside and glanced around. Empty.

"Bill! This is not funny."

She padded over to the bed and flicked on one of the lamps. Bill wasn't hiding in the shadows. She tiptoed over to the bathroom, pausing at the door, and then sprang out.

"Boo!"

The bathroom was vacant. She flipped off the light.

"Okay, you can come out now."

She headed back into the hall and peeked into the storage room and the two other bedrooms — all empty. Finally, she jogged upstairs, positive she heard the floor creak under Bill's weight, but no one was there.

She wrapped her arms around herself, feeling alone in her parent's house.

She hustled back to the dining room.

"Quit it, Bill. I'm warning you."

From the game room, she heard a clicking sound. As she approached the edge of the pool table, she saw the mechanical nativity winding down.

She knelt to examine the scene. The third Wise Man— the one she'd stepped on—was there, the clothes whole and looking as though it had been painted today. But the face. It didn't look the same.

Her heart froze.

It was Bill's face.

She let out a little yelp and jumped back. Her heart banged against her ribcage, ready to leap out any second.

She forced herself to breathe easy, calming down.

She stepped closer. *Damn, if that doesn't look like Bill,* she thought. A glance at Joseph told her it didn't just look like Dad—it was Dad. Down to the little mole on his neck. And Mary, too. Totally Mom.

"Okay, is this some kind of joke?" There was no answer. "You guys got me, all right." She scanned the area around her. The various quilted figures from the nativity wall hangings glared at her with empty eyes.

When she returned to the nativity scene, she could swear that some of the figures had shifted. Had the shepherds been looking at her before? She reached out to touch the third Wise Man, the one that looked so much like Bill, but paused and furrowed her brow. She glanced in the wooden box. The shattered remains were missing.

"How did they do that?"

She bent closer to examine the figures. Looking at the Wise Man felt like she was looking at a costumed version of her brother, a perfect copy of Bill. Too much like him, in fact. Her gut clenched. The figures of Joseph and Mary quivered as though resisting the spring inside. Then the eyes of the Wise Man jerked open. They weren't mechanical eyes. They were Bill's eyes.

Marissa screamed and lashed out at the nativity, striking it with her fist. Two of the Wise Men fell to the floor. She instantly pulverized them, stomping on them repeatedly.

Finally, better senses took control, and she stopped crushing the tiny figures underfoot. When she took a step back, two very different remains littered the floor. The first Wise Man showed shattered ceramic shards over a metal skeleton. The other looked different. Some sort of pulpy red liquid oozed out. She bent over to examine it. Under the fractured shell, she saw blood, torn muscle, and bits of bone. The face she recognized. It was Bill's. She'd smashed him, crushed her own brother underfoot.

Marissa glared at the nativity scene. Now she didn't have to imagine. The figures of the shepherds, the angel, and the lone Wise Man all swiveled to look at her. The angel flapped its wings and leaped into the air. The other figures also came to life, scurrying away from their posts.

She seized one of Mom's glazed pots and brought it down on top of the nativity. The pot smashed into wicked-looking shards. She grasped a massive three-foot nutcracker and beat at the nativity. One of the arms sheared off after the second blow. The head snapped away by the tenth.

She abandoned the mangled nutcracker and staggered away. Bits of the broken figurines lay scattered amidst the wrecked pot. She noticed that the figures of Joseph and Mary were also split open, revealing bloody interiors.

Marissa held one hand up to her mouth. Tears, hot and stinging, filled her eyes. She retreated, wanting to escape the ghastly scene. Her back banging into the dining room table jarred her to her senses. She would get in the car and drive away.

But before Marissa could reach the front door, the angel from the mechanical nativity hovered in the air before her. She raised one hand to swat it, but then the other figurines caught her eye, hundreds of nativity scenes set all around the room. Were they moving, too? She felt their gazes—wooden, ceramic, painted, and unpainted—all staring at her.

The angel dove forward, and Marissa threw herself against the wall, knocking down a quilted scene of baby Jesus. The angel zoomed past. She rushed for the door, pawing at the handle. Every second that passed she imagined the other figurines crawling off the shelves to get her. Yet a glance told her that they were still motionless.

The lock clicked, and she flung open the door. Racing to the car, her feet slid on the icy cement. Her parka was still inside, and globs of semi-melted sleet plopped onto her shoulders and head. As she dashed for the car, a thought seized her. *The keys!* Had Bill had left them in the ignition? She threw open the driver's door and groped around the steering column. The keys jangled. *Yes!*

She grabbed them and twisted. The car started up immediately. Thank God for preventative maintenance. She yanked the door shut.

Her gaze flicked back to the house. Any second, an army of figurines with robes and crooks would pour through the open doorway. Her heart thumped in her ears, drowning out the engine.

When she had the car turned around, she stomped down on the accelerator. The tires spun on the slick driveway but finally found purchase. She hurtled down the access road, taking the turn onto the asphalt strip at top speed. The Audi skidded to the shoulder, the tires popping on the rocks along the drop-off.

She pumped the brake.

The car rocked over the embankment, threatening to slide into the woods.

Her fingers tightened on the steering wheel. The tears came in a flood. She couldn't control them. One hand flew up to cover her face. She cried for Bill and Mom and Dad. She cried for the sheer horror of it.

A cracking sound caught her attention. She peered through her fingers. A star marred the windshield. A stray rock must have hit the glass. Had that been there when she'd stopped? Probably. She hadn't been thinking clearly. The sight of the damaged glass steadied her. She gripped the wheel again and put the car in gear.

Something shot at the windshield and hit the same spot. She jumped back in her seat, her heart revving. That was no rock. The angel figurine hovered on the other side of the glass. The crack spiderwebbed across the windshield, the hole in the center now large enough for it to poke its diminutive head through. It stared at her for a moment and then leaped up into the night air.

Marissa floored the accelerator. The engine gunned, and she nearly drove off the embankment. She yanked on the steering wheel and swerved onto the road. As she drove, she kept glancing toward the sky, unsure when the angelic kamikaze might strike next.

Then she spied it.

Somehow the angel had gotten in front again and was speeding toward her. She jerked the wheel to the right. The fender scraped along the rock face. The Audi rebounded off the wall and careened across the two lanes and off the other side.

Marissa screamed.

For one brief moment, the night sky filled the windshield, the stars looking like glistening drops of dew.

Then the Audi struck the tree — a detonation of splintered wood and crumpled metal. A globe of white eclipsed her vision. As the airbag deflated, she could see the windshield. Teeny cubes of safety glass dotted the dash like shimmering snowflakes. Her body caved under the weight of her injuries. She fought off fatigue.

Rain cascaded down through the shattered windshield onto her face, but she craned her head toward the sky.

The angel landed on the crumpled hood with a *plink* — its ceramic form pulverized and the frame underneath distorted. It folded its wings and marched straight for her.

She tried to squirm away, but her body was slow to respond. As her consciousness faded, she felt the tiny figurine grab her by the lips.

Then the blackness took her.

~~~

Marissa blinked awake. Her muscles ached, and she could hardly move. Had Bill found her and brought her back home? But why had he left her in the game room? She could just make out the dining room table with the cardboard box Bill had brought. She tried to look down, but her neck felt stiff. The extent of her vision showed her that she sat on the pool table. She shifted her gaze left. A giant nutcracker sat beside her—impossibly large. In fact, everything in the room seemed gargantuan.

A sickening chill coursed down her spine.

She was *in* the nativity scene. Mom, Dad, even Bill stood back in their places.

Her heart crescendoed, creating an unbearable tattoo inside her chest.

Marissa wanted to scream, but the sound died behind her frozen ceramic lips.

I Must Go

Scott J. Couturier

Fall begins briskly & it ends in rot—
what is it that I have forgot?
To light the bright candles—no, no.
My pumpkin's grin already glows.

Perhaps I forgot to appease the dead,
restless & rotting in their coffin-beds?
But no—my offerings are all laid out.
It is not this I have forgot about.

Bright leaves roar like living flame
as they glorify in Autumn's fame:
full moon ascends, a garish glaring red.
The trees are gilded, as if they bled.

Is all our harvest brought in at last?
Winds howl, a chilling specter cast
from out furthest Hyperborean north:
cold will rule these lands henceforth.

See, the strawman trembles too:
all meddlesome crows long ago flew.
Gourd-guardian of fallow earth,
he reigns over death as he did at birth.

Holiday Leftovers

Fields are swathed in a spectral mist –
have I locked all doors, my crucifix kissed?
Something unseen at the window scratches:
a rogue spirit up from those blighted patches.

I know I have forgot some vital thing.
Witches cackle, high on the Hunter's wing.
Huddling down, I whisper fearful prayers,
yet the monist God remains unawares.

Instead, Cernunnos hears my plea,
& pipes rejoinder in reedy melody.
My blood froths as his alluring call
summons me forth to Black Mab's ball.

Tonight the Horned God dies anew:
his ichor the dead earth shall renew.
Spilled at slaying, his seed will bring
about pale snowdrops of early Spring.

Briskly, I adorn myself in dew.
Like gemstones gleam moon's residue.
With reddish berries I stain my skin,
soul surrendered to a bewitching sin.

Fall begins briskly & it ends in rot—
what is it that I have forgot?
Never now will I in surety know:
the Great Night beckons, & I must go.

Machines in Motion

Benjamin C. Kinney

Eszter spent her first battle in breathless fear, not of some errant shell or cannonball, but of the engineers. She followed them through trenches choked with smoke and rust-red mud, expecting them to see through her at any moment. Sooner or later, they would realize the new girl wasn't so clever after all. Sooner or later, they would know what she was.

She held the toolbox steady and watched the three engineers work on the humanoid hulk of a fallen automaton. Kúlisch buried his hands wrist-deep in the engine's pumps and ducts, his trim goatee wet with condensed steam. Nahlah crouched, her dark wiry body twisted as she angled a screwdriver up into the back of the automaton's neck. Corporal Lujza sat to the side with an armor plate in her lap. Smoke and soot painted her coat the same color as her hair. A scowl creased her face as she laid new silvery thaumic wires into the charred armor plate.

Nahlah caught Eszter's eye and offered her a screwdriver. Eszter rose, and then froze as Lujza grabbed her arm. Lujza shook her head and shoved the armor plate into Eszter's hands. Her mind went blank, but her body was already moving. She tucked the armor under her arm and grabbed a wrench from the toolbox. She had only glanced at the fasteners that would join armor to chassis, so she had to pluck out a handful of bolts and hope she had guessed their sizes correctly. She realized she had no prayer for this, and the thought sent a rush of worry and exhilaration up her spine.

Kúlisch lifted his hands clear of the machine. Nahlah leaned across and slid her screwdriver deep into a gap between engine and chassis, her glove braced against gears. She turned the screw, grimacing in concentration. Machinery clicked, engaged--and jumped. Nahlah yanked off her torn glove and wrapped a rag around bloodied fingers. She stumbled away, and Eszter's shock dissolved into a guilty exhalation of relief.

Eszter wrestled the armor plate into place, and bit back a curse as metal rattled against metal. She shoved down the plate, then forced herself to let go. She dropped in the bolts and wrenched them tight. Lujza elbowed her aside and connected the thaumic circuits with a few final lengths of wire.

Kúlisch snapped a flag in front of the machine's lenses, and the automaton rose: seated, then kneeling, and then standing. It swept smoked-glass eyes across the engineers, then raised and lowered the small-bore cannon of its right arm. Eszter strained to hear its engine, but the cacophony of battle muted it as surely as every other sound.

The automaton took position alongside three of its kin, and infantrymen formed up behind. Eszter tried not to read the faces of the soldiers in their mud-stained white coats and once-blue breeches. Instead, she watched the engineers. They were both staring at her: Lujza with grim satisfaction, Kúlisch with raised eyebrows. Eszter lowered her gaze, gathered the tools, and followed the engineers to their next corpse.

My hands won't shake next time, she told herself.

~~~

The sunset light stretched out their shadows ahead of them as they approached their corner of the sprawling camp. Eszter watched Lujza's stride, the way the woman's boots slapped the mud on every step, the way she gained her speed from stride instead of haste. Someday Eszter would figure out how to copy that fearless gait.

Lujza glanced backward, and caught her stare. Eszter froze, and the two of them halted as the other engineers moved onward. Once they were alone, Lujza said, "You saw what I did for you back there?"

Eszter glanced down at her hands, her skin raw but whole. "Thank you for stopping me. She was trying to give me the dangerous work, wasn't she? I didn't realize."

"If you have to reach in deep, do it before the engine's fixed. Save your hands for something worthwhile." She narrowed her eyes. "You did well today. I should apologize," she said without a trace of regret.

"For what?"

"For being surprised. I should've expected you to be a fast learner. Jews are supposed to be cunning, aren't they?"

Eszter's blood halted in her veins. There was nobody close enough to overhear, but still she whispered. "Don't speak of it, Lujza. Please! You mustn't let anyone know."

"Why not? You think the army doesn't take Jews? No, I suppose it doesn't. Their loyalties don't lie with Hungary, after all. But our squad has three foreigners and three women in four people—nobody cares where engineers come from." She smiled like a hungry woman set before somebody else's meal. "Nobody cares unless someone complains to the officers."

"But you wouldn't do that." Eszter buried her hands in her greatcoat pockets, so Lujza wouldn't see them clench into fists.

"I brought you here, why would I get rid of you?" Lujza's hand descended on Eszter's shoulder. "Remember that." She turned away, leaving a smear of red mud on the shoulder of Eszter's coat.

Eszter's stomach tightened at the thought of following meekly behind Lujza. *She doesn't upset me*, Eszter told herself. *I just need a minute to stretch my legs before dinner.*

She turned aside and meandered among the grey canvas barracks tents. She scarcely noticed the soldiers until a voice called out, "Hey, engineer! Come sit with us!" She instinctively reached up to adjust her kerchief, but all she could do was pull her peaked cap more tightly over her hair.

She found the engineers around their cookfire. Kúlisch prodded a pan full of meat, and Lujza opened a flask of liquor. Nahlah sat across the fire, bandages wrapped around two of her fingertips.

Kúlisch spoke to Lujza in a Slavic accent, maybe Polish. "You haven't told Captain Sipos about the new girl yet, have you?"

Lujza shrugged. "I'll tell him when the battle's over. For now she's got Bertók's old tent."

Nahlah studied Eszter with a smile like a sugared lemon. "Glad you could join us, new girl." She flashed her bandaged hand. "Don't worry, you'll get your scars soon enough."

Eszter searched for the right words, but she got no chance to speak them. Lujza grinned like a lion defending her kill, and said, "It took you a month to measure bolts that fast. Keep on getting yourself cut up, maybe the surgeon will marry you and get you out of our hair for good."

Nahlah laughed sharply, and she and Lujza began to banter like husband and wife who hated each other slightly less than they hated the thought of divorce. Kúlisch offered the bottle to Eszter. While he was sitting down, she could hardly tell he was a few inches shorter than her.

He said, "You stuck through your first battle, good start for an assistant. Brave and stupid, two fine qualities for all of us in the army. Where'd she find you?"

She didn't found me, I found her, Eszter wanted to say. But Lujza would hear it, one way or another. "I lived in Budapest my entire life. And through the siege."

He lifted his eyebrows. "And?"

Eszter shook her head. "And that's all. Nothing left for me there." Nothing left she would accept, at least. The liquor burned her throat like acid and apricots, the way pálinka should.

"All right, point taken." He shared a knowing smile. "But if you don't want to talk about your past, you need some good lies to tell."

She traded the bottle for a hunk of bread and a warm plate of canned beef. Her best meal in months, but she clutched the knife until her fingers hurt. *I can endure this,* she told herself. In the last year, she had starved, she had lost her brother, she had abandoned her fellow Israelites;

what more did it cost her to live without pride? As long as she could stay among the machines.

The fire grew low, conversation slowed, and Eszter slipped off to her tent. Alone at last, she shed her coat and threw herself onto dead Bértok's cot. Exhaustion saturated her bones like metal fatigued beyond its limits, but her mind kept ticking. The bolts still rattled in her hands; Lujza's threats and promises still loomed over her head. Eszter rolled onto her side. If she wanted to sleep, she would need to finish one more task, despite the risk. After all, it was Friday night.

She fished two stubs of wax from her meager pack and lit the candles, her body bent over the flame so no one would see the light. This wouldn't be the first time she worked through Shabbos, but in the old rhythms of her whispered prayer, she might find a little bit of rest.

~~~

At dawn, Eszter's squad joined the mobile artillery on the south flank. Six-wheeled carts launched shells into the distance, shrouding the ground with sulfur and smoke. Every fifteen minutes, the guns would roll themselves to a new position before the French artillery could find their range and return fire. Usually, it worked.

The engineers let Eszter carry tools, tighten connections, and watch them do the real work. She tried to understand every choice they made. Why won't an 8/5 gear power a three-inch pivot joint? How long do you have to wait between laying down overlapping thaumic wires? How do you identify the replacement modules for the automata's cognitive mechanics? She memorized each question so she could scavenge for answers later among Lujza's leavings.

Another squad relieved them at midday, and the engineers divided up the burden of materiel worth returning to camp. Lujza argued with Nahlah over a disabled mortar, while Kúlisch set off with an empty coal cart and the temptation of a moment out from under Lujza's eye.

Eszter hurried after him. "Can I—" She halted, her voice distant and muffled. No, her ears exhausted from the battle. She tried again. "Can I try directing the cart?"

"Of course!" Kúlisch beamed. "Here, take the baton, go on. Wave it like this if you want the cart to go faster, like that to slow down. To make it turn, twist like this and then point."

Eszter rolled the baton in her hand. It was a hollow metal tube inlaid with the silver lines of thaumic circuitry. Back in Budapest, Lujza had said that thaumic science was to magic, as chemistry was to alchemy. To Eszter's eyes, the silver plexus was a book written in a language she could not yet read. This, at last, was a Talmud worth deciphering.

Kúlisch said, "A lot of girls try to sign up just because we'll take them. Chasing after some soldier boy, usually. But those girls don't pay attention like you, and Lujza talks like you have a real knack. Think you might join us for real?"

Eszter's heart coiled with hope, a clock wound full. "I will. I've made my choices. And like I said, there's nothing left for me back in Budapest."

"Ach. What happened?"

The mainspring in her chest unwound, its power dissipated. She could not mention the pogrom that took her father, nor the humiliations her brother had refused to endure. But she could tell a piece of truth, and make it sound like the whole.

"Our apartment building burned down at the end of the siege, after the French diggers came up."

Kúlisch grimaced. "I'm sorry to hear it. Still, at least we have the frogs on the run now. It's been fifty years, but who knows? Maybe Napoleon has finally run out of steam. Here, slow the cart down, the depot's right over there."

Eszter reoriented the cart, and after a few tries she sent it rolling toward the coal depot. Kúlisch reclaimed the baton and led her among the quiet tents.

She asked, "Can I really join like this? Don't automaton engineers need some kind of training?"

He shook his head. "It's like working in a factory. Start next to someone senior and learn as you go."

"Even thaumics?"

"Ah, for that you'd need real training. A year, Lujza says. Looking to follow in her footsteps, are you? You may well have what it takes, but you'll have to start at the bottom with us. Don't worry. If I tell the captain you're good with a wrench, that'll be enough to get you started." He swept an appraising look across her face. "I'm glad you're staying. A girl like you would brighten this company up a bit. You're a pretty girl, and an honest one too. Not like some people we know, yes?"

Eszter's heart beat faster, for more reasons than she could name. "I'm sorry, Kúlisch. I'm not looking for something like that right now. I just want to be an engineer."

He frowned. "You don't have to obey Lujza, you know. She's only a corporal." He chuckled, shook his head. "Whatever she told you, forget it. I'll put in a word for you with the officers. They won't let us fraternize with soldiers, but they can't keep two engineers apart. My tent's a lot more comfortable than a dead man's, I promise." He took a step closer and looked up at her with his jaunty smile.

Eszter glanced around at the maze of tents, empty of anyone who could hear a shout for help. She extended her arm, but she couldn't bring herself to push her hand against his chest. "Please, don't. You've been kind to me, but you don't know me."

Kúlisch dipped his head. "Well, fair enough. Perhaps I'm getting ahead of myself. I hope I didn't offend you." He took a step back and offered a trim little bow, without ever losing that confident smile. "Consider my enthusiasm as a compliment, yes? And if you ever—"

"Kúlisch, you pint-sized bastard!" From thirty feet away, Lujza's voice sliced through the echoes of distant battle. The stout older woman strode toward them, her uniform spattered with coal dust and blood.

Kúlisch turned his smile toward Lujza. "Corporal! Is something wrong? I hope that mortar didn't bite you, I warned you about the bolts."

Lujza shoved him away from Eszter. "Don't play games with me, you six-inch shit. Keep your jealous little hands off of her."

"Calm down, Lujza. I'm not bothering her. Tell her, Eszter. We were just talking, that's all, right?"

Ezster opened her mouth to speak, but the answers fought each other in her throat, and no sound emerged.

Lujza slammed her fist into Kúlisch's stomach, and the air rushed from his lungs with a grunt. Lujza crossed her arms and watched him gasp for breath and then straighten.

He worked his jaw as if a splinter of bone had stuck between his teeth. He glanced at Eszter and then let his gaze fix on Lujza. "My apologies. Lujza."

Eszter dropped her hand from her mouth before Lujza could see it. Lujza turned away from Kúlisch, grabbed Eszter's arm, and guided her away.

Lujza said, "If anyone talks to you when I'm not around, you tell me, understand? Come on now, girl. Put on your gloves, we have scrap duty for the afternoon. You can ask me a few questions while we walk."

The engineer's hand on her elbow made Eszter feel safe, like a treasure under lock and key. *But I need to walk at my own pace*, she told herself. She pulled her arm free. Lujza maintained her stride, and Eszter had to hurry to keep pace.

Lujza glanced back and smiled like a child eyeing an errant marble. "Don't get lost, girl."

A dozen memorized questions hung on the tip of Eszter's tongue, but she held them back. More important than any scrap of knowledge, she needed to make sure that Lujza wouldn't tire of mentoring her.

"Thank you for your help back there," Eszter said. She probably even meant it.

~~~

The boneyard was a wide low heap of scrap and riches, the size of a house smashed into kindling. Eszter took a spot at one edge and began to sort. Again and again, she took a hunk of mangled metal, studied it, tested it, and placed it one of her own little piles. Occasionally she found a serviceable mechanism, or a fragment inlaid with intact thaumic wires. More often, she pried apart broken machinery and extracted some salvageable component, an unbroken gear or piston. Even pieces with French measurements could be pressed back into service. Mostly, she found scrap metal, and tossed it behind her so a conscript could cart it away to be melted down in some distant foundry. The scrap, at least, might make it back to Budapest.

Lujza sat ten yards away, but the distance might have been ten miles. Eszter worked at her own pace, her gloved hands deep in the guts of the fallen. Every shattered mechanism gave her an excuse to study or to wonder. A pair of warped pistons let her test the interplay between form and friction. A broken gear train outlined the story of all its lost and scattered pieces, and all the things she might someday make it do. At one point, the words of the shekahcha rose unbidden into her head, a sentence of thanks for the world's beauty. She could not recall when last she'd said that prayer.

"You the new girl who's been following Squad Eleven? Eszter something?" An unfamiliar voice broke her reverie. Eszter registered the late-afternoon light, the sound of distant shells, and the sullen young man in a sergeant's uniform. He rolled a truncheon in his hand, back and forth.

"That's me, yes. Can I help you?" *I have no reason to fear,* she told herself. *My secret is safe, it has to be.*

"Captain Sipos sent me to get you. Come along now." He beckoned with his truncheon.

She glanced toward Lujza, but the older woman shook her head and returned to her work. Eszter was trapped against the iron, with place to go save where this sergeant might take her. She stood, and followed the sergeant back into the domain of men.

~ ~ ~

The captain's tent had four poles, and room enough for bed and office both. Captain Sipos sat at a table strewn with notes and blueprints. He had a bushy face, with sideburns and moustache, pierced by clear blue eyes.

"Sit," he said, without looking up from his writing.

Eszter found two chairs, but one had Kúlisch already sitting in it, his arms crossed. He offered her an apologetic little smile.

Sipos handed a note to his orderly, who stepped outside and left the three of them alone in the tent. Eszter tried to sit up straight. She wished she had cleaned some of the mud and grease from her clothes. She wished she had a uniform that fit.

Sipos said, "Specialist Lengyel here says he was attacked by one of the other engineers. By Corporal Lujza Rigó. He said you witnessed it. Did you?"

The two stares made Eszter's heart curl up like a snail. "They had a disagreement, sir, but it didn't seem important. I don't know what to say."

Sipos said, "Specialist Lengyel, back to work."

Kúlisch raised his eyebrows and glanced at Eszter, but she focused on the captain's brass buttons. The tent flap rustled, and then fell quiet.

Captain Sipos said, "Soldiers can brawl if they want, but I'm in command of engineers—a gaggle of women and undesirables who need a sterner hand. I decide what's important here, girl, and the important things are these." He ticked off on his fingers: "Discipline among my engineers. Knowing whom I can trust, and whom is unworthy of service. And your answer to my question."

She started to speak, and then halted. Kúlisch had treated her kindly, but for his own motives. If she wanted to rid herself of his insistent smile and insistent questions, she held the tool to achieve it on her own.

"They argued, but she didn't hit him, sir. He's lying." A bitter taste rose in the back of her mouth. She swallowed, and it was gone.

"Very well. I'll do something about this." He wrote another line, signed his name, and then sealed the letter. "But I'm not finished with you. Come closer." He looked her up and down for the second time. "So you're Lujza's latest foundling. There are things I tolerate from that woman, because she's one of our best engineers. She picked you up in Budapest, yes? I grew up in the old town, up the hill in Buda. Where are you from, girl? And what's your full name?"

"Eszter Révay, from Prater Street," she lied, a name and address from outside the ghetto.

"Prater Street? My favorite cukrászda was just around the corner from there. Did you go to the Széchenyi? You have to stand with Jews sometimes there, there's no avoiding it so close to the ghetto. But you'd hardly notice, the bad ones stay behind their walls. Besides, it's worth it for the krémes. You never went? Ah, a pity."

He gestured her back to her chair. "Our little troublemaker Kúlisch said you have some real talent. That you could make a good engineer someday, maybe even in thaumics. Is that what you want?"

"It is, sir." A burst of heat and lightness spread through her chest like an engine's first breath of steam. "More than anything."

"I assume you need the army to pay for your training, so if you want to learn thaumic engineering, it'll be a five-year enlistment." He shook his head. "You don't know what you'd be getting yourself into, Révay. You're young, you're polite, you're pretty enough, and evidently you're smart; you can do better than waste your youth in oil and mud. Save yourself some callouses, go back home to your family. Besides, if I let you sign up, you'd never get to try that krémes."

Krémes. A pastry she could never afford, from a city she might never see again. This question, at least, she could answer honestly.

"I wouldn't anyway, sir. At the end of the siege, a lot of the diggers came up in the Erszébetvarós ghetto. There's not much left of the neighborhoods around it. And my family is all in the army or gone."

Sipos put a hand against his face, his index finger pressed against the hollow of one closed eye. He took a deep breath, then lowered his hand and started writing another letter. "Well, if you're certain, I'll keep you on as an assistant until we've pushed the French back past the Balaton. Then we'll send you north for thaumics training. Best of luck and God bless, Junior Specialist Révay. Hungary and the Coalition could use more girls like you. You're dismissed."

Eszter stood up, but a knot tightened in her stomach. Lujza would hold so much more power, now that Eszter had earned a prize worth losing. The walls of the ghetto loomed around her still.

"Sir." Eszter swallowed, her mouth dry. "There's something else, if you have a minute?"

Sipos' pen paused above the paper. "Make it quick."

"It's my squad, sir." She spoke slowly, trying to plan one step ahead of her words. "There's a reason why Kúlisch wanted to get Lujza in trouble. I think they used to be lovers, but now he's with Nahlah, the Arab woman. If you discipline Kúlisch, it'll put those two at each other's throats. Or mine, now." *Truth is the seal of the Holy One*, the sages said. But she would not let guilt stop her tongue, not when one more lie might save her.

He pointed his pen at her. "This is why I care so much about how my engineers behave. I was afraid your squad might fall into such things after Bertók died. But if they're just jealous, you all can sort it out yourselves." His pen descended and scratched out a word from his note. "Don't waste my time, Révay."

The words clicked into place like a bolt into its fastener. She could forge the truth, and her heart, into tools of their own.

"It's not just bad moods, sir. Lujza's trying to ruin me. She's started spreading rumors, making up lies. Telling people I'm a Jew."

"I see." Sipos frowned. "Well, perhaps it's time to split up that squad up after all. I'll make sure Lujza knows she won't get away with any rumormongering." He crumpled up his letter and started anew. "Go get your things, then give this note to Lieutenant Orosz. He'll find a place for you."

~ ~ ~

Eszter stood outside Captain Sipos' tent as the cannons and sun faded for another day. Back home, in her burned-out apartment and the shattered ghetto, it would almost be time for havdalah. The end of Shabbos, the border between the sacred and the mundane, between Israel and the nations of the world. The cycle of another week, beginning anew.

She could see her tent from here, and she spent a few moments watching a nameless figure start a cooking fire. If she did not return to that tent, she could escape the lot of them.

She would have to abandon what little she possessed: some threadbare old clothes, a tin of friction matches, and two stubs of wax.

It's better this way, she told herself. *I want to bring nothing with me.*

Barcelona Sandals

Lynn White

Standing in the Andorra snow
shivering in our Barcelona sandals.
Glad of a lift down to Foix
as darkness was falling.
And the driver knew a hotel,
Hotel du Centre.
Very grand
and full
of people looking down
long noses.
But the driver knew the owner
who was a kind man,
a nice man.
So we shouldn't worry
about the cost, he said.

A lovely room
and in the morning,
breakfast!
We must eat
the owner said.
Warm bread and jam.
Coffee with hot milk
which tasted sour.
But I don't like
the taste of milk,

anyway,
so most likely
it was sweet.

And then the bill.
But there was no bill.
Save it for the journey,
the owner said.
A kind man,
a nice man,
who believed
the driver's story,
whatever it was.

A few years later,
we returned to Foix
and went to find
Hotel du Centre.
But it wasn't there.
No one knew it.
It didn't exist.
Did it ever exist?
Did any of it happen?
Or did we somehow
share
a memory
from our
imaginations.

Good Science

Michael Wertenberg

"I'm going to call you Gobbles, and we're going to be gobbly good friends."

Gobbles seemed to take to the name as she pranced around her pen repeating it loudly and proudly.

"Howie, come on inside," Mom called from the kitchen.

Howie gave Gobbles a hug. "Don't be scared, Gobbles. Once the family gets here, they'll see how beautiful and nice you are, and they won't want to eat you."

"Howie," Mom called from the kitchen, "be a good boy and help your mother get the house ready for our guests."

Howie was a good boy, and he helped his mother get the house ready. Then Howie turned in for the night. But Howie couldn't sleep. Instead, he retrieved his flashlight from under the bed and slipped under the covers with his latest copy of *Tales of the Incredible.*

~~~

Uncle Johnny was the first of the Likearts to arrive, three days before Thanksgiving. "Let's have a look at that turkey," he said immediately after setting his bags down and giving Mom, Pop, and Howie a hug. He was led to the back of the house where, from the window, there was a clear view of the pen. "Oh, she's a beauty alright."

Howie smiled. *I knew he would find her beautiful, too.*

"Howie, be a good boy," said Mom, "and go get your uncle a glass of water."

Howie was a good boy, and he got his uncle a glass of water. "What are those for?" asked Howie, pointing at the bottle of pills Uncle Johnny was struggling to open.

"The ol' ticker ain't what she used to be, I'm afraid," answered Uncle Johnny.

"And those pills can help?"

"Yep." Uncle Johnny opened the bottle and poured two brown pills into the palm of his hand. "Gets the ol' ticker tickin' again."

"Howie," Mom said, "go brush your teeth and wash up. It's bedtime."

Howie made no fuss, as he was anxious to get under his covers and read the end of *Tales of the Incredible*. He was fascinated by the mad scientist who used large machines, wires, and electricity from the lightning storm to get the corpse to come alive.

It would have been a whole lot easier if he'd had some ticker pills. But I suppose you make do with what you have; good science is good science.

Howie finished reading the comic book and went fast asleep dreaming of lightning and scientists and corpses.

~ ~ ~

Aunt Betty was the next of the Likearts to arrive, two days before Thanksgiving. She wasn't so keen to see Gobbles. "I don't need to see it prancin' around in a pen. Just happy to see it on my plate."

"But she isn't going to be on your plate," said Howie.

"Oh, no?"

"Nope," responded Howie. "This year, we're having chicken for Thanksgiving. Gobbles is part of the family now. Ain't that right, Mom?"

Mom turned to Pop. "Why couldn't we have gotten a store-bought turkey like a normal family?"

"Since when have we been a normal family?" said Pop then he turned to Howie. "Now, why don't you be a good boy and go get your aunt a glass of water."

Howie was a good boy, and he got his aunt a glass of water. When he returned, yellow triangle-shaped pills were spread out on the table before Aunt Betty. "What are those for?" asked Howie.

"At my age," said Aunt Betty, "my muscles and joints aren't what they used to be."

"And those pills can help?"

"Gets the blood flowin' and gets the old muscles and joints workin' right again." She popped two pills in her mouth and washed them down with a glass of water. "But they're not for young boys. You hear me?"

"Howie," Mom called from the kitchen, "go brush your teeth and wash up. It's bedtime."

Howie brushed his teeth, washed up, and went to bed, wondering if the mad scientist had had yellow triangle-shaped muscle pills, maybe his reanimated corpse would have been nimbler and been able to outrun those pesky villagers.

~~~

Uncle Raymond and Aunt Mary were the last of the Likearts to arrive, the day before Thanksgiving.

"Who are you?" asked a visibly upset Aunt Mary. "And what are you doing in my living room?"

"I'm your nephew, Howie. And this here's our living room. You're at our house, Aunt Mary, for Thanksgiving."

Aunt Mary didn't look none too pleased with his answer, and Howie was confused.

Mom pulled Howie aside. "You're going to have to be patient with Aunt Mary. Her memory's not what it used to be. Now be a good boy and go get her a glass of water."

"So she can take pills for her ticker, or for her muscles?"

"Not exactly, dear. Aunt Mary takes pills for her—" Mom tapped her head with her index finger.

Howie was a good boy, and he got Aunt Mary a glass of water. But Howie was also a curious boy, and he stayed and watched Aunt Mary take her purple brain pills.

~~~

"For the pre-Thanksgiving dinner," announced Mom, "I've prepared a chickpea soup."

The Likearts all sat around the table, all except Uncle Johnny Likeart.

"Where's Uncle Johnny?" asked Howie.

"Uncle Johnny's busy," replied Pop. "Now, pass me the salt, Son."

Howie passed Pop the salt, but he was uneasy. He recognized the tone in Pop's 'Uncle Johnny's busy', something suspicious and secretive, like when he told Howie that Pickles had gone 'to a farm upstate.'

Suddenly, his stomach tightened. It twisted and pulled. And his heart started beating fast. Howie stood up. "I forgot to feed Gobbles. I'll be right back."

"Sit down, Son," said Pop, and there was nothing suspicious or secretive about that command.

All the Likearts ate their soup, all except Howard Likeart.

"What's the matter, sweetheart?" asked Mom. "Don't you like the soup?"

"No, I don't like it! I don't like it at all!"

~~~

That night, Howie didn't brush his teeth, and he didn't wash up before going to bed. He didn't retrieve his flashlight from under the bed, and he didn't read his copy of 'Tales of the Incredible'.

Instead, he shut his eyes and dreamt of a reanimated corpse lumbering around the house scaring his family and punishing them for what they had done to Gobbles. But the corpse he dreamt of was nimbler, stronger, and much smarter than that of the mad scientist, because Howie had given it brown ticker pills and yellow triangle-shaped muscle pills and purple brain pills.

~~~

Howie woke up before the sun. He woke up before the other Likearts. He tiptoed through the house, through the cold, and through the dark. He crept up to the kitchen window to have a look at the pen, the empty pen, the Gobbles-less pen.

Howie was sad, and Howie was angry. He opened cupboard doors. He looked in the pantry. He even went outside into the cold November morning to have a look in the shed. *What have they done with Gobbles?*

He returned to the kitchen, opened every door, and went through every drawer, even those far too small to hide a turkey. When he closed the refrigerator and turned to peruse the room, all the furnishings faded into the background, all except the oven whose sleek metal cast stood out from the wood countertops.

Howie trembled; his heart raced. He inched toward the stove, reached out with much apprehension, and just as he was about to place his hand on the door handle—

"What you doin' up so early?"

Howie jumped and spun around to catch sight of a groggy, disheveled Uncle Johnny lumbering toward him.

Howie stumbled back, caught himself on the handle of the oven door, and tried to regain control over his breathing.

"No peeking," said Uncle Johnny, motioning to the oven. "She'll be ready soon enough. You'll smell it."

Howie swallowed the lump in his throat and slid away from the oven.

"Can't blame a young boy for being excited for Thanksgiving, now can we?" said Uncle Johnny. "Tell me. What's your favorite Thanksgiving dish? I bet it's pumpkin pie, isn't it?"

Howie nodded. He tried to respond, but the words stayed stuck in his throat.

Uncle Johnny walked up to him and reached out with an open hand ready to grab. "Excuse me, there."

Howie jerked his head to the side, avoiding Uncle Johnny's hand by a split second.

Uncle Johnny pulled a glass off the drying rack behind Howie and shuffled over to the sink.

Howie stammered. "I su- I suppose I'd bet- better get back to bed."

"Nonsense. You're up. You might as well have breakfast with me. You set the table and take a seat. I just gotta take my pills then I'll pour us some cereal."

Howie set the table and took a seat. Uncle Johnny fetched the newspaper from the front steps, joined Howie at the table, took his pills, and poured them some cereal. Howie ate while Uncle Johnny read the headlines out loud. When they had finished, they were joined by Aunt Betty.

"If you'll excuse me," said Uncle Johnny as he stood from the table. "I do believe I have some work to do to prepare for the big feast." He dropped the newspaper on the table and picked up the two empty cereal bowls.

"I'll clean up, Uncle Johnny."

Uncle Johnny smiled. "Aren't you a good boy?" Uncle Johnny left the bowls. Uncle Johnny left the newspaper, and Uncle Johnny left his bottle of ticker pills and went to prepare for the big feast.

Howie was a good boy. Howie served his Aunt Betty breakfast. He brought Aunt Betty a glass of water so that she could take her yellow triangle-shaped muscle pills. And Howie cleaned up.

Aunt Mary and Uncle Raymond were late to rise. They said good morning to the others then went straight to the living room to read.

"Shall I bring you some tea and toast?"

"Why, that's mighty kind of you," said Uncle Raymond.

Howie was kind, and he brought Aunt Mary and Uncle Raymond some tea and some toast. And he sat with them as they ate and drank and Aunt Mary took her purple brain pills.

"Aren't you such a good boy?" said Aunt Mary.

And Howie was a good boy. And Howie cleaned up.

~~~

Uncle Johnny had work to do to prepare for the big feast, and he helped Mom in the kitchen.

Howie, too, had work to do, but he stayed down in the basement away from all the grown-ups. He left a few pills in each of the three pill bottles he'd cleaned up but poured out the remainder onto the desk then crushed them into a powder: the brown ticker pills, the yellow triangle-shaped muscle pills, and the purple brain pills. He added water, creating a yellowish-brown liquid, and filled the turkey baster with it.

Hang in there, Gobbles. A bit of good science and we'll undo this mess.

"Howie," Mom called from the kitchen, "be a good boy and come help your aunt set the table."

Howie was a good boy, and he picked up the turkey baster he'd taken from the kitchen drawer, slipped it in the inside pocket of his vest, and went to help his aunt set the table.

"Well, aren't you a handsome young man?" said Aunt Betty. "All dressed up for Thanksgiving dinner."

Howie smiled.

~~~

The Likearts sat around the dining room table. And there were mashed potatoes and gravy and string beans and cranberry sauce. In the center of the table was Gobbles, head cut off, and set in a pan of yellowish-brown juice.

Pop spoke. "Before I carve this beautiful bird, let's go around the table and say what we are each thankful for." He motioned to Mom on his right. "Honey, would you start us off?"

Mom was thankful for family and friends.

Uncle Johnny was thankful for the freedom he enjoyed in the country he loved.

Aunt Betty was thankful for the peace she felt surrounded by the people she loved.

Aunt Mary was thankful for such a caring husband.

Uncle Raymond was thankful for such a strong and resilient wife.

Howie was thankful for the chance to see his favorite aunts and uncles. He was thankful for modern science: thankful it could provide Uncle Johnny with pills to make his ticker work and pills to help Aunt Betty and pills to help Aunt Mary. Howie was thankful for new beginnings and for friendships that could overcome adversity. He stared at Gobbles while he spoke, waiting for her to move, waiting for her to wake up.

There was no lightning storm outside. But Howie was using good science, and he was certain good science didn't need lightning to work. Still, Gobbles wasn't moving.

But I gave her the good science juice nearly an hour ago. It should be working by now.

Howie continued. He was thankful for the nice house he lived in and the nice clothes he could wear. He was thankful for his teachers, which he named individually. Still, Gobbles did not wake up.

Finally, Howie ran out of things he was thankful for. *Maybe it just takes a little time for good science to kick in.*

But Pop wouldn't wait any longer. He stood up, brandishing a large carving knife and a metal poker thing. He stabbed Gobbles in the back, cut off pieces of her, and set them on the plates that were passed to him. While he served, Mom used a large spoon to scoop up some of the yellowish-brown juice to cover each slice.

Howie filled his plate with green bean casserole and cranberries. And, as Pop was carving another slice, Howie, out of the corner of his eye, thought he saw Gobbles twitch.

It's working! The good science juice is finally working!

"I'm so thankful," said a delighted Howie.

But the other Likearts didn't give the juice the time to take effect.

"Mmm, delicious," said Uncle Johnny.

"Succulent," said Aunt Betty.

"Truly divine," said Aunt Mary.

"Devilishly good," countered Uncle Raymond.

Howie wanted to shout, "Wait! Five more minutes, please. She'll come back to life. Good science just needs a little more time to act." But instead, he sat silent, saddened, and frustrated as he watched his family fork down his feathered friend.

"I have to say, there is a peculiar aftertaste to the turkey," said Pop, and his eye twitched.

"The juice has a bit of a bite," said Uncle Raymond with his shoulder in spasms. "Did you use whisky or another liquor?"

Each Likeart, with one peculiar tick or another, made a comment on the strangeness of the taste and the strangeness of the color, but this did little to slow them down. In a matter of minutes, each Likeart had helped himself or herself to seconds and thirds, and all that remained of Gobbles were a few bones marinating in a yellowish-brown juice.

Uncle Johnny's shoulder spasmed, and he shot up, clutching his chest. "I don't feel so good."

Mom clutched her jaw to keep her teeth from grinding. With her other hand, she clawed at the tablecloth. Her fingers began to bleed, but she continued to claw, biting and licking her lips and pulling and scratching the skin of her neck.

Aunt Betty took a knife and stabbed the green beans. "They won't sit still." And she stabbed. "They won't sit still!" And she stabbed and she stabbed.

Aunt Mary clenched and unclenched a fist while her other hand clutched the blade of her knife, squeezing until a trail of blood ran down her arm to pool on her plate.

Uncle Raymond stood and grabbed Uncle Johnny. "You alright there? Where are your meds?"

Uncle Johnny patted each of his pockets in a panic. "I don't know! I don't know what I've done with them!"

"Everybody calm down!" Pop's voice shook the room. He pounded his fist on the table, rattling the cutlery against the plates.

"Stop yelling! You're always yelling!" Mom shouted.

Pop pounded his fists.

Uncle Johnny clutched his chest.

Uncle Raymond put his hands in the cranberry sauce, scooped up a handful, and threw it against the wall then wiped his fingers on his face.

Aunt Betty stabbed the green beans.

Aunt Mary released the knife she'd been squeezing and grabbed Aunt Betty by the wrist. "Leave the green beans alone!"

"They won't stop moving!"

Aunt Mary seized the knife by the blade. "I said, leave them alone!!"

Mom grabbed Aunt Mary. Pops shouted. Uncle Raymond threw a bowl against the wall. Uncle Johnny grabbed Uncle Raymond. And Aunt Betty stabbed the green beans.

There had always been family arguments at Thanksgiving dinner, but this was too much, even for the Likearts. Amidst the confusion, Howie collected the Gobbles bones off everyone's plates, put them onto his plate, and backed away from the table.

Aunt Mary wrestled with Aunt Betty, and Aunt Betty kept on stabbing. "They won't stay still." A geyser of blood hit Uncle Raymond in the face.

There was blood and stabbing and mashed potatoes and gravy.

Aunt Mary threw herself onto Aunt Betty.

There were insults and punches and cranberry sauce and pumpkin pie.

Uncle Raymond threw a plate against the wall. Pop threw himself onto Uncle Raymond. Uncle Raymond stuck the metal poker thing in Pop's throat. "You're always yelling!" shouted Mom, and she stuck the carving knife in Aunt Mary's chest.

There were knives stuck in necks and forks stuck in faces and cornbread and yams and pecan pie.

Howie took the pan with the yellowish-brown juice off the table. Something else to be thankful for: nobody had knocked over the pan and spilled its precious contents. He dumped the bones he'd collected into the pan.

There were bodies on the table and bodies on the floor and Gobbles bones piled in a pan.

Howie looked at the bloody chaos around him and shook his head. *It's going to take a whole lot of good science to undo this mess.*

Holiday Baggage

Ann Gibson

When we got back I emptied my handbag.
On top, the much used purse and wallet,
and a supermarket bill I'd paid.
Underneath, a restaurant receipt with my name on it,
the empty sun cream, sand-scratched sunglasses,
two pairs of untouched reading specs
(I can't read in the sun),
the car hire agreement you arranged by phone
with my credit card
and, of course, the petrol station bill.
At the bottom, to be thrown away,
the debris of sugar cubes,
salt, pepper and serviettes you gave me
and the realisation that
I need a new, less expensive bag.

Holiday Leftovers

A Cup of Holiday Cheer

KC Grifant

"Double venti half pump pumpkin spice soy latte no whip?" The barista smiled at Samantha as he guessed her order, his eyes like mocha flecks.

"You remembered!" Samantha hadn't missed a day at the coffee shop since the start of seasonal drinks. "Let me get a pumpkin loaf too."

"You got it," he said. "Will that be all for you today?"

"Ooooh how about a gingerbread loaf for later?"

"Great. Anything else?"

Samantha shook her head and hummed along to "It's the Most Wonderful Time of the Year" playing over the speakers. When he handed her the bag of pastries, she paused.

"There is one other thing..." Samantha began.

"No word yet," the barista said. After checking to make sure there was no one behind Samantha, he leaned in conspiratorially. "But keep an eye on our social media. I *hear* they may be rolling out Holiday Cheer as soon as this week."

Samantha squealed. The new mystery drink had been hyped since *last year*, and she had entered every online contest to be one of the early tasters to no avail. As she waited by the pick-up counter, she pulled up the company's social streams. She had set up an automated alert for her phone whenever a new post went up but still liked to check. Nothing, except for an announcement that a limited-edition holiday tote would be given out when the drink became available.

Samantha was a connoisseur of holiday drinks from all of the major vendors. She knew whose eggnog latte had a touch more nutmeg, where to find the best-balanced gingerbread spice drinks, and *the* place to get the most whipped cream topping for a peppermint mocha. But the new holiday drink promised to be something that would blow the others out of the water.

This week, she told herself as she took an approving sip of her latte, savoring the caffeine and sugar.

It was silly to be so excited about a drink. She knew that; yet there was something unabashedly fun about getting caught up in holiday festivities. And if a drink could lift her spirits for a few bucks, it was worth it, she thought as she headed out of the coffee shop and back into the mall, crammed with shoppers and Christmas and Hanukkah décor.

A lot of people bemoaned the holiday crowds. Samantha reveled in it. Like a seasoned sailor on familiar waters, she maneuvered seamlessly between the currents of people, mouthing whatever Christmas song was blasting and shooting smiles at anyone wearing holiday accessories.

As luck would have it, her phone alerted her a few minutes later to a new post. Holiday Cheer would be available tomorrow at all locations, supplies limited. *Finally.*

The next morning, she was standing at the dark café door at 4 am, a full hour before opening. She once waited 18 hours in line at Comic Con to see the cast of her favorite show, so this was a piece of cake.

First in line, Samantha thought in satisfaction and tweeted it a moment later before playing a promotional video for *#HolidayCheer*.

"What's *in* this?" One of the taste testers, a brunette showing a little too much cleavage, raved. The video didn't show the actual beverage, only the tasters' reactions.

"We call the special ingredient Holiday Cheer, after the drink," the company representative said with a wink. "Think of it as the new Coca Cola. You can't place it, but something in it makes you feel better amidst the stress and chaos of the holidays. Holiday Cheer can get you where you need to be."

Once the video ended, Samantha switched to her very detailed and *very* long Christmas task list. She did it all in a joyous frenzy: printing her own clever-but-sweet cards, correlating 100% recycled wrapping paper with matching bows and tags, organizing her work's Secret Santa, and considering each present she would give with the solemnity of a saint. She baked dozens of cookies and presented them, cellophaned and topped with ribbons, to benefactors like the FedEx guy and the staff at her gym. And as for holiday parties, this year was a record—she had no less than *nine* to attend already.

"I'm like Mrs. Claus," she'd joke with her friends.

All she was missing was a husband and house so she could take cheesy family photos and deck out a yard with enormous inflatable decorations and lights. Oh, *the lights.* She had outlined her studio apartment with blue icicles, bulbous glass balls and the smaller white blinkers, all in a feverish cornucopia of flashing colors. If she ever lived in a real house, she would get so many lights that the surge in her electric bill would be a badge of pride, one people would shake their heads over in affectionate disbelief.

She even knew what she would tell her future kids about Santa. She wasn't religious—religion was so serious!—but she would explain how Christmas tales reflected the spirit of the holidays, tapping the very best and most generous side people had to offer. It was like a veil settling over everyday life. For about two months everything was different. Special.

At last the doors opened, and a cheer rose up behind Samantha from the line that spanned out to the parking lot. She felt like the head of a proud snake as she led the other customers toward the counter. Baristas worked with machine-like precision, placing down one cup after another topped with signature red-and-white swirls in anticipation of the orders.

The employee who rang her up smiled through his piercings. "Ready for some holiday cheer?"

"I am *brimming* with holiday cheer," Samantha said. "I've been waiting for this since *last* year." He looked appropriately impressed and handed her the exclusive tote—a mini canvas bag printed with red bells and a splash of silver glitter.

"I love it!" Samantha shrieked then lowered her voice. "Thanks." Nothing matched the utter satisfaction of a free, high-quality item. That, coupled with being one of the first customers to try the coveted drink, was a double whammy of reward signals for her brain.

At last the warm cup was in her hand. It was more beautiful than she had expected: flakes of crushed candy cane rested atop the striped swirl of whipped cream, along with brighter crimson specks she couldn't place. A miniature gingerbread man rose artfully in the mountain of fluff capping the caramel-colored beverage.

Samantha pressed through the crowd into the mall, walking rapidly toward her favorite holiday display with her free hand guarding the drink. In the mall's west wing, a giant snow family surrounded a dining table piled high with gifts. There, in front of a heap of sparkling fake snow, Samantha posted a quick selfie with the tote and drink before taking her first sip.

Heavenly. She swirled the blend of holiday spices on her tongue, trying to place the delightful combination. Nutmeg, certainly, and the barest hint of cinnamon. Was that molasses? She took another sip and a warm glow spread through her chest. Placebo? No, she definitely felt good, like after a few sips of spiked eggnog.

"Holiday cheer," she murmured, nibbling at the gingerbread man. Her head buzzed at the temples, but not in a drunk way. Rather, everything seemed especially clear, sharp as ice. "Silver Bells" blared over the speakers and she could almost feel each note chime and hover in the air like something liquid and humming. The song sounded so striking she actually turned to check if there were real bells behind her.

Samantha smiled. All of the people passing her looked utterly divine, like characters in a movie, bundled and busy as life-sized ants scurrying through the tunnels of the mall. Parents toting two girls in animal-themed pushcarts grinned at Samantha simultaneously.

Holidays really are the best, Samantha thought, downing the rest of her drink. One of the girls dropped something out of the back of her pushcart and Samantha darted forward.

"Hold on! You lost—"

It was one of those little elf-on-the-shelf dolls, a skinny, green-clad Santa's helper. As Samantha's hands closed around its soft cloth body, its head turned to look at her.

The elf laughed. *Battery-operated,* Samantha thought. But its laugh was mean, a shriek that seemed to laugh *at* her.

"Oh you are in for a treat," the elf said, its eyes rotating in its sockets.

"*My toy,*" one of the girls hollered. She was standing outside of her pushcart and her pupils were as red as Santa's suit.

"*Here.*" Samantha thrust it at her and rubbed her own eyes. The girl must have a medical condition.

Or maybe it was Samantha. A dark red hue seemed to hover at the corners of her vision, even after she blinked. Over the speakers, "Silver Bells" ramped up, faster and faster in a demented version of itself.

Am I having a stroke? Samantha dropped the cup of Holiday Cheer. It rolled past her furred boots, dripping a little leftover whipped cream. Something scurried out of the cup before it disappeared into the display.

Samantha jumped as the music screeched louder. *"Silver hell... silver hell... It's Christmas time... if you're shitty."*

"That's not right," Samantha said, her voice sounding far too panicked to her own ears. "It's silver *bells.*"

Something caught her eye, distracting her from the erroneous song lyrics. The snowman family was moving. The mall had hired actors to stand in instead of mannequins, Samantha realized.

"Fun," she told herself after a shaky breath. She'd watch the show while she got her bearings.

The snow family—a male, female, and three child-sized figures, all with coal-like eyes and carrot noses—gyrated as if they were on motors and locked their eyes with Samantha's. The snowman tipped his bowler hat and grabbed the ball that made up his lower torso with twig-like hands. He tossed the torso ball up in the air as the rest of him floated and reformed. The snowwoman ripped off her apron and likewise detached a piece from her body, lobbing the white globe to a smaller snow child who caught it and threw it back. Soon the entire snow family was exchanging and flinging snowballs, all while keeping their gazes fixed on Samantha.

Samantha clapped uncertainly. Something about the way they threw their snowballs seemed inexplicably vulgar. She shrieked as an icy clump of snow smashed into her face.

"What the hell?" She tried to sound angry but her voice trembled as she shook out pieces of ice from her collar. She looked behind her and nearly screamed. Shoppers passed by in a blur, as if they were in a sped-up video. Their heads turned to snarl at Samantha, their mouths crammed with pointed mistletoe.

Samantha's fingers wound around the canvas handle of her limited-edition tote as she tried to ground herself. But it was too late. The world seemed to peel back a fine veneer, as if a sheet had been ripped away to show the rot beneath. Berried ivy raced around the storefronts, growing thick and filling the air with the smell of must and decay.

The snow family was gone, but in its stead swarmed small figures, streaming over the hard snow that had taken over the display. Ants?

No, they were gingerbread men. Three dozen at least, led by the one that had adorned her cup of Holiday Cheer. As they neared they smiled, their teeth glinting silver spikes. The leader bled black where Samantha had tasted its arm. Several of the humanoid cookies donned candy canes sharpened to long points in place of limbs, like a profane experiment in cross-candy fusion.

She didn't actually scream until they started climbing her boots and jeans, nipping with their teeth. One lifted its pointy candy cane arm and stabbed her in the wrist.

Samantha flung them off and ran. She tried to go to the parking lot or even the coffee shop to get help. Instead, she found herself at the center of the mall, the exact spot she didn't want to be. She skidded to a stop at the giant fir tree swaying under the weight of super-sized silver and gold ornaments.

Santa's workshop, a blinking sign exclaimed next to the tree. A half-man, half-reindeer behind the sign snarled and paced, eyeing her as if it wanted to charge.

I am glimpsing another realm, she thought. *One of Dante's circles of hell. A Silver Bell Hell.*

The children in line glared in unison, eyes as red as brake lights. They looked angry or hungry, she couldn't tell which. But none of them moved, too afraid of losing their spot in line. Samantha prepared to run again when she spotted Santa, his back to her.

The looming red-and-white figure turned. Samantha was terrified at what monstrosity she would see above the Santa suit. What was there was far worse than she could have guessed: a blank slate, completely white, as if his face was a blizzard onto itself. That terrible void sucked all of the strength out of her and she fell to the tiled floor, crying.

"Why doesn't he have a face?" she sobbed to herself. Despite lacking features, his head was cocked toward her. Listening. Or waiting.

The faceless Santa took a step toward Samantha and spread his arms, too long to be human, as if he was welcoming her to his lair. The world shifted, spinning like it was in a blender, with him at the epicenter. He threw his head back in a silent laugh.

Samantha turned away from the maelstrom as a burning sensation made its way up her throat. A great glob of peppermint foam flaked with crushed candy cane, tinted yellow from her bile, forced itself out.

She threw it all up, right into her exclusive special edition holiday canvas tote bag.

#

Samantha woke up the next morning in her apartment with a blurred memory and headache. At first she figured it was a hangover, but as she waited for her mind to clear, hardly any memories of the previous day came to her.

Did someone roofie me? She wondered, rubbing at a sharp ache at her wrist. She remembered the mall and Holiday Cheer and feeling sick—

Nightmares. She had had nightmares but couldn't recall the details. Samantha tried to blink away the feeling of dread that had settled into her chest.

By the end of the day, she had convinced herself it was a 24-hour bug or, quite possibly, an allergic reaction to Holiday Cheer. She kept to her apartment for a few days to be safe.

While she stayed in bed googling articles on allergies and food, Samantha stumbled across someone's personal blog ranting that synthetic flavors could, in a small subset of users, evoke inexplicable psychotic episodes, similar to a trip. One of the links on the blog led to an ode to psychedelic drugs, raving about how they let users see the world as it truly is, the layers of dimensions beneath everyday reality. Samantha shuddered and closed the website, quickly turning back to her many Christmas to-dos.

A week later, Samantha was back into the spirit of things, whatever sickness she had had gone. Except—the next few times she glimpsed a holiday-themed coffee cup, the music started to warp into a demented version of itself. She would quickly will it away, sweating beneath her festive sweater, until it passed.

She gave up coffee shortly after.

Tricksters

Amanda Cecelia Lang

8:57 p.m.

I linger on the steps of my front porch, hugging the candy bowl with a heaviness in my chest. The last of the trick-or-treaters crunch down my leaf-littered lawn, returning to the shadows of the sidewalk. Teenagers, tricksters, they jostle each other, hooting and whooping it up—and good for them! I'd join them if I wasn't seven decades north of my childhood. I shuffle past my clan of shakily carved jack-o-lanterns. I'll keep the candles burning a while longer. Maybe there will be stragglers. The gang of candy-bag ruffians I ran with back in the day never went home before midnight.

Grinning at antique memories, I settle into the creaking wooden bones of my rocking chair—hidden deep enough in porch shadows to give any visitors who tip-toe up my walkway a nice healthy scare. If there *is* anyone left to scare. The street beyond my oak trees rests in moon-dappled peace. But an old man can hope, can't he? One more glimpse of sneaky mischief, of snickering monster-shaped shadows streaking through front yards. This was the hour when the old gang used to switch out pillowcases full of Pixi Stix and Atomic Fire Balls for sacks of soap and toilet-tissue pilfered from our mothers' powder rooms.

Ah God, do I miss those guys. Squares by day, hellions by night. Good old Emerson with his giddy sense of humor and out-of-this-world throwing arm—he could chuck a roll of TP higher than any kid I knew. And sweet-tooth Charlie who belly-crawled through yards and giggled like a ten-year-old madman at every prank we pulled.

These days they're elderly men in their graves. Emerson ended up the butt-end of a heart attack, and Charlie got suckered by a stroke. Death snuck right up on the poor bastards, only nobody was laughing in the end.

Of course, back in the day, we thought we'd laugh forever, live forever. Hell, some Halloweens it seemed as if the good times might just roll on and on. Treats and scary stories and tricks. Hot damn, the mischief we caused! And me as our mastermind, always one prank ahead, hip to every trick in the bag.

The neighborhood never saw us coming—not even dressed as spacemen and masked cowboys and skeletal grim reapers in inky-glittery robes. They'd wake up November 1st to find their windows soaped and foggy, their trees and yards haunted with slow-wavering streamers like the tattered remains of bedsheet ghosts. And Halloween would last another day.

Somewhere down my street, a young lady shrieks. Sharp and sudden—maybe at a goblin or a vampire leaping out at her from behind a parked car. It's the perfect goof for when the walk home turns spooky.

I listen for a second scream, for bursts of laughter, but the spiced autumn air settles back into silence.

With a sigh, I balance the candy dish on the porch railing and flip the switch on my transistor radio—same model I had as a kid. Another tradition, I dial in K-103's annual Halloween radio drama, already in progress. The gang and I used to live for these old shows—crackly and creepy over the airwaves, my radio clipped to my belt as we capered through sleepy yards and blackened streets.

Tonight's story is a classic: the proverbial escaped maniac on the loose with a mask and a hook—the kind who terrorizes nubile couples necking in backseats. They're even playing it as breaking news, complete with buzzing police bulletins. I chuckle. Might fool the kiddies, maybe even spook some folks into locking their doors. But old pros like me are wise to the gotchas of the season.

As the newscaster interviews snappy police detectives and weeping survivors, I indulge in leftover chocolate bars and watch pumpkins and porchlights blink out across the neighborhood. One after another, signaling the time for treats has expired.

Somewhere closer, comes that second scream. A high-pitched shriek, it echoes between the houses.

On the radio, the newscaster's brisk vocal fry darkens in tone: *"In the interest of public safety, please, Miss, tell our listeners what you saw tonight..."*

A melodramatic pause darkens the staticky airways, then: *"We were driving home from Lookout Hill,"* says a voice reminiscent of poodle skirts and strawberry phosphates. *"There was someone lying in the middle of the road. My boyfriend pulled over, and we got out to help. But it was just a scarecrow. Someone's idea of a joke. We dragged it off to the side then climbed back into the car. But the keys were missing from the ignition! That's when we heard the most awful sound... a* tap-tap-tapping *on the undercarriage. Someone was hiding beneath the car! My boyfriend and I slammed our doors just as a dark shape crawled out from underneath us and rose up outside my window. A tall, gangling man with a machete!"*

Chuckling again, I shake my head—in my day it was a hook.

"He wore a tattered burlap sack over his head, same as the scarecrow he left in the road. Black stiches for eyes and a crooked grinning mouth. He tapped his blade on the glass and tilted his head, as if to say 'Gotcha!' We weren't going anywhere, not without the keys. He was almost playful at first. Circling the car, tapping his sharp steel blade along the hood and roof and windows. Tap-tap-tapping *right up until he—"*

My porch light blacks out. The radio buzzes to silence.

A power outage? Oh, good grief! And just when things were getting hairy.

Streetlights and glowing windows go black all down the block until the whole neighborhood rests in black-and-grey gloom and breath-held anticipation. The only light is the sallow, flickering glow from my jack-o-lanterns.

I throw a sideways glance at my dark and silent radio, and my pulse goes jagged. That radio runs on batteries, so how the heck did it—

A sharp sound cuts across the neighborhood.

Tap. Tap. Tapping ...

The sound drifts along the street and through the oaks in my front yard, makes the hairs on the back of my neck prickle on end.

I creak forward in my rocking chair, squinting at the murky, night-stained lawn and the empty sidewalk where—

TAP-TAP-TAP! Someone knocks on my front door.

I startle, gasp, nearly fall out of my seat, heart clenching like a fist.

A short grim reaper cloaked in an inky-glittery robe stands alone on my welcome mat. The plastic scythe is his small pale hand is just like the ones they used to sell at the corner Five-N-Dime. The kid withdraws it from my door.

"Snuck up on me there, didn't you?" I laugh the laugh of old fools and clutch the candy dish against my pounding, hammering chest. The trick-or-treater turns to face me in my rocking chair. Beneath his reaper's hood, he wears a cartoon skull mask with an exaggerated grin and gleaming white-and-black eyes.

"Nifty costume, kid. Had one like it myself once." I haul myself up onto boney, uneasy knees and wobble toward him. Sweat prickles my forehead despite the crisp autumn air, and an eerie heaviness returns like a sack of tricks to my pounding chest. My left arm trembles, tingles, ready with the candy bowl. Lucky kid, I think I might dump it all into his pillowcase and call it a night. I just need those three magic words ...

But the little reaper tilts his head at me, silent.

He reaches out with his plastic scythe and *tap-tap-taps* my breastbone.

"What the hay, kid?" I try to chuckle, but my voice has gone gravelly.

With a swish of his cloak, the kid rushes out into the yard—and *oh!*

My eyes widen like moons. The candy dish tumbles from my hands with a clatter.

Oh, how strange. How impossible and strange!

My yard is haunted.

Hundreds of gauzy toilet-tissue streamers hang from the oak trees, tendrils of a simpler time. They sway in a lazy breeze and part like a veil to reveal the dark silhouettes of candy-bag ruffians watching me from the sidewalk. My heart pounds and pounds with sharp pangs of nostalgia.

The old gang.

Sweaty-icy awe prickles my spine and antique skin, and I stagger forward and grip the porch railing.

The old gang—these days, they're elderly men in their graves.

Yet I'd know those cowboy hats and space helmets and giddy Halloween troublemakers anywhere. They face my house with devilish, glinting eyes and sagging pillowcases full of treats.

Or is it tricks?

I clutch a hand against my pounding chest. *Pounding, pounding,* and the nightscape spinning. I need to sit down. But I'm afraid to look away from yesteryear, from the ethereal spectacle haunting my front yard—afraid if I turn around this living-dream will end and darkness will sneak up on me.

Impish and gleeful, the tricksters disperse into my yard, boyish shadows sneaking through the ghostland of gossamer white streamers. Emerson in his space helmet tiptoes with slow, exaggerated footsteps, while Charlie in the cowboy hat drops down and belly-crawls through the fallen leaves.

All the while, the pint-sized grim reaper looms on the sidewalk. He points at me with his cloaked hand and taps his plastic scythe against the pavement.

Tap-tap-tapping. The sound is surreal, it floats through the yard, echoing all around me.

Sneaking up.

I tighten my grip on my chest.

Tap-tap-TAP!

A machete bursts through my ribcage.

Blood sprays out, splashes the jack-o-lanterns—and my hand closes around the blade. I can't believe it. Razor sharp steel. It slices through my fingers, but I try to hold on even as the jelly goes out of my knees.

I collapse to the porch, old meat and bone and nostalgia.

"Gotcha," the maniac in the scarecrow mask says and yanks his machete free.

Should've seen that coming. Of course, in my day, it was a hook ...

Dying laughter wheezes through the frothing, ragged hole in my chest. With a playful tilt of his masked head—stitched eyes, warped burlap smile—the maniac steps over me and blows out my jack-o-lanterns.

It should all go black.

But instead of flickering to darkness, the nightscape flares around me. Misty and white, as if someone soaped the windows of my soul.

The scarecrow maniac stalks back into the night. *Tap-tap-tapping* his bloody blade down my porch steps, strolling past oak trees laced with spectral streamers and out into the neighborhood. Somewhere farther down, sirens rise and red-and-blues strobe against the houses. Help is coming, but that side of the street seems suddenly silly and far away—like how childhood was once long lost.

With the maniac gone, the coast is clear. Charlie and Emerson storm the porch around me, whooping and hooting and giggling like tiny madmen.

I try to protest as they grab my elbows and haul my old bones upright. My head droops, but as I squint down at what should be my slashed and ancient torso, cold awe tingles through my chest and bones and spirit.

Oh, how impossible and strange!

I stand cloaked in a robe of inky glitter, and my tiny, ageless hands grip a plastic scythe and a pillowcase.

All around us, those tattered gossamer streamers ripple and sway, never darkening or fading. Excitement and sweet terror swell inside my chest as I caper down the steps of my blood-splattered porch. Still can't believe I fell for that—a machete.

But I can only laugh.

The night is young again.

The neighborhood will never see us coming!

A gang of mischievous shadows, we jostle and jest and live it up, out here on the sidewalks of our endless Halloween.

Don't Count Your Eggs

Or, Springtime in Belville

Elle Hartford

You know what's great? *Not* sharing a bed with a great big hairy magical dog. William, my canine companion and winner of Belville's Loudest Snore award, had recently taken to complaining that his cushion in the window seat of our apartment was "too scrunched." Despite the fact that *he* had been the one to do the "scrunching"—he practically lived in that window seat—apparently *I* would be the one to bear the consequence of the scrunchiness, as William had opted to take over my bed until I replaced his favorite cushion. In fact, it wasn't just me: the entire town of Belville, or at least everyone present for what would come to be known as the Spring of Terror, would suffer for William's commitment to his beauty sleep.

I rolled on to the floor on the morning of Belville's Ostara Egg Hunt feeling like I'd been trampled by gigantic bunnies all night long. The one good thing about it was that, seeing as I'd already been pushed half out of bed, I didn't have far to fall.

William stretched. "Keep it down, will you, Red?"

"Oh, I'm sorry, did my discomfort wake you up?" I glared over a mountain of blankets at the big black dog.

He sniffed. "You're never going to win the egg hunt with that attitude, you know."

"Then you should be sad, because if I don't win the prize money, I'm not getting you a new cushion."

"Belville's Ostara celebration isn't just about winning money," William told me primly. "The winner also gets to guide the 'rebirth' of the town square and oversee the spring equinox feast."

"And tend the ritual beacon and be remembered for ages to come, yada yada yada," said I, stumbling into the kitchen for a glass of water to—hopefully—clear my head. It would probably take something stronger than water to do the trick, but I'm a hopeful person. "You sound like Gloria. As far as holidays go, Ostara's nice, but really it's just a celebration of spring. I don't see the big deal."

"You're participating, aren't you?" William pointed out.

"Only because I need money for all your 'spring renovations.'"

"How festive." William rolled over on his back, thoroughly messing up an already messy bed.

I sighed and downed my glass of water. "Listen, mister, 'rebirth' doesn't come cheap. On top of your cushion, I've got new plants to buy, a new line of spring potions for the shop, not to mention new sheets—"

"How about you get yourself a watch? Because if you keep standing there complaining, you're never going to be ready for the competition in time."

~~~

William could be annoying at times, but he could also be right. The sun had barely risen, but plenty of noise drifted up from the park outside the apartment windows. Thanking my lucky stars that it promised to be a warm day, I threw on a sundress and sandals while simultaneously sopping up the blackest of black teas with a bit of yesterday's bread. Normally I stick to lab coats and tunics, but with a dress, I didn't have to worry about matching separate pieces of clothing. The way I saw it, the egg hunt wasn't about frivolities: it was about focus and speed. In order to win, all I had to do was find as many brightly colored eggs as possible before lunch.

Not all residents of small-town Belville shared my practical approach to the day's festivities, though. Even

William had been infected with holiday cheer. While I stepped out the front door, he bounded off ahead of me like a rabbit late to a party, shouting something about 'help.' Before I could puzzle this out, the owner of the beauty shop next door called out to me.

"Nice to see you taking this seriously, Red."

"Gloria." I locked my shop door—no one would be doing any business during the festivities—and turned to face my neighbor. She stood a head higher than me and on top of that, a plume of red feathers rising from her head gave her an impossibly regal—or perhaps warlike—air. "Happy Ostara," I yawned.

"Since this is your first year, you might want to sit this one out. Leave the search to the professionals," she continued.

Definitely warlike, I thought, looking over her black egg-hunting outfit accessorized with heavy boots. "Uh-huh. I thought this was supposed to be fun?"

Gloria scoffed. "'Fun' is for the kiddie crafts and games afterwards."

"But it's a celebration."

"It's a test."

"A test for what? When do you ever need purple egg-spotting skills in real life?"

"A test," Gloria insisted, grinding her heel into the cobblestone street, "for determination and ingenuity. Which you'd need to preside over a ceremony for rebirth."

I was torn between pointing out that, as far as I could tell, the only real 'rebirth' involved was deciding which annuals to plant in the town square and the realization that if I said this, Gloria might well consider it an invitation to fight. And I was wearing my only decent dress. *Is it worth it to ruin my outfit in the scuffle just to one-up Gloria?* I was saved from making this difficult decision by another bright voice.

"Rebirth is very important in the phoenix community, right, Gloria?" Scholar and bookseller Luca, in his habitual dusty robes, grinned expectantly at us both. He practically skipped up the street to join the growing crowd, bright green eyes shining against his dark skin. At first he seemed like a child waiting for lessons to begin, but in the next moment he launched into a lecture of his own. "You see, Red, ceremonies like this are very common across Pastoria, but the degree to which they're held in regard varies from place to place. In Pine, for example, they go so far as to paint all the shopfronts pink and replace all the town flowers with daffodils, while I've heard that down in Hollow it's really just an excuse to have a dance under the moon. Here in Belville, our tradition began with the inception of the Ritual Fire, which isn't really a fire at all but is instead a symbol of—"

"Oh my gods," Gloria cut in. "You're going to talk right through the starting announcement. What are you doing, trying to sabotage us?"

"I just thought that Red might like to know—oh." Luca watched Gloria stalk away, his head to one side. Then he turned to me. Whether because of his lecturing or Gloria's attitude, the crowd had left a wide berth around my front steps. All backs were to us as people crowded into the grassy, tree-dotted Square, their attention fixed on the ritual fire at its center. I shrugged at Luca, thinking, *And here I barely made it out my front door. I should have brought along a mug of tea.*

Luca, apparently embracing the spirit of the day, decided to start over. "Hi, Red," he beamed. "Want a daffodil? I've got a whole boxful back at the bookstore, the post office got me confused with some scholar over in Pine. Can you do anything with them, for your shop? They might be lucky. I should have looked up daffodil potions but instead I stayed up all night reading about—"

"Sure, thanks." I hastened to accept the yellow flower Luca had produced from somewhere in his wide black sleeves. Reluctant to carry it all morning and bereft of pockets, I tucked it behind my ear. This was mistake number one (or maybe number two, if you count not baiting Gloria); I have since learned that daffodils worn by the heart bring good luck, but when they're worn anywhere else, the nature of the luck is up for debate. "We don't use a whole lot of daffodils in alchemy, but you could use them on Gloria somehow. Throw them in her way and distract her from being such a force of nature, maybe."

"Like Atalanta and the apples." Luca's eyes twinkled. "So you're really going to go for it, the competition, I mean? I think that's great. I usually just find two or three. Gloria has the record—a few years back she found forty-one of them. There was a big controversy because she *thought* she found forty-two but it turned out one was just an acorn that had gone all moldy and Officer Thorn said—"

"Atten-*tion!*"

Said Officer had climbed up on a barrel in the middle of the Square, her green orcish head and broad shoulders bobbing just below the lip of the spring beacon. Though ostensibly she yelled at the entire crowd—which looked to be just about everyone who lived in Belville, plus their uncles and aunts to boot—I could have sworn Officer Thorn stared directly at Luca and me.

"You all know the rules," Thorn continued. Luca's anecdote died in his throat. "No fighting. No sabotage. No throwing smaller persons up into trees to retrieve eggs. All eggs must be found and captured under your own power!"

"Why is she saying 'captured' like that?" I whispered to Luca. "The eggs don't actually move, do they?"

"No, not normally."

"'*Normally*'?"

"Well, there was one year where a bit of a fracas broke out. 'The Great Egg War,' some of the people around here call it. According to a reliable source, someone said something about someone's mother and then someone else responded with a pie lobbed at another person's face, and then everyone was throwing the eggs, not to mention the pastries set out for the banquet—"

"ALL EGGS," Officer Thorn resumed at a bellow, "must be collected in the regulation baskets distributed to your homes and businesses yesterday. Any eggs found in any other container will be disqualified!"

A small wicker basket with a red ribbon emerged from behind Luca's sleeve. This prompted me to look frantically for my own green-bedecked basket, which I found after I'd kicked it over; earlier I'd set it near my feet so I wouldn't forget it. *Oops.*

As I bent to retrieve my basket I noticed that Luca's already held something that looked suspiciously like a book.

"All eggs are hidden within town limits, *not* in shop or home interiors. We'll have no housebreaking this year, you hear? I had the Witch make up a security spell, special." Officer Thorn looked meaningfully around the crowd, and then declared, "You have between the first horn now and the second horn at lunch time to complete your search. Ready. Set. Go!"

The sound of a horn rang out across the Square, making most people duck as though they could avoid the oncoming noise. Luca positively radiated at me.

"Best of luck, Red!"

~~~

Focus and speed, I reminded myself, pushing aside thoughts of scuffles and egg-throwing. I stuck to my plan. I'd decided days ago that my best chance would be to go after the hard-to-find eggs stashed all over the outskirts of town; all the easy-to-find eggs sitting in the central Square would get picked up by the massive crowd. The way I looked at it, getting trampled by a bunch of egg-hunters wouldn't help my chance to win the prize money.

Besides, when I say speed, I mean *speed*. Have I mentioned yet that, due to some magic in my ancestry, I can run super-fast?

It's hardly cheating when Officer Thorn said herself that you had to rely on *your own power* to find the eggs.

I'd raced up and down the alley behind my shop twice for good measure and returned to the edge of the Square with a good half-dozen eggs by the time William caught up with me.

"You can't help me," I warned him, heading off whatever he had been about to say.

"I'm not helping you," he retorted. "I'm helping *me*."

"What?" I paused. Something in the self-satisfied tone of his voice triggered alarm bells in my mind. I've looked after him long enough to know when William is up to something.

Looking down at my arcane dog, I noticed something new about him. He had a basket of his own strapped to his back, secured to a very frilly white-and-blue saddle.

"What in Beyond are you *wearing?*"

"Try a Cheep," said William, panting at me with a gleam in his eye. "A new treat from the bakery. Made fresh this morning."

"A *what?*" Further inspection of the basket revealed that it did, indeed, hold piles of pastel-colored... somethings. In my surprise at the frills, I hadn't noticed them before. Keenly aware that precious egg-hunting seconds were ticking by, I leant over to look at William's basket. Sugarly blobs of yellow, pink, and white resembled fat little birds.

"A Cheep," repeated William. "Try one."

"Why?"

"Because if I get people to eat them, I make enough money to buy myself a new cushion. Seeing as you're too cold-hearted to provide me with a safe and comfortable home."

"That is *not* what you told the bakers, is it? William! That's ridiculous."

"What's ridiculous is this basket," William replied, grumbling. "I tried just dumping all the cursed things into the nearest bush, but it didn't work. There's magic on it. You have to actually take one and eat it or else I don't get credit. So take one already!"

"Welcome to the world of working for a living," I told him. And because he'd started to glow ominously, and I didn't want to be known as the worst dog-parent ever, I took a pink Cheep gingerly between two fingers. "What is it made of?"

"Beats me," said William. "I think they're gross. Eat up. See you!"

He rocketed off toward the nearest group of egg-hunters, a family whose young ones immediately began clamoring over the "Cheeps." I scrutinized mine. I do love William, but everyone has their limits, particularly on days of high-stakes competition. Deciding it wasn't worth the stomachache, I tossed the Cheep over my shoulder into the ritual beacon. The sugar crash would only slow me down later.

~ ~ ~

One bright orange striped egg teetered on a lamppost.

One red and blue mottled egg trembled above a window.

Two neon green eggs burrowed among the flowerpots outside the police station.

I'd just finished fishing a fluorescent yellow-checked egg off of a gutter when I realized that strange noises were coming from the Square.

As I paused to count my eggs, I listened with one ear. A bit of yelling, I thought, and some thunderous applause. Maybe Thorn had started a game for the people who were tired of egg-hunting? *How much time do we have left, anyway? Maybe William was right when he said I need a watch.*

"Twenty-five. Not too bad," I murmured, pleased with myself. Glancing up at the sun's position, not yet overhead, I decided I had time to race back to Market Square, check my progress, and then do a sweep along the lakeside edge of town to look for more eggs. There were bound to be some left hidden in the sand. Unless, of course, they'd been squished...

Antsy to get a move on my search, I barely slowed down when William caught up with me at the Square.

"Thorn ran off down a side street," he said. "Take another Cheep while you wait for her."

"I'm not waiting."

"Take two for your egg-hunt, then."

A *crash* rang out from somewhere behind the shops, and I paused. "What was that?"

"No idea," said William. "Are you going to take a Cheep or not?"

I scanned the area for anyone sensible to talk to, and my eye caught a spot of black among the revelry. Luca's hooded head swayed gently from side to side as he leaned against a nearby tree, reading. I grabbed two Cheeps from William, feeling them squish unpleasantly in my hand, and headed over to Luca for some actual news.

"Is Thorn entertaining the masses?" I asked him, at the same time doing my best to pawn a Cheep off on him. He waved the sickly confections away politely, which was probably for the best, since they seemed to be glued to my hand.

"I already had one. They're, um, not too bad, but they need something, I think. No, Thorn has her hands full. Apparently someone brought along a magic creature of some kind to help them on their search, and it got loose."

"Really?" I wondered what kind of creature it might be. A griffon? Those were known for good eyesight. Maybe a minor dragon, good for finding treasure? "And you're here reading instead of watching another historic egg hunt?"

"Oh, I plan to collect lots of information about it later," Luca promised. "But I find it's best not to get in Thorn's way. She says I'm... what was it?"

"Accident-prone?" I guessed, chuckling. "Well, alright then. I'm going to keep hunting. Any idea how much longer we have? Ugh, I've got to get rid of these darn Cheeps before they're permanently stuck to my hand."

"Probably an hour or so. You aren't going to eat them?"

"No. I burned the last one."

"You brought matches along?" Luca looked impressed. "Of course, you're always so prepared. Look, did you see my book? That's *my* kind of preparation. A treatise on seasonal symbols. Did you know that beacons like the one we have were once thought to give life, and were kept going all year long? Also apparently some cultures used them for cooking special ritual meals. I've just started that bit now, and it says—"

"Tell me about it later, okay, Luca?" I smiled at him, still scraping granulated dyed sugar off my palm. "I'd like to hear all about it, promise, but now's not the time."

"Right, right. Good luck hunting! Last I heard, Gloria had twenty-nine."

Darn. I sped toward the lake as fast as I could, pausing for the briefest of moments to shake the Cheeps off my hand and into the ritual fire. If I felt any guilt about using Luca's magic beacon as a Cheep disposal, it was vastly outweighed by my competitive drive. I needed to find at least five more eggs!

~~~

The thing about egg-hunting is that the whole idea of it is so incredibly silly that it throws you off-guard. The actual idea of celebrating a new season and new life makes sense, and eggs certainly fit into that, but why should the eggs be hiding? Not to mention that if you find a bright red and purple polka-dotted mystery food in the wild in real life, the *last* thing you should do is scramble it up with mayonnaise and put it into a salad. Or a sandwich. My point is, when you're already engaged in an activity that you *know* is ridiculous, your radar for ridiculous-and-potentially-dangerous occurrences gets all messed up.

I'd made it about halfway down the beach with three new eggs nestled in my basket when it finally occurred to me that the noise assaulting my eardrums wasn't wind.

It sounded more like screaming.

So much for luck.

At that point I'd gotten myself shin-deep in sand, following the trail of something brightly colored which I suspected my fatigued mind had made up. I looked up and down the beach before pinpointing the source of the sound. It came from town. In fact, it was coming directly at me. Townsfolk were barreling down the street, arms pumping, egg baskets akimbo. Eggs flew left and right like rainbow bullets.

"Get inside, get inside!"

"But what if *it* followers you?"

"You can't get inside, the Witch did a spell!"

"Ahhhh!"

Over the confused screams, I started to hear that rumbling noise again. But this time I realized it wasn't clapping. It had a rhythm to it. A rhythm like footsteps.

Very big, very loud, very scratchy footsteps.

A huge pink blob loomed above the heads of the crowd.

"Into the lake!" they cried.

In an instant they were all around me, running past me, like I was the finish-line post in the county race. I clutched desperately to my basket, trying to make sense of the situation. But it's awfully hard to make sense of anything when the world is whipping around you in a blur and everything smells overwhelmingly like s'mores and something that looks like a giant sparkly chicken is headed your way.

"Look out, look out, look out!" cried the townsfolk.

I cursed under my breath. "Is that a..."

"Look out for the giant Cheep!!"

~ ~ ~

"Windows at the feed store broken. Outdoor stalls at the farmer's market smashed—and they had just finished setting those up, mind you. Gunk all over the streets. Two of the Green's kids got stuck together, and one of the druids *still* can't smell anything but marshmallow. Not to mention the absolute *ruin* they made of the banquet table!"

Late into the evening, when the mayhem had finally broken down into what can only be described as the most dramatic sugar crash of all time, Officer Thorn paced up and down the central aisle of my potions shop. I remained safely behind the sales counter. Outside, in the twilight, teams of townsfolk dutifully mopped up pastel eggshells and tugged sticky strings of sugar out of trees before commerce resumed tomorrow.

"It's the worst Ostara ever," Officer Thorn declared.

I cleared my throat. "Well, I don't know about that. At least no one insulted anyone's mother. And when you think about it, a baby chicken growing into a—"

"*Nothing* from you, thank you very much," Officer Thorn interrupted. "Where were you when I was trying to lasso a ton of crazed pillowy bird, that's what I want to know. Some unofficial assistant you are!"

I'd been flat on my back in the sand watching an upside-down giant sugar-chicken disintegrate in the lake, most likely. But I said nothing of the incident. Instead I wondered what effect all that confectionery would have on the local fish.

"I still can't figure out how they did it," Officer Thorn continued.

"*Who* did it?"

"No word on that either. Must have been the bakers, I thought, since they made those tiny ones. You saw William with them? Terrible sales-dog, by the way. But the bakers swear they're innocent, and I'm inclined to believe them." *Probably because they fed you full of cupcakes while making their statement,* I thought, but again kept quiet. Thorn went on, "Given the disruption to the hunt, I had a thought it might be Gloria. You know, sabotaging the competition."

I frowned. "Seems a bit extreme—"

"But how would a beauty salon owner find the time to make something so huge and then bring it to life?"

With the beacon, I thought, remembering Luca's interrupted lectures on the topic.

My blood ran cold as I then recalled that *I* had thrown my Cheeps into the beacon.

"Um," said I, shivering in my sundress. "How many were there, exactly?"

"A pair," said Thorn, wheeling on her heel as she paced. "Or maybe three. You said there were reports of one that chased a crowd into the lake?"

"Yeah...about that..."

"Nonsense, all of it," declared Thorn. She heaved a heavy sigh, the shiny buttons on her uniform glinting in the dim light of the shop. "Luca's got one for the books this year. D'you reckon *he* did it, for a spot of amusement?"

"Luca's had enough trouble lately," I said. The daffodil tumbled out of my hair as I shook my head. "Actually, I think *I—*"

"You're right, I suppose. It *must* have been the bakers, then. Or William." Thorn rubbed her chin thoughtfully. "That dog of yours is always up to something. And you must admit he *did* want to get rid of them. Maybe he put a spell on them!"

"Officer Thorn, I really don't—"

"Of course you wouldn't. No one ever suspects their nearest and dearest. You said he's over at the home goods store picking out a cushion? I'll just wait and have a little chat with him, then."

"Yeah... A cushion..."

I twisted the flower petals in my lap, my brain a whirlwind of thought. The most coherent line of thinking ran like this: William had pawned off all his Cheeps on unsuspecting tasters in order to get that cushion. If he found out I hadn't eaten mine and therefore hadn't helped earn him any sales credit, he wouldn't just accuse me of being cold-hearted; he'd declare all-out war. I'd be lucky to have another restful night's sleep ever again.

Right then and there, I decided my secret would go with me to the grave.

"You know what," I said to Officer Thorn, "some mysteries just won't be solved."

And this was one I wouldn't lose a wink of sleep over.

Future Tourism Promo for Antarctica

Kurt Newton

Tired of the heat?
Has Level Red Stagnation got you down?
Well, book your next vacation to Antarctica!

Due to global warming
our once chilly little outpost
has become the destination capital of the world!

You'll enjoy year-round skiing & snowmobiling.
Tee off at one of our summer golf courses
where the daylight never ends!

For the kiddies there's Penguin Village,
a place of enchantment and thrill rides,
where the penguins dress like Disney characters.

Stay at one of our five-star ice hotels,
and select from the delicious menus available
at our all-you-can-eat sushi bars.

And for newlyweds, try one of our winter packages,
when the aurora is the only light you'll see.
So romantic.

Holiday Leftovers

With the North Pole melting
and water levels rising everywhere,
Antarctica is the last best hope for that weekend getaway.

So book a flight now!
Before another piece of the ice shelf
breaks away and floats off into the sea.

Limited time offer.

Xmas Letter

Stephen Schwei

Season's greetings to one and all,
friends and family, short and tall.
It's been a busy year once again
so time to get out my paper and pen.

We hope everyone has been quite well.
We have so much of our news to tell.
Nothing like the holidays I swear
to put us back in the mood to share.

Aunt Mabel had one of her legs removed
to stave off flesh-eating bugs, she improves.
She's returned to her usual jovial self,
cracking jokes like an irrepressible elf.

Uncle Frank bought an old Toyota sedan
after smashing his new Porsche into a van.
It's a little more sedate, we know,
intended to get around, and less for show.

Timmy's transition is now complete.
He's Tammy no more, still happy and sweet.
He just might graduate high school this year
then off to find himself a career.

Holiday Leftovers

Susie is no longer a hypnotist,
switching gears as a numismatist.
We guess she's happy, hard to say,
buried in musty coins all day.

Billy has stopped wetting his bed,
so our trips have gotten the go-ahead.
His therapist has done such wonders,
now he only pees when it thunders.

On our third cruise earlier this year,
we met a couple we found so dear.
We bought a house big enough for us all,
come visit and meet Sally and Paul.

They bring great passion into our lives
and help maintain Martha's beehives.
If two can live together cheaper than one,
imagine four of us and what can be done.

The Costa Rican jungle has been so great
though sweltering all day until it gets late.
Panthers run wild here like squirrels there,
we just carry our guns everywhere.

It turns out being fired has its own rewards
I have much more time than I had before.
My lawsuit against my boss didn't get very far,
but we manage ok after I sold my car.

Martha says she misses her office. Right!
Nothing to complain about to me each night.
She has taken up making all of our clothes,
but we don't need much the way it goes.

If you have a chance, drop us a line.
We hope you're all doing just as fine.
Stop by if you travel to San Jose.
We're three hours south and a ferry away.

Best wishes for all each and every holiday!

Heebie Jeebies

John Wolf

Something clung to the chilly air, something harsh and spiced like the smoke from burning leaves. It might have come from the golden remains of the harvest blown from the turned soil, rich and ripe as graveyard earth. But there was something else. An unseen dry charge lingered, only growing stronger as the reddening sun shrank below the horizon. It tingled on the nose of every princess, monster, and superhero running out of their homes and into the street. Halloween had come, staking its sugary claim on this special night.

Margie hated it.

"You going to be alright?" Herb struggled with Ryder's Buzz Lightyear costume.

Margie tried giving a reassuring smile. It seemed to do the trick. Ryder, ready for Space Command, dashed out into the growing evening.

"You two just go have fun." Margie hefted the candy bowl in her arms. "I won't starve. Go on now."

Hurrying Herb out the door didn't help. It only reminded him.

"Wait a minute. Wait just a minute."

He reached behind the door and fished out the skeleton. CVS had a sale the day before, one Herb declared "Too good to pass up." This particular paper skeleton, a real steal for only five bucks, glowed ghoulish green in the dark and came with crazy googly eyes.

Their grandson had approved. "Cool!" Between Ryder and Herb there was no negotiation.

"Lemme just," Herb muttered to no one in particular while he fiddled with the sticky backing. "There." He stood back to admire the handiwork. A cool breeze rustled down Ohio Street and sent the skeleton into a demented jig, eyeballs waggling on tissue paper optic nerves, bony mouth grinning at the street.

If anything, the single skeleton was a welcome de-escalation. There was always one decoration. Margie Roberts would never let herself be deemed a sourpuss or party-pooper. A few years back, there was a cemetery of plastic gravestones. Last year, a fog machine and spooky sounds CD. The porchlight stayed off every year, fat load of good. Children could sniff out a candy bowl blocks away. Margie thought it must be instinctual, like geese flying south for the winter.

"Grandpa!" Ryder called from the sidewalk. Witches, no more than third grade height, ran past him. "It's starting!"

Herb zipped up his jacket, patted the front pocket. "Got my phone." That was hardly a comfort. Herb still hadn't quite figured out how to work the darn thing. Even with the bigger buttons.

"Go on," Margie urged, "bring me home a Caramel Apple!" Her laughter cracked like peanut brittle, and she couldn't ignore the worried face Ryder wore. It said it all:

Grandma was weird.

Herb always tried to make light of it, called it her "Heebie Jeebies." It had another name before they married: Nerves. Doctor Ramsey had a more formal name; something somebody could scratch onto a prescription pad: "General Anxiety Disorder."

The knob shook a little as she closed the door. Then it was just Margie, her candy, and the whiteboard on the entryway table. On the plain white surface were columns for "Homemade" and "Store-bought." Neither Margie nor Herb had decided on stakes, but Herb thought it might be something fun to pass the time.

Margie knew he really meant, "Keep the nervous wife occupied." Herb already had one point for Store-bought.

Margie didn't think that was very fair, him buying Ryder's costume and all, but she let it slide. It wouldn't be such a bad idea to keep score and worry less about being alone.

She thought of those witches: lumpy, green faces, pointy hats, and flowing cloaks. One cloak sparkled with sequined moons and stars. On the other, a black cat's glowing, green eyes. No way those came from CVS.

"Ha!" She quickly slashed two points beneath Homemade. Now the evening could get interesting. Margie looked at the clock. A measly five minutes had passed. Worry quickly gnawed at her backbone again.

Cocoa.

She took the steaming mug from the coffee table and took an eager sip. The sweetness pushed away any and all trouble like a magic spell. Cold, lonely weather was never a problem so long as Margie had a working stove, cocoa powder, and milk. She took another sip, breathed. The clock chimed half past five. It always ran slow no matter how carefully Herb wound it. Running slow wasn't the problem.

It will be fine, she told herself. *It will all be fine.* Herb and Ryder would soon be past Ohio, down Broad Street, and at the Fun Fair. They'd trick-or-treat, laugh, win a few prizes, bob for apples even. Laughing too much and moving too fast to think about their kooky old lady back home.

The doorbell rang. Margie started, spilling some of her drink. She stood there, sucking on her finger and struggling to decide what best got cocoa stains out of carpet.

The doorbell rang again. Margie put down her mug on the entryway table and picked up the candy bowl. Mountains of Whatchamacallits, Hershey bars, and others crinkled in their wrappers. One more breath to steady her hands, and she opened the door.

Margie choked on her scream. The peeling face on her doorstep oozed fluids nearly every color in the rainbow while a single, fat gray worm wriggled out one punctured socket. The other held a ruined, jellied eye glowing like a dying coal within the bony face.

Princess Elsa and the zombie held up their pillowcases and sang, "Trick-or-treeeeat!"

"Oh," was all Margie could say. The children held their cases up a little higher. They had started early. The pillowcases already bulged with an entire treasure trove's worth of candy.

"Oh," Margie said again and plunged her free hand into the candy bowl. A good fistful of candy went into Elsa's bag, and then another for the zombie.

They sang out again, "Thank you, Mrs. Roberts!"

The zombie lifted his mask. A wide, living, grin spread across his face. He lisped between incoming adult teeth, "Ith juth a mathk, Mithuth Roberth! We made it in clath!"

"Yes," she replied. Margie was surprised by her even tone, especially with her heart hammering in her chest. "Very nice, Jake. Go catch your sister now." Jake Talbot whirled to find Elsa halfway down the sidewalk, spinning around and belting out verses of "Let It Go."

"Crap! Bye Mithuth Roberth!"

Margie slammed the door shut. The wind howled against it, sending Herb's paper skeleton into another horrid dance. She plucked out a Jolly Rancher and puckered up at the sour taste. She wished she hadn't requested a caramel apple. Even if Ryder remembered through the sugar high, it wasn't like Margie's teeth could really take that kind of punishment. It really wasn't fair. Kids and grown-ups seemed to always get such a big kick out of Halloween. The kids with their candy, the adults laughing and hollering at parties.

Only, Margie never liked dressing up to scare people, and having company over as an adult just stressed her to the breaking point. She could have candy whenever she wanted, why did the rest of the town have to lose its mind for 24 hours?

Margie set the candy bowl down and breathed. It was all just a stupid holiday. A stupid, stupid holiday! But there was the scoreboard to think about. Sure, Elsa had come straight from Target or Walmart. Margie gave a point to Store-bought. Jake's mask had really been something. Just what was Miss Lyman teaching them in art class? Margie slashed a point beneath Homemade. Still in the lead. Margie helped herself to a celebratory sip of cocoa.

~ ~ ~

Wind whistled a pitiful tune as the clock kept time. The paper skeleton found the beat and boogied. Every time its limbs scratched and scrabbled at the door, Margie thought of giant spiders, hands caked in grave dirt, or other abominations.

She turned up the volume on Seinfeld. The clock kept ticking. She finished her cocoa, got up for a refill, and suddenly remembered the cherry brandy tucked away above the fridge. When had they last opened it? The big storm last summer? Or getting snowed in that one winter?

It didn't matter. Margie decided a little zip in her Halloween treat was better than a caramel apple or Jolly Rancher. It was a hard reach up the fridge, and Margie thought she really ought to use a footstool instead of going on tiptoe. While fumbling around for the brandy and thinking on footstools, an oil-black shape slithered across the glass face of a nearby cabinet.

Margie spun, thin hand on her chest, and stared out into the living room. The brandy momentarily forgotten, her mind raced with possibilities. An intruder, Satanists, burglars, kids with an armory of toilet paper. The living room beyond the breakfast nook remained empty.

Something outside, probably. Definitely. All the doors and windows were locked. How could it be anything inside? It had to be outside. What was outside? A leaf probably, there were tons blowing around. It was autumn! No, it was Halloween when all kinds of things bumped in the night. Fine, so it was some bratty kid having fun scaring an old woman half-to-death. Maybe it was Ryder? No, they'd never come home early.

Audience laughter boomed off the living room walls, echoing throughout the house, mocking Margie. Just a big old scaredy cat. Couldn't take a trick, couldn't ever have fun. A family passed on the sidewalk, clearly visible through the large living room window. A now much too large and far too fragile living room window. Margie understood what a piece of bacteria felt like beneath a microscope.

She went to the window, flicking on every single light switch she passed. She didn't care if the electric bill for next month shot a hole through the roof. She imagined each cluster of swirling shadows dropping dead with a flick of the switch. The lights would probably draw more trick-or-treaters, but that was fine. Suddenly, Margie could do with a little company. It might even help her score a few more points on the costume board.

The shape flashed by the living room window again. Margie yelped and ducked back from the glass. She raised her hands in defense and only struck cold window. The pull cord felt slick in her sweaty hands, but she finally yanked it back and Halloween night vanished from view.

Should have gone with them, should have gone with, Margie thought over and over in time with her buzzing heart. But with the blinds down she could breathe a little better. Now it seemed entirely possible she hadn't really seen screeching monster's intent on devouring her whole fly by her window. It now seemed plausible it was just another family going by, or an overexcited trick-or-treater rushing across her lawn. But whatever was outside had been dark. Darker than night, swifter than any third grader hopped up on sugar.

That settled it. No more trick-or-treaters tonight no matter how much they pounded on the door. Margie would only open it for Herb and Ryder. Those two wouldn't mind the candy surplus. The three of them could live off of Dots and Mr. Goodbars till the sun came up on November when the world made a little more sense.

Seinfeld gave way to Wheel of Fortune where Pat and Vanna were ready to help the contestants win Spooktacular prizes. Margie clicked off the television on her way back to the kitchen. The lukewarm chocolate still lacked for an adult beverage. A little of that to calm her nerves, maybe a little phone chat to pass the time, and Margie could relax.

Only without the television's racket, the *scritch scratch* of paper skeleton arms just about crawled right inside Margie's ears. It sounded loud as Mr. Dickinson's marching band. She decided next year it would be only simply jack-o-lanterns. Herb could fight her all she wanted, but Margie would put her foot down. And that horrid little thing hanging on her door tonight? Straight. In. The. Trash.

Margie let her mind wander to sadistic thoughts as she went to open the door. Maybe the skeleton would fit in her paper shredder. Maybe it was safe to burn. Then a screeching piece of the night sky came alive and flew in through the open door. There wasn't time to be scared or scream. The best Margie could do was let out a strangled, "What?"

She caught the candy bowl on her way down, rear end and bowl connecting with the tiled floor at the same time. The bowl wobbled crazily for a few seconds more and went silent and still as the grave.

Margie kicked the door shut with her legs and turned her back to it. Her eyes danced from one living room corner to the next. All she saw was eggshell white paint and a startling amount of dust bunnies. There weren't many hiding places left with almost every light in the house blazing. What shadows remained crawled to life. Margie watched through wide eyes as the dark patch beneath Herb's easy chair writhed across the carpet on thousands of smooth, shiny legs. The meager bits of shadow lurking in the fireplace dangled and swung from the ashy bricks like tentacles.

Then just like that, Margie couldn't breathe. Simple as someone flipping a switch in her lungs from "ON" to "OFF." Margie gasped, dry tongue heavy as lead in her mouth. White dots grew over her vision. It didn't matter if what she saw wasn't real. She couldn't afford to think that way. She couldn't understand how it could be so cold inside while pools of sweat formed in her armpits.

Doctor Ramsey's voice came to her:

"This is just fight or flight turned to 11. Fight or flight. Nothing wrong with your nerves. "Nerves" isn't a real condition. You just need to breathe. Breathe. Count. Count. Breathe."

God, she could kill Ramsey. A jury of her peers couldn't possibly convict.

Margie finally caught a stray gasp of air, clutched it and held on for dear life. She counted, turning the release and intake of air back into a regular rhythm. At least that worked. It didn't change her feelings on Ramsey though, or chase away the raw panic carving a ragged hole in her chest.

What the heck had flown in? What had she let into her house?

Those creepy bits of living shadow still lurked in the corner of Margie's vision. She didn't dare close her eyes and wish them away, not if there was a real something lurking in her house. But she could look up at the ceiling. Her perfectly average, off-white ceiling with a black, quivering square folded up into one corner.

Now Margie screamed.

The bat screamed too. It wasn't much, but it let loose all the same. Its fuzzy head unsheathed from beneath rubbery wings and frantically scanned the room. Jittering, black eyes landed on Margie. Her hand shot up to her mouth and capped anymore noise. They waited there, Margie and her evening caller, just the two of them in a staring contest. Margie kept staring and reached back over her shoulder for the doorknob.

It all played perfectly in her mind: Open the door, shoo out the little bugger, let it fly, fly, fly far away from her house. If it didn't Margie would fly, fly, fly far away across the street. Let Herb find her at the neighbors.

Margie sang under her breath, "Shoo bat, don't bother me, shoo bat, don't bother me, smelly, smelly rat don't-"

The bat dove off the ceiling and swooped overhead, a flurry of bristly hair and wings. Margie met floor and scrambled across back towards the kitchen. Halfway across the living room carpet, she turned and crab walked till she met the opposite wall. There would certainly be a goose egg back of her head tomorrow.

Some of the neighbors teased Margie and Herb for keeping a rotary dial. Margie didn't know what a hipster was and she certainly didn't care. All she cared about was the way her shaking fingers fit into each wheel, allowing her to smoothly dial Herb's number. She could dial it from memory. That was one thing old age hadn't begun its assault on at least.

Her eyes never left the bat. It perched atop the doorframe like a living gargoyle. Every second number or so it would stick a tiny pink tongue out from between jagged fangs and hiss. The thought of hurling the phone at the bat had some appeal. But then common sense asked Margie, how would she make a call?

Finally, Herb picked up.

"Hello?" Along with Herb came cartoony howls and moans from the Fun Fair's haunted house. He shouted again, "Hello?" Someone or something on the other end screamed in fear or delight. Margie could spit.

"Herb!" She rasped, "You need to come home. Right. Now!"

The connection cleared a little as Herb put some distance between himself and the Halloween hijinks currently underway on the other side of town.

"Margie? What's wrong?"

The bat hissed again.

"Herb! Come home now!"

"What happened? Are you alright?"

"A...bat." She choked out the last word. The plastic handset crackled in Margie's grasp. "A bat got in the house. Come get rid of it!"

The next laugh wasn't from a school spook house or excited kid. Coming from Herb, it hurt more than the back of Margie's bruised head. The sounds of good-natured ghouls, ghosts, and monsters grew back over the phone.

"Is it trying to bite?"

Margie's brain about short-circuited with irritation while Herb went on:

"It's probably just as spooked as you are, hon. Leave the door open and I'm sure it'll leave. Probably."

"It's right over the door," she meant to say but all that came back was an angry croak.

"Got to go, Margie. I don't want to lose Ryder in all this. Home soon!"

The click echoed over anything else. The bat bobbed its head up and down, cackling from its safe perch above the door as the old lady cowered in the corner of her own flipping house on Halloween Night.

Cold tingled around Margie. Solid, ugly, cold rage. Her back stopped aching. She forgot all about the goose egg on her head. The bat's beady eyes met hers again, only this time Margie met them with a scowl. She laid the phone back in its cradle like it really was the antique the neighbors teased her for. The mug of hot chocolate next to it had grown cold as Margie. This observation only threw more kindling on the strange, icy flames billowing up inside of her.

"You." She finally spat out from behind her teeth. The bat quit bobbing and laughing. It crawled a little further up the wall, putting just a little more distance between them. As if afraid. Margie smiled, really smiled, for the first time that evening. The bat's puckered snout drew back for a full reveal of its needled teeth and wicked fangs. Margie kept smiling.

If Herb wouldn't be back anytime soon, then what? Margie Roberts didn't enjoy Halloween, but liked crouching helplessly in a corner even less. Her heartbeat rose with her.

"You just get out."

The bat cocked its head from side-to-side. Good. Maybe it could understand.

"You little stinker." Margie moved forward till her aching knees met the coffee table. She walked past it and the up-ended candy bowl, willing each step closer and closer to the door. The bat never left her sight. Another few steps. Then her feet met the tile floor of the entryway. Just another few steps. One hand crept out and slowly came to rest just over the doorknob. The bat still studied her with its unblinking, black gaze.

So close to the doorknob, but Margie's hand refused to come down on it. The cold metal repelled her like a magnet. Margie tried breathing and counting again, tried looking away from the bat, tried inner criticism.

"Come one, just do it, you wiener."

In the end, another of the bat's jeering hisses did it. Margie glanced back up, grit her teeth, and slapped her hand down. The bat responded by unfurling its wings, filling the white wall like a bank of monstrous thunderheads. Only this time, Margie didn't scream. She backed away and launched her empty mug before common sense could intervene. The crash of ceramic against wood and cloud of shrapnel did better than any exercise Doctor Ramsey could come up with.

The thought of the future mess never even registered. Or the fact that she missed her target by a mile. There was little time for that. Margie's nighttime caller flew overhead and made a beeline straight for the kitchen. Tiny claws ran ragged trails across wood cabinets. Muted thuds and crashing glassware came soon after. The little bat was still having a grand old time on Halloween night.

Margie kicked the candy bowl again. She dived, surprising even herself with the speed and flexibility. Maybe those yoga classes really did help. Shiny tin foil wrappers and cardboard boxes were crushed underfoot. The crunch of breaking Heath Bars and Butterfingers was like heaven. It made Margie think of snapping bones. The bat screeched out in delight from the kitchen. Margie answered with a howl of rage and charged towards the kitchen, empty bowl out front of her like a shield.

A vase lay tipped over and cracked on the kitchen counter, dripping stagnant water onto the floor. The cabinets, shined and polished for company, now bore crazy zigzags of claw marks. Torn open cocoa packets lay scattered on the counter like tiny body bags. Adorable, chocolate-dusted tracks led to the fridge. Margie went hunting.

"Come on," she cooed and rapped her knuckles against the bowl. The hollow *GONG* echoed over the ticking clock, the spooky wind, everything.

"Come on."

GONG.

"Come on."

GONG.

Something rustled in the cabinet atop the fridge. The door up there hung open just a crack. Had she forgotten that? Margie raised her candy bowl and readied to pounce. The cabinet door creaked and she leapt back. The red cap of the brandy bottle appeared, and then, bit by bit, the fuzzy head crawled into view.

"Get down from there!"

The bat obliged. But this time Margie was ready. The bowl let out another *GONG* as the bat collided inside it. Margie had no time to celebrate. She rushed the bowl straight into the wall. No satisfying crunch of bone, no horrific squeal of pain. The bat had wisely tucked inside and remained safe from impact. It sure wasn't having fun anymore. Claws scraping on metal made Margie's skin break out into gooseflesh. She looked to the nearby mudroom door and suddenly the plan became so simple.

"Fly around in there all you want." She held the bowl firm against the wall and drug it across to the door. Herb had planned on using the dim, concrete mudroom as a workshop. If by work he meant store boxes and dust, it was a home-run success. It also made a fine cage.

Margie flung the bowl and its contents out into the mudroom and slammed the door shut.

"Keep it!"

And like that, it seemed she was cured of Nerves or Heebie Jeebies or whatever Ramsey felt like calling them. She thought that was a pretty great deal. No pills, no classes, just have an arrogant, flying rat lay siege to your house and fling him into the mudroom. Boom! Problem solved!

Margie leaned against the fridge door and gave silent thanks for the cool surface. It felt so good, she barely heard the bat's angry squeaks or rustle and thud of falling boxes.

"Fly around in there all night, fella." Margie reached up on tiptoe and found the brandy without looking. The bottle's contents lapped against the cap like breakers on the lake. Her first swig went down easy as water. A shiver of a completely different kind swung through her on the second one. She slid down the wall and kept sliding till rear end hit floor. On the third swig, Margie finally understood why she and Herb had kept the same bottle of booze in nearly the same place since moving in almost 25 years ago. The stuff tasted less like brandy and more like cherry-tainted motor oil. By the fourth it wasn't so bad.

It did nothing to make the messy kitchen disappear though. As dread left her body, weariness crawled in. Herb and Ryder would think she'd gone nuts. The squeaks faded away behind the door. Margie shut her eyes.

They sprang back open as the mudroom door shook with a dreadful impact. Then a wild series of blows followed, like someone throwing tennis balls one after another. The bat's squeaks of protest rose over the thuds, but kept rising till they reached a high-pitched wail. Margie wailed back and ran for the front door, catching a shard of broken mug on her heel.

The merry chimes of the doorbell sang out before Margie could clear the living room. The chimes put an end to the chaos in the mudroom and Margie's near heart attack. Someone else was finally here. Herb and Ryder back already maybe. A lost trick-or-treater. The darn census taker. Margie didn't care, so long as she could get help from a real live flesh and blood person. Someone else could deal with all the crazy nonsense happening tonight.

The doorbell came again. The strange cries from the mudroom door came with them.

"Coming!" Margie limped to the door. "Please wait!"

She hoped there was at least one adult waiting on her doorstep. God only knew how a bunch of little kids would react to a bleeding, limping woman swinging open the door.

"Good evening," the man answered.

"Oh my!" The woman extended a manicured hand to Margie's shoulder. "You look awful!"

Margie took the observation and hand without a moment's resistance. She did not shake, only let her hand rest in the woman's like a piece of roadkill. The woman's ruby lips twitched and gave a try at smiling. The man did about as well as the woman.

"Are you alright, ma'am?" That at least sounded sincere coming from him.

Margie cleared her throat and gave a strangled clicking sound instead of words.

The man quickly added, "May we come in?"

The "yes" that finally escaped Margie was meant for the man's first question, but did for the second one as well. A real two-for-one like at CVS. The woman pointed one long, black fingernail at the skeleton as she passed through the doorway.

"Spooky!" She laughed, "Oh, I love it!" She quit laughing when one of her high heels speared a Heath bar. "Oh dear!"

"It, it..." Margie slowed. The clock counted for her. Once. Twice. Then the events of the night poured out in a mad rush. She ended the story by leading the man and woman to the mudroom door.

"I locked it in here."

The man held up a slender hand. "Yes, we know."

"Huh?"

Something heavy crashed onto the mudroom floor. Margie jumped, clutching her shirt with white knuckles. The woman patted her shoulder, gave it a strong, gentle squeeze.

"It's alright, ma'am. It's alright. We will have a talk with him."

Before Margie could muster another mighty "huh" or ask who or what, the woman pounded on the mudroom door.

"Toby!" The cries stopped as soon as she spoke. "Tobias Matheson! Are you decent?"

She rolled her eyes with impatience as feet shuffled on the concrete floor.

Margie's injured foot throbbed while her mind spun and spun. She wasn't really sure which bothered her more. The man offered her a jelly glass of water. Margie took it and immediately discovered it was not water, but instead more brandy. On the rocks even. The ice did little to help the taste, but the brandy did wonders for her spinning head.

"Tobias." The man joined the woman by the door. Side-by side again, they reminded Margie a little of the American Gothic family.

"You've done quite enough, son. Come now." A whimper came from beyond the door. The man continued: "No, we're not mad. Your mother and I were just scared. You scared this nice lady too."

The last word came out as a placating, "Toooooo." It did the trick.

The door opened a crack. Wide, dark eyes stared out at them. Then the child stepped into full view. He shivered before them despite his thick, black sweater and trousers. Margie guessed he was no more than six or seven. Just about Ryder's age. Just about perfect for a little trick-or-treating.

Doctor Ramsey's voice crept back in, telling Margie to "breathe" and "think logically." Margie told Doctor Ramsey to shove a sock in it.

"Toby, Toby, Toby," the boy's mother moaned and rocked the boy back and forth. He climbed into her arms and nestled his head in her neck. "There, there my love," she sang. "Thank goodness you're safe." Her placations faded as she left with her boy.

The man sighed, shrugged at Margie. He looked into the mudroom and sighed again.

"His first Halloween." The man shook his head, ran a hand through his dark hair. "We never counted on the sugar rush! Goodness gracious!"

Margie's stomach turned at the man's wide, red grin and too-white teeth. It was like he had chomped down on a big pair of wax candy lips. He placed a chilly hand into the small of Margie's back and led her into the living room.

"All we wanted was a nice night out." Margie wasn't so shocked at the man's hairy palms or overly long ring finger. It even had black nails too.

Margie glanced out the door into the front yard. Toby's feet, and the rest of him, hovered just off the ground. The evening mist swirled in little pools beneath him. His mother tugged on one arm of his sweater.

"Come down! People might see!" That sugar rush really was something.

The man smiled wider still and orange streetlight glittered off twin sets of curved canines.

"Holy. Shit." Margie fainted and fell back atop a pile of broken candy.

~~~

"Shh, let's go unpack it in the kitchen."

The words passed through a tangle of poisonous cobwebs thrumming in Margie's skull.

Oh God, I have a hangover. At 72.

There was a true holiday miracle. The back of Margie's throat was slick with cherry aftertaste and her tongue felt like it needed a good shave. She groaned and creaked open one eye and then the other.

Herb came to the recliner and took her hand. "You alright, hon?" She tried to nod. "Can I get you something?"

"Coffee." The word escaped her in a growl. Herb hustled back to the kitchen quick as a nurse in the ICU. Ryder stood nearby. His plastic pumpkin wore a crown of candy, another successful Halloween night.

"Watch out for broken glass," Margie croaked without thinking. Then it all came back. The bat flying. The American

Gothic couple. Toby. Fangs. Each memory more harsh than the last.

"Herb! Herb!"

It hadn't been a dream. It couldn't be. The instant Margie's heel touched the floor, a warm jet of pain traveled up her leg. Only the bloody sock was gone, replaced with clean slippers. Tight bandages secured her injured foot.

"What glass, grandma?" Ryder's Space Command boots stood on unblemished tile.

"What you holler about?" Herb returned from the kitchen, two mugs of coffee in hand. Margie took the offered one, hoping the bitter warmth could shock her back to reality and was soon disappointed. She went back to the living room window and tried not to limp. Something fluttered down as Margie lifted the blinds, and for a single instant the bat was back. The bat that could be a boy if it wanted. A boy with sharp teeth, pale skin, and nothing on his mind tonight but tricks and treats. Like a million other children out there in the world tonight. Mostly like them anyway.

Then it was just a fluttering piece of folded paper again.

"See you took care of the bat, huh?" Coffee delivered and job done, Herb wandered back into the kitchen. "Where's the brandy, darling?"

Margie ignored him and unfolded the paper. It wasn't any kind she or Herb kept around the house. A rich, dense cream-colored parchment. No one putting a grocery list on this. The blue cursive embedded in the paper was just as fancy.

Ma'am,

My family and I, Tobias in particular, extend our deepest apologies. We try to teach him our days of home invasions and other such deeds are things of the past, but children can be so difficult. As further apology, we have mended what mess our son made. Any irreparable damages will be paid for in full. However, I must insist that you in return keep this unpleasant business to yourself. Privacy is very important to our family. Rest assured, we will not trouble you again. I expect you to extend us the same courtesy.

Gratefully yours,

D.

"What is it, Grandma?" Ryder's face had turned the color of off-cheese.

She tucked the note away in her back pocket. "Trick-or-treaters, sweetie."

Later, Margie would cuddle with her grandson beneath blankets and watch Frankenstein and Dracula back-to-back. They didn't seem so scary anymore. Margie took down that silly skeleton though. She was through with both tricks and treats for another year. Then there was only one last thing before settling in to wait for November's first light.

Margie took the marker and added three blood-red slashes beneath Homemade.

Holiday Leftovers

Rest Stop for the Stars

Maxwell I. Gold

Every year the same old thing, I'd follow the path where the Stellar Things dream, and the laughter of dead galaxies trickled along the waning lightyears; but I couldn't help myself.

I longed for relief from those effervescent, darksome waypoints. Occasionally, I'd come across the concrete and plastic ruins of old cities, I smiled, reminiscing at the changing landscapes, how different it looked every time, every trip.

So bright were the fires of tomorrow, when the dust of yesterday trailed behind me while visions of crumbling cities, rusted cars, and frightened peoples gazed up to see me glowing in an awful, purple night.

Every year, the same old thing, but stars often must move on, eventually.

The Tree Hunt

Marissa James

Grady's family had always gone Christmas tree hunting. The day after Thanksgiving he helped Mom pack sandwiches spilling leftover cranberry and stuffing, hot cider and slices of pumpkin pie, while Dad and his aunts Amy and Pat packed the real supplies.

Most families went to one of those U-Cut places, where trees were raised like livestock: densely packed branches, perfectly straight trunks and conical silhouettes. The more squeamish went to a pre-cut lot and lugged a tree home, cold and already drying out.

A Doug or Grand fir would do fine, but every year Grady's family drove up the deep-rutted forest roads before dawn in search of Noble habitat.

Within the snowline they donned red and green camouflage in mistletoe print. Each adult carried a pack with fruitcake-pellet bait, shiny bows for diversion, and popcorn string snares, as well as a felling axe and a handsaw. Chainsaws were quicker, but better for U-Cut lots. They were too bulky, too noisy, for a clean cut on a feral tree. And unsportsmanlike, besides.

"Carry this for me?" Dad asked and held out his handsaw.

"Sure." Grady took hold of it, but Dad didn't let go.

"You remember how to use it, just in case?"

"I remember," he said, and grinned nervously as he slung the D-shaped frame of the saw over a shoulder. His aunts chuckled and nodded, perhaps remembering when they were first trusted to carry the tools. Grady had observed a half dozen hunts, had helped afterward trimming branches and bucking stumps, but hadn't cut a tree yet. Maybe this year, Dad would let him try.

Then again, with how wild some of the trees got, he wasn't sure he could do the job fast enough. He clutched the saw tighter and pushed the thought away.

They set out, silent and sweetly minty with the candy cane pheromones they'd daubed on to cover their scent.

Aunt Amy shook the jingle bells, and they all paused to listen. Grady wasn't sure exactly what it was about the trappings of Christmas that called the trees so strongly when they were at that age. It was as though the holiday spirit was infectious for evergreens as well.

In the hush that followed, he heard it: the distinct rustling of branches, shivering in the same rhythm as the bell.

Grady followed Dad through snow and underbrush. His aunts went the opposite way. Circling was often the best bet—if the tree focused its attention on one hunter, the others could take it by surprise.

Trees may be rooted to the spot, but they were wily. One year Uncle Carl got a lashing when he stepped too close. Even the slimmest branches struck with whipcrack speed and ferocity and from every angle at once. The bright pink welts across his arms and upper back lasted for weeks; the bark splinters took even longer than that to work their way out. Needless to say, Uncle Carl never joined another hunt.

Ahead, the clearing opened. The tree stood in its midst, branches shivering in tune to the jingle bell call. It was a Doug fir, thin and scraggly in the understory of its much older fellows. An undeniably wild thing in every rangy branch and sharp-ended needle. Dad shook his head; not a Noble, after all. Perhaps they'd been overhunted in this area. A shame.

Across the clearing, string lights twinkled as Aunt Pat inched out from cover, decked in glittering tinsel and baubles. Further along, Aunt Amy emerged in similar decoy décor, still jingling to offer a doubled distraction. A sparkly garland trailed between them.

The tree shivered when they got within a handful of paces, refusing to be soothed by the bells. Aunt Amy switched to verbal assurances, a steady, soothing stream of "Ho, ho, hos," that worked much as they would have on a spooked horse.

When the tree had calmed, both aunts whipped up the garland, looping it around the tree's lower branches and pulling them back to expose the vulnerable trunk.

Dad leapt out of hiding, axe ready, and Grady followed with the saw gripped tight.

The tree erupted in a furious struggle, needles flinging free like projectiles at their faces, even as Dad skidded in on his knees to deliver the first blow. Both aunts began a verse of "O Tannenbaum" in hopes of distracting it.

Grady stood just out of range of the branches, as he'd been taught, waiting to hand the saw over once Dad got halfway through the trunk.

A long branch slipped loose of the garland lasso and smacked Dad hard across the face. He ducked against the battering onslaught; the axe slapped out of his hold.

Grady looked at the widening gash in the trunk, the saw in hand, his caroling aunts. If he moved fast, he could duck in, hand Dad the saw, duck out—

Or, he could do it himself.

He lunged into the fray, set the serrated blade to the cut, and began to saw.

The tree thrashed, raining needles, swinging at him with all its might. Grady was small enough that the branches couldn't quite reach him—not with the force they wanted.

As he sawed deeper, the thrashing slowed. Dad, holding branches out of the way, nodded, a proud twinkle in his eye, and Grady severed the trunk.

The tree fell to the forest floor in a sigh of branches. As his aunts helped Dad get up, Grady touched the stump, surprised at the bittersweet mix of relief and regret that filled his chest. When Arbor Day came around, he'd be sure to plant saplings in its honor.

Dad pulled him out of his thoughts and into a big hug. Aunt Amy and Aunt Pat propped up the tree to take his picture with it.

Despite its straggly branches, irregular trunk, and odd growth pattern, Grady beamed alongside his tree.

The air smelled of pine and candy cane and the perfect Christmas.

The Perfumer in Purgatory

Alicia Hilton

I was a perfumer in Purgatory, peddling aromatic wares; the sandwich board placard I wore over of my crimson robe advertised travel size atomizers. The hottest sellers were spicy florals—best at snuffing the stench of death. The priciest fragrance, a blend of frankincense, patchouli, ambergris, cloves, and coyote secretions, was extolled for its powers of repelling cloven hooves. Not demons, certainly not the Dark Lord, just goats, gazelles, and sheep. Customers never read the fine print.

Ding, ding, ringing my bicycle bell, I reported to work, skidding to a stop beside the dock where pontoon boats were tied, along the shore of the river of fire. Since I'd been toiling as the Purgatorial Perfumer from 1949 to 2043, you'd think I would've gotten numb to their desperation, but my customers' bloodshot eyes and pleas for mercy made my stomach churn. I donned the placard and took up my post beside the perfumer's stall, unlocking its tall metal case.

"Single file, single file, no pushing, hold the handrail when you disembark," uniformed ushers shouted, directing the colorfully robed passengers with jabs from their taser prods. Demonic ushers were the only purgatorial employees authorized to inflict corporal punishment. Clerks, like me, were lackeys, working off our sins.

The neon sign on the closest boat flashed a warning, reminding me of The Rules:
1) Greet customers with a smile.
2) No name-calling
3) No spitting

4) Leave the Maiming to the Demons

Most of the moral infractions that I'd committed when I was alive were typical for a thirteen-year-old—cheating in social studies, temper tantrums when I got my period, and my bedroom was usually a pigsty, but I'd never tortured animals or hurt people, except for the accident.

~~~

It was nearly midnight when I arrived at Wesley Anderson's house.

Sandy was hiding behind the shrubberies. I switched off my flashlight and crouched beside her.

Wesley Anderson's three-story colonial was the nicest house on the block. He didn't need that much space, since he was divorced, and his kids had grown up and moved away, but he was the kind of jerk who liked to show off his wealth. If he wasn't so rich, and the mayor's brother, he would've been arrested for molesting Sandy.

Sandy said, "Maybe this isn't a good idea?"

I said, "We can't let him get away with it. He deserves to be punished!" I opened my satchel and pulled out a bottle. The cap was on, but I could smell the gasoline. I'd brought a strip of fabric to make a wick.

Sandy started sobbing, digging her hands deep into her frizzy hair.

I patted her shoulder. "Everything's going to be okay."

"No it's not!" she said. "My father talked to the police again. They said there's no evidence—his word against mine."

Seeing how miserable she was made me want to cry. I blinked back tears and said, "You want to go home? I can do it." Sandy lived at the other end of the block, in a smaller ranch house.

She sniffed and wiped her eyes. "I'll do it." She pulled a box of matches from her pocket.

"You're sure he's alone?" I said. Mr. Anderson usually drove a fancy Tucker convertible, but there was a Jeep parked in the driveway.

Sandy nodded. "The Jeep's his."

My hands were shaking when I shoved the rag inside the bottle. When the Molotov was ready, I handed the bottle to Sandy.

Wind blew out the first match. I lit another match, and the wick ignited. Sandy hurled the bottle on the driveway, next to the Jeep.

The bottle shattered. *Whoosh,* flames shot into the air, enveloping the front of the Jeep. I smelled rubber burning.

I said, "Let's go!" and ran to the sidewalk. The heat from the fire was intense, and I was afraid of getting caught. When I looked back, Sandy had stopped at the end of the driveway. She was watching the Jeep burning.

"Come on!" I said, but Sandy didn't move.

I thought of running back to get her, but Mr. Anderson walked out of his house. He was holding a shotgun!

Boom! The blast tore into Sandy's chest, knocking her down. She landed on her back, with her arms spread out like an angel's wings.

"Sandy!" I shouted, but she didn't answer. I was too far away to see whether she was breathing.

Mr. Anderson squeezed the trigger and shot Sandy again.

The porch lights on a house partway up the block turned on.

With tears streaming down my face, I ran into the dark.

If I hadn't escaped, Mr. Anderson probably would have killed me too, but I haven't forgiven myself for abandoning Sandy.

At least Mr. Anderson was arrested, but I never got to see his trial.

~~~

I didn't pick my penance because I liked selling sweet-smelling perfumes. Most of the purgatorial perfumes reeked, but it was easier to get promoted from deck swabber to perfume sales than it was to become one of the artists who painted murals on the cavern ceilings. And only those who spoke Greek and Latin became confessors.

A clove-studded sachet bought fifty-three minutes of talk therapy. My confessor said, "Fretting about the past is as productive as trying to mop a never-ending stream of offal." Good advice, but encouraging platitudes didn't improve my mood. Time was the best healer.

As decades flew by, fashions changed, but human behavior didn't— newcomers arrived in spandex instead of suits and fedoras, but envy, greed, and lust were still the most popular sins. Penalties for moral transgressions, and the resulting screams, were timeless. After a while, you got used to coexisting with monsters.

The borders between Purgatory and Hell were more fluid than people think. Demons inflicted punishments in the land of limbo, as well as in Hell. Howls, wails, gnashing teeth, thrashing tentacles—it all became background noise, almost as easy to tune out as a boring social studies class.

~~~

Penitent souls who wanted to observe what was happening in the living world, as well as in Heaven and Hell, could bathe in the Oracle Pool. It wasn't as exciting as impersonating a ghost and haunting people who were still breathing—only angels and demons got to do that. And the Oracle Pool was infested with flesh-eating eels, and bats roosting on stalactites would crap on your head, but when you're lonely and depressed, you'll do just about anything to connect with someone who's not doomed.

The deeper I swam, the more I'd learn. Flashes of light illuminated the murky water, revealing images that were projected like a movie. If I held my breath until my lungs were about to burst, I'd hear snatches of conversation.

When Neil Armstrong landed on the moon, I watched him say, "That's one small step for man, one giant leap for mankind."

Watching astronauts was surreal, but it was hard to watch Sandy getting along so well in Heaven, walking through a meadow with other angels. That should have been me; I was the one who stood up for her.

Two-and-a-half percent of Earth's population bypasses Purgatory and goes straight to Heaven when they quit breathing. Their names were displayed on daily dispatches, as inspiration for lost souls like me to behave.

Names of the sinners who were sent to Hell weren't announced, but the mayhem was hard to ignore.

Cato, the warden in charge of Purgatory since Julius Caesar ruled Rome, governed by carrot and stick. Not literally, you wouldn't get whacked upside the head with a stick if you screwed up. The penalty for breaking important rules was much worse.

"Excuse me," I said, pushing past huddled newcomers who were gawking at a man being dragged by Cerberus. The giant, three-headed hellhound chomped into the poor guy's butt, tearing off a chunk of flesh.

I wiped sweat from my brow and averted my eyes. Gore made me queasy.

In a few moments, the copper bell that hung from the cavern ceiling would ring, announcing that the market had opened. I used the heavy key that hung from a chain wrapped around my waist to open the perfume display. Some of the bottles were dusty. I shined them with a rag, then pushed up my shirtsleeve, and scratched the inside of my left elbow, picking at a crusty, red patch. My eczema was flaring up, but I kept smiling.

Rule Number 1—*Greet customers with a smile.*

Steam from bubbling lava made it impossible to see the end of the queue, but from the sound of the crowd, there must've been at least a thousand passengers disembarking the boats. As they got closer, I smelled sweat and the pungent stench of vomit, blending with the ever-present tang of sulfur. Flu season was dreadful, not because I worried about barfing until I keeled over— you could only die once.

During viral outbreaks the number of new arrivals would triple, even quadruple, and my workday was extended, with only an extra bowl of veggie rice as compensation for the overtime. After thirteen hours of haggling, with only two pee breaks and one snack, exhaustion would make me hallucinate. It was tough to separate freakish visions from reality, since the ushers that patrolled the market were demons and other unearthly creatures.

Though it was almost the middle of the 21st Century, Cato, the Purgatorial Warden, refused to approve credit transactions, and it would've been too complicated to accept paper currency, so bartering was the norm. Silver, gold, platinum, and jewels rarely crossed my palm.

When I was a newbie, the pathetic trades made me cringe. A woman who hobbled on one stiletto pump, her other foot bare, with the big toe missing, had nothing to trade, so she offered to confess about three times she'd lied to a friend, in return for a sample size vial of Chanel No. 5 *eau de toilette.* The first fib wasn't bad, "Your haircut looks great," but then she said, "I recommended you for the promotion," and "It's not my fault you got fired!"

She was crying so hard, I patted her on the back and told her everything would be okay. Providing a sympathetic ear and a sweet-smelling placebo was the least I could do for lost souls, quaking in terror at the prospect of eternal damnation.

~~~

After shilling perfumes, colognes, and incense to panic-stricken mobs for decades, it wasn't easy to keep following the rules, but smiling when I was miserable was better than having blisters on my butt from being tased by the ushers.

Folks who approached my stall were nearly always contrite, shuffling forward with their heads bent, but it was tough not to pre-judge, when each newcomer's attire told the story of how they'd died.

Color-coded robes spun from the softest spider silk were issued to all of the dead who boarded the boats, and passengers were eager to freshen up and don their new garments. Royal blue for cardiovascular disease. Mustard yellow for cirrhosis. Taupe for lung cancer. Neon pink for hemorrhagic fever. Eggplant for strokes. Puce for influenza. Burgundy for homicide victims. Racing green for appendicitis. Sunny yellow for leukemia. Teal for hepatitis. Orange for arsonist. Hot pink for rapist. There were so many different hues, sometimes I had to consult my pocket chart, but I never forgot what my crimson robe meant—murderer. It was so unfair.

Sandy probably would have had a long life if I'd refused to give her the bottle with the gasoline, but I was a victim, too. When I asked if I could have burgundy stripes on my robe, the demons laughed.

~~~

Gabe wasn't a perv, and he never hit me, or my mother. Considering the horror stories that I'd heard about other stepfathers, I thought Gabe was a nice guy, especially since he didn't ignore me, like the previous men that Mother had dated. In fact, he seemed to adore me. He even suggested that he become my legal father, and he hired a lawyer to file adoption papers.

When Mother's diabetes got so bad that her hands were shaking, Gabe filled the insulin syringes, and gave her the shots. He was so gentle, she hardly ever got bruises from the injections.

"I'm lucky that you're a doctor," Mother said.

Our neighbors thought that Mother was lucky, too. When WWII ended, there were so many war widows, and it was hard to find a good husband, especially a successful endocrinologist like Gabe. And Gabe got along with everyone—the macho sports fanatics, the nerdy accountant, the snobbish lawyer, even the crotchety old lady who lived down the block. Gabe found her lost terrier when the little dog escaped from the yard.

Twenty-three months after Mother married Gabe, she passed out while she was driving, and rammed her Packard into a tree. During Mother's funeral, I overheard Gabe talking to Aunt Mary.

"Jane belongs at home, with me," he said.

It was strange living in the house without Mother, but Gabe and I settled into a routine. When I forgot to take out the trash or let the pile of dirty laundry get too big, he'd scold me without yelling.

Gabe was a crappy cook, but I should've known that something was wrong when I started getting stomach aches.

When I woke on my fourteenth birthday, I smelled bacon wafting from the kitchen.

Gabe greeted me with a smile. "Happy birthday, honey."

There was a platter of bacon on the table. Bran flakes for him, and a bowl of hot oatmeal for me, topped with fresh strawberries.

"Wow!" I said. By this time, I confess, I had all but forgotten about Sandy.

"A birthday's a special day." He patted my head. "You want OJ?"

"Thanks," I said. I grabbed a piece of bacon. It was crispy and delicious, not even burnt on the edges.

"Try your oatmeal," he said. "I added cinnamon."

He'd also added poison, but I didn't realize that until I'd collapsed, writhing on the floor. At least my death was quick.

Maybe I should've felt flattered that Gabe killed me for life insurance money, instead of just because he was sick of raising someone else's kid, but when he arrived in Purgatory, I wasn't ready to show mercy.

The life insurance company had tipped off police, and Gabe was arrested. An argument in the prison yard led to him being shanked. After he bled out, Gabe spent only a day in Purgatory before I asked Cato to banish him to the Seventh Circle of Hell. When he wasn't gagging on poisoned oatmeal, poured into his mouth from steaming troughs, he was assigned janitorial duty, collecting used syringes.

Somehow, my act of revenge didn't get me one step closer to Heaven.

~~~

The Lord works in mysterious ways. That saying is totally clichéd, but I think it may be true.

By the time the front of the line had reached my bike, I'd opened the stall where I set up my wares each morning. In my left hand, I gripped long-handled barbeque tongs, for plucking bottles from the top shelf. That's where I stashed the most expensive scented oils. At least once a year, a desperate fool tried to shoplift. Thieves were always caught, and the punishment for stealing Cato's property was to be transformed into a lizard. Down the trapdoor they would plunge, slithering through the darkest caverns of Hell. It was a cruel, solitary fate, but better than the future that awaited violent sinners.

A woman wearing a crimson robe, marking her as a murderess, gave me a saccharine smile and pointed at a rose-colored crystal atomizer on the top shelf. Her selection was potent musk oil, laced with jasmine and coyote urine, one of the luxury scents. She said, "Will you trade for hair?" Gesturing to the little girl standing beside her, she grabbed the child's ponytail.

When neither is in a state of grace, sometimes the victims accompany their murderers into Purgatory. A murder-suicide will fit the bill.

The girl's hair was a pretty shade of light brown and was frizzy, like Sandy's. Suddenly the offer made me want to bludgeon the murderess with the barbeque tongs, which would've been a violation of Purgatorial Edict Number 4—*Leave the Maiming to the Demons.* I didn't have the right to decide a killer's fate. Yeah, I'd wanted Gabe in Hell, but that seemed so long ago now.

The girl didn't say anything, but her eyes watered. She couldn't have been much older than six when she took her dirt nap. She hadn't changed into a robe, and was dressed in a muddy parka, matching pale pink mittens, jeans with a tear in the left knee, and sneakers. It must've been the outfit she was wearing when she was buried. Obviously, without a coffin.

A tear rolled down the girl's face, leaving a wet trail in the dirt that coated her cheek. Something underneath the girl's puffy jacket squirmed. The girl hugged herself, pressing her arms against the wriggling lump.

"Do we have a deal?" the murderess said.

I said, "I'll take your hair, not the child's."

The woman patted her coiffure. It was an obvious dye job, the roots several shades darker than the rest of the long tresses. She pressed her lips together, as if she was pondering my offer.

My auburn ringlets were shorn close to my head. Wearing a wig wouldn't be practical, but if the murderess insisted on giving me her hair, I'd shear it, and toss the blonde mane in the flaming river.

The woman's smile turned to a sneer. "Blonde's not your color, honey. Platinum would make you look sallow."

No one had called me "honey" since Gabe.

The lump underneath the girl's parka *meowed*.

I said, "Is that a cat?"

The girl shrieked, "No, Mommy. Don't hurt Princess!" She clutched her arms tighter to her chest.

The meow became a *yowl*.

The girl tried to hold her jacket closed, but a furry head popped up above the neckline, and butted against her chin. It was a calico kitten. Someone had burned the poor kitten's face, singeing both ears.

Glancing to my left, I looked at the ushers. A Leviathan, one of the monstrous leech creatures, had bitten off a man's foot. He was bleeding on the dock, flailing like a fish out of water. Another usher, a Siren with the head and chest of a woman and the body of a bird, jabbed the wounded man with a hypodermic, administering a sedative.

The little girl's cat *meowed* again. Glimmering feline eyes stared at me.

I said, "I'll take the kitty."

More tears trickled down the girl's face. When she unzipped her jacket, the little cat *purred*, the sound making a loud rumble for such a scrawny feline. There were wounds on the animal's chest, shaped like cigarette burns.

The murderess pushed her daughter aside, preventing me from taking the cat. She laid a hand on my arm and said, "Just the tail? Two atomizers if you want the whole pelt."

A short man in line behind the little girl stepped forward, as if he was going to intervene, but he shook his head and retreated, pushing past two elderly ladies wearing puce-colored robes.

The murderess tightened her grip on my arm, bruising my flesh. Her fingers were as cold as the icebergs that barricaded Heaven's Gate.

The neon sign on a boat closing toward the dock flashed its warning.

1) Smile
2) No name-calling
3) No spitting
4) Leave the Maiming to the Demons.

I stomped on her foot with my steel-toed boot. She shrieked and let go of me.

"Stop!" I said, but she lunged at the stall where all of the perfumes were displayed. Giving the metal case a shove, she rammed it into my bike. Bottles *smashed*, spraying a hail of shattered glass on the rocky shoreline. One of the jagged shards pierced my right calf. I yanked out the broken glass. A trail of blood trickled down my leg.

The murderess grinned at me. "Oops," she said.

Three ushers raced towards us. A Leviathan was in the lead, leaving a trail of slime.

Grabbing the little girl, the murderess held her up like a shield. "Touch me and I'll toss the kid in the river."

"Mommy, don't hurt me! I promise to be good," the little girl cried, her face twisted in anguish.

If it had been an ordinary river, the girl might survive, but a plunge into the flames would incinerate anything, within seconds. The girl wouldn't die again, since she was already dead, but there would be nothing left of her body but ash, floating in Purgatory for eternity, with no chance of earning a place in Heaven.

Squirming in her mother's arms, the girl dropped the kitten. The feline landed with a *yowl*, and scrambled past the elderly ladies, to hide behind a boulder.

I took a step closer to the murderess. "No one's going to hurt you," I said.

The murderess glanced to her right, watching the ushers. Kretus, Cato's most trusted henchman and leader of the Minotaurs, had overtaken the Leviathan. Kretus pawed at the ground and bent his head, brandishing his horns. He said, "Put the girl down."

"No," the woman said. Backing away from Kretus, she moved closer to the river.

The crowd of gawkers parted, clearing the path to the docks.

While the murderess was distracted, I advanced. Before I could chicken out, I leapt on her back.

The blow made her stumble, but she still clutched the girl. The child's shrieks became a wail.

The sound echoed through the cavern, feeding my fury. Clinging to the woman's back with my thighs, I used my left hand to jab her face with the tongs. I missed her eyes, hitting a cheekbone.

Teeth dug into my wrist, making me scream. We landed in the mud with a *thunk*.

The murderess tried to wriggle away, but I clung on with all of my strength, and bit her shoulder.

The fall must've knocked the child unconscious, because she'd stopped crying. It was impossible to see whether she was bleeding, because her mother regained her feet, blocking my view. She moved toward the child.

There was nothing else to do. With a rush and tackle, I drove her—and myself—toward the river. I felt the flames right through her as our feet left the dock.

The heat was so intense, I never felt the calloused hands that grasped my back, lifting me high in the air. Windmilling my legs, I tried to run for safety, but Kretus hugged me tight, against his chest. I never heard the screams of the murderess, only the sound of Kretus's hammering heart, pounding in my ears. Portending my doom.

~~~

People who claim that finding the path to Heaven is as easy as following a white light don't know what the Hell they're talking about.

If I said, "Kretus carried me to a magical escalator," that would be a lie.

If I said, "You can only earn your wings if you break a Purgatorial Edict," that would be a lie.

If I said, "Growing wings feels like having dozens of nails hammered into your shoulders," that would be a lie.

If I said, "Heaven is a field of buttercups where murdered girls play with a kitten," that too would be a lie.

Or maybe all of these things are true. Maybe Heaven is an idyllic place where no one feels pain, everyone noshes on ambrosia, and all of the pretty flowers don't cause seasonal allergies. The bottom line is— those who've climbed, crawled, swum, flown, or teleported to the pearly gates eventually learn what it takes to join us. Believe it or not, there are no rules governing the Upper Sphere like those in Purgatory, only eternal truths. Ethos Number 1— *Love flowers in self-sacrifice.*

No sweeter scent have I known.

The Christmas Zombie

Marissa James

Every year the Christmas Zombie came, bringing not just the seasonal scents of pine and cinnamon, but also the aroma of fresh meat.

Grrg had waited and waited; finally, fresh meat! Christmas morning was still hours away but already he imagined the warm flesh on his tongue, the juices flowing between his teeth. Last Christmas, his first in undeath, he'd had no hopes whatsoever—there was nothing in the world that he wanted except brains, and Santa Claus seemed unlikely to bring those. But the Christmas Zombie had come instead, and so he and his parents had feasted on a sweet (though leathery) little old lady.

The long months of dog food, courtesy of their neighbors the Cambleys, would have made him weep if his tear ducts remained functional. Still, Grrg knew undeath was even harder on his parents. Dad's commute to join a flesh-crazed mob got longer every day, and he rarely managed to bring home more than pre-gnawed long-bones or stiff roadkill anymore. No, it was the dog food that really sustained them: beef-flavored, or chicken pate, or sometimes the Cambleys would leave a few of those cans with the big chunks of actual meat.

They were lucky to have such understanding neighbors; most breathers' minds, confronting undeath, swung compulsively to extermination, decapitation, conflagration. But since Grrg first encountered the Cambleys' youngest

227

son, Ripley, and didn't eat him, they'd understood. Just like Grrg's family wasn't wholly dead, they weren't wholly bad, either. And while Dad went out rending breathers limb from limb in ever more distant neighborhoods, Mom stayed home scrubbing the floors just as in life, and fending off the odd undead menace so the Cambleys could save their bullets. Because if you couldn't depend on your neighbors, then who was there?

He'd even play with Ripley sometimes. Ripley's parents and four siblings were too old to understand the boy's lonesomeness, but Grrg wasn't. They were just kids, and when they played catch (admittedly, Grrg wasn't the best at it), Ripley's delectable nature didn't even cross Grrg's maggoty mind.

Which proved he'd been good this year; if anyone had earned a heaping bucket of sweetmeats, it was Grrg.

In the living room, a creak. Then, wafting through his bedroom door, the unmistakable scent—bloody and intense, mingled with cocoa and nutmeg. He peered into the living room; a shadowed figure was placing glistening gobs of flesh and organ meat into battered-yet-festive boxes, sticking lids on them, then limping over to place them, one at a time, by the fireplace.

That limp was familiar—Dad's limp, from when he'd closed his leg in the car door once.

Dad was the Christmas Zombie? Grrg's desiccated heart seemed to skip a beat when he realized what this meant: there was no such thing as magic in the world.

And yet—and yet there was, for where had his dad possibly gathered those brains and livers and a dozen succulent eyeballs from?

Dad straightened, saw him in the dawn light of Christmas morning, and gurgled him over. Grrg shambled out, arms stiffly forward, and they caught each other in an undead, yet warm, embrace. Dad smelled of filth and gore and Christmas.

The best Christmas ever.

Next door, Ripley let out a bloodcurdling scream.

A Daffy Holiday

Irene Radford

"Please, Daffy, can you please shop for the kids for me?" G begged across the cell phone ether.

As usual. I sighed. "We aren't married anymore. You need to do your own shopping with your own money." I slammed the door of my coffee shop/bakery with extra vehemence so he'd hear the level of my frustration. I hated Christmas shopping in the crowds. The tinny speakers on every street corner. The lines, the crowds, the stress. And that was just here in town. God help me if I had to go to the mall.

"Come on, Daffy. You have my credit card."

"Just give me one reason you can't do this yourself?" I did not know, nor did I really care where he was or who he was with. Our divorce had been final for three months.

"I'm in Vienna," he said. "And no one is with me." He answered my unasked question. "This case is taking longer than I expected. The perp is a stronger magician than what he put on his Guild registration."

They always were.

I could at least walk from my shop to enough small businesses to make the shopping easier. No staring down an oversized pickup to get the last parking spot within a thousand yards of the mall entrance.

There were no cars on the street today. The shop owners had come to an agreement with the city council and shut down the narrow street on the holiday weekends. Street venders from local groups raised money every year by selling hot cider on the streets, roasted chestnuts and such to add to the festive atmosphere. It was a special time, but it was still the last weekend before Christmas with crowds. The sounds of Christmas carols rose over the rustling voices of the shoppers. In the open air the overworked and inadequate speakers were tolerable.

I fingered my wallet, wondering what his credit balance was. Our ten-year-old Shara could tell me with a few clicks on her computer.

Having a hacker genius in the family had its uses. Especially when G was hunting down a criminal and needed to trace a flow of money but couldn't go through official channels. Being Sheriff of the International Guild of Master Wizards had led, not only G, but the whole family into strange places.

I stared through the window of Tommy's computer shop at the ten-bazillion terabyte external hard drive Shara swore she needed.

I knew I should walk into the store, pick up the box and pay for it with the credit card. It was more tempting when I knew I was paying probably twice the on-line price.

Shara was a good kid. If she said she needed it, she probably did. But—because I'm her mom—I knew that she secretly wanted something else. Something she really didn't need.

And sometimes you needed to let a ten-year-old be a ten year old. Not just a cog in the family wheel. Too many Christmases in my parents' home meant new socks rather than fresh make up or even a gift certificate to get my hair cut properly. I turned away from the electronics display window. The store I wanted was further up the street, deeper into the blocked off area of narrow streets and deep overhangs of cheap apartments for owners or college students above the storefronts.

I felt the forgotten bite of winter as I walked past the giant welcoming displays into the open entry way to the open-air shopping district. A waving Santa with his kettle stood ringing a bell, exhorting charity from the passing people. It must be hard in the plastic world to coax cash out of people's wallets.

I stepped out of the flow of foot traffic to check my purse and nearly stumbled over a homeless man crouching out of the wind in a nook that offered precious little shelter. I didn't recognize him as one of the regulars who camped by the dumpster behind my shop, but he'd been on the street long enough for dirt to become ingrained in the worry lines around his eyes. His knitted cap frayed and his camouflage jacket was ripped at the shoulder seam. The smell of stale bacon grease, but not booze, hanging around him took me back to my childhood.

Mom served beans and rice flavored with textured protein bacon chunks three times a week. I hated those beans and told Mom that loudly and frequently. "Just eat your dinner." She never snapped at her ungrateful child. I blushed, even in the cold wind, when I remembered it. She worked as a bookkeeper while she studied for her accounting degree. Dad pastored at a small church in an empty store front. Between them they barely paid the bills. Food sometimes came in boxes left in the church on Sundays with a note. My dad, bless his heart, would sometimes keep the beans and rice, but never the canned meats.

"If you'd drink generic coffee instead of that imported crap we could afford hamburger!" I would complain at my Mom. Good coffee was her vice, and it was Dad that brought it in. She never asked. I was a rebellious ass in those days.

I started to walk past the homeless man. When he flashed me a smile that lit up his gaunt face with hope. I scooped the change from the bottom of my purse. The clank of a quarter and three pennies in the cup drowned out the off-key bell of the nearby Santa. The money to Santa might feed this man tomorrow, but he looked hungry today.

"Sir, please stay here a moment." I slipped back into the traffic stream and crossed the street. Habitually, I touched the wooden spurtle in the back pocket of my jeans, my wand. In case you're wondering, a spurtle is a wooden kitchen tool designed for stirring thick Highland oatmeal, and it was a gift from my grandmother.

The smell of baking bread from the sandwich store replaced the other unwanted odors.

Calm spilled through me. I knew food. I'm a baker. More than a baker, a kitchen witch, and I knew what the man outside needed.

"Shirley, got any pre-made sandwiches?" I called to the owner of the store in the back. As tempting as the fresh bread and freshly assembled sandwiches were, the college-age servers would take too long assembling a sandwich to order. They'd chat and be friendly too. I loved that. I employed similar kids and taught them that friendliness built customers, and loyalty. But I was in a hurry.

"In the fridge behind the soda machine," Shirley called through the pass through. "Help yourself, they're from this morning and getting a little stale."

I grabbed two, a ham and cheddar and roast beef and provolone, each with a good helping of lettuce. I grabbed an apple too. Soon I was back outside, my offerings in hand.

"Thank you, ma'am. Bless you." He flashed me his charming smile again. At one time he'd likely been handsome. And he wasn't as old as the dirt lines on his face suggested.

"You are welcome. May I ask what you did before you... you fell on hard times?"

"I was a financial analyst."

That made me step back and take stock. "What happened?"

"The crash of '08. I caught my boss with his hand in the cookie jar. He went to jail. I was out of work and just as fast the word was out, I couldn't be trusted."

I felt the tugging. Twenty-eight cents and a couple sandwiches wasn't going to cut it. I fingered the spurtle. It was warm and smooth.

I squatted in front of him. "Look, I own *Magical Brews* two blocks over." I pointed down the street. Here's my card. If you can wash the floors and do some cleaning. I'll pay you minimum wage and give you some food and let you use the place to clean up. Show up and do the job right and I'll give you a recommendation so you can get a real job. Maybe not in banking or financial services, but better than begging in the cold wind with a tin cup."

He took the card in his grubby hand and peered at it closely. I guessed he needed reading glasses.

"Thank you ma'am, Ms. Daphne."

"Please, everyone calls me Daffy." Except my parents. They didn't like nicknames.

"Ms. Daffy. And I'm Noah. I'll be there at five sharp today and every day. May all the saints and angels bless you today. And every day. Have a safe and joyful Christmas."

I left him savoring his coffee, not certain any saint or angel would bless a witch. But the thought was nice.

I looked back and waved to him. He set aside his coffee to wave back.

Suddenly I was back in my parents' kitchen watching Mom close her eyes and take her first sip of coffee in the morning. She sighed and all the tension drained from her face and shoulders. Then she opened her eyes and smiled at me. For once I knew she had no reason to find fault with my hair, my posture, the length of my skirt, or anything else. I relaxed too and enjoyed the enticing aroma of freshly ground and brewed coffee. Maybe excellent coffee for Mom was worth beans and rice with fake bacon three times a week. Her love of coffee had given me the nose for a good blend when I opened my own shop.

The warmth inside me allowed me to ignore the wall of noise from shrill voices and tinny piped music. My route took me past a discount clothing and consignment emporium. There! Right there in the front window I spotted precisely the party dress Shara wanted. She hadn't talked about it much, but I knew from a single chance remark... "I wish I had a new party dress to wear to Amanda's party on Christmas Eve. One that fits right." She'd recently grown two inches, a precursor to adolescence and other changes.

I flagged down Zoe, the owner, and pointed to the shimmering confection of chiffon over satin, full skirted with a light petticoat, heart-shaped neckline and three-quarter sleeves. "Do you have that in any color but red?"

Red would do. But with her pale skin, Shara really needed a less vibrant color, otherwise people would see only the dress and not *her*.

"All we have is the red." Zoe said. "But... I don't know if it will do, but we have another one on the consignment rack. It's from the summer collection but a similar style." She beckoned me to follow her to the back corner of the store and a circular rack with a small "Clearance" sign sagging above it.

"Here," she held up a misty, sea green dress in Shara's size. The iridescent chiffon overlay glinted green, then blue, then into a shade of lavender and back again to the pale green.

"It's perfect. Why is it marked down below normal clearance?"

She put her finger through a side seam of the chiffon. "The price of taking on consignment items."

"I can fix that." I looked at the original price—almost as much as the external hard drive. The exorbitant numbers had a red slash through them and a new reasonable price. That had another red slash and a lower price.

"I'll take it."

A warm glow started in my tummy. This was what holiday shopping should be like. And I hadn't had to use any of my newfound magic.

Now what should I get twelve-year-old Belle and fifteen-year-old Jason?

From the speakers, yet another version of "Jingle Bells" squeaked out. An electric guitar wailed in distress from an abusive musician. I touched the wand in my back pocket as I concentrated on blocking out the music. The whine faded. But as I relaxed, another sound intruded.

A young woman, barely out of her teens stopped an older woman and begged for help. "Have you seen my son? He's only three. A little boy wearing a red Santa T shirt and green pull up pants."

Losing a child was a mother's worst nightmare.

"I'm sorry, sweetie. I haven't seen him. Look, there's a security guard. Maybe she can help you," the older woman said and beckoned to the uniformed woman to come hither.

I'd lost Jason in the mall when he was about three. He'd gotten tired and climbed out of his stroller to curl up for a nap among a pile of colorful towels on a low shelf beneath a display table.

Children can disappear in a heartbeat.

This time I grabbed my wand and held it out as I turned a wide circle. The piece of turned and polished wood telescoped out from the size of a fat pen to the foot-long cooking tool that fit my hand perfectly.

I'm more than a kitchen witch, I had to remind myself. *I transform things.*

Give me sugar, butter, eggs, and flour and I can turn them into amazing deserts. Now I had to transform a little-boy-lost into a little-boy found.

Once I had a focus, I listened for the distinctive whimper of a lost child.

I heard a tiny giggle instead.

"I think I found him," I said to the anxious mother. Then I pointed to a circular rack of winter coats outside the store. Two tiny feet, clad in tennis shoes that blinked red lights around the heels, poked out from beneath a black jacket with a brown faux fox lined hood. "He's playing hide and seek." Then I held a finger to my lips.

We tiptoed up to the rack. I slipped behind it, my back to a display window. The mother stationed herself by the wiggling feet. "Where's Bobby?" she asked me in a coaxing singsong.

Giggles erupted from the depth of the jackets.

"I can't see Bobby anywhere. Do you think he ran away to the North Pole with Santa?"

That prompted full-out laughter.

"Why there's Bobby!" the mother laughed as she clamped a firm hand around his ankles.

"You finded me!" Bobby chortled as his mother dragged him free of his hiding spot.

"Thank you," the mother said as she pulled Bobby into a fierce hug.

"As long as he's safe, no thanks needed."

"You've given me the best Christmas present ever." The mother wiped away a tear. "I'm Tiffany." She stood up with Bobby still clutched tightly on her left hip as she held out her hand to me.

"I'm Daffy. And here." I shook her hand and held out one of my cards with a coupon on the back for a free coffee drink with the purchase of a pastry."

"Thank you again. I hope your Christmas is the best ever."

The music blasted my ears again.

I suddenly knew what Jason wanted for Christmas. He'd been working for months turning our attic into his own private ballet studio. With the floors refinished and five tall mirrors, originally designed to grace the back of closet doors, he could practice up there to his heart's content. Only the twelve feet of head space beneath the roof ridge restrained his jumps and leaps to normal human levels. He needed nice clothes—another growth spurt in the family—for a series of auditions with professional dance companies. He had tights and Ts and soft shoes. But if he made it beyond the dance portion of the audition, he needed slacks and dress shirts for interviews.

What he wanted was speakers for the music loaded onto his phone—everything from classics to African drums.

And there they were, a compact wireless box in a high-end executive business store. I'd called it CEO Haven from the day they opened even though they had an official, and pretentious, name, *Executive Extensions.*

I remembered the enormous relief I'd felt when I found Jason all those years ago. I wanted to give him those miniature speakers because I loved him so much. Then as I grabbed a sealed box containing speakers from beneath the display I found the last gift on my list. A chess set for Belle sitting on a lower shelf behind me.

The board was made of alternating squares of ebony and blond maple. But the pieces themselves, were what made the set perfect—carved Chinese characters in a soapstone made to look like ivory and jade.

Ivory and jade. Belle's magic wand was an ivory hair stick with jade charms shaped like the chess classic Bishop and Queen. I couldn't imagine a more appropriate gift. She considered Math Olympics games. Chess she took seriously.

With a huge sigh of relief. I avoided close scrutiny of the credit card charge.

When I emerged from CEO Haven into the street again, the canned music blasted me with more "Jingle Bells" in the form of an out-of-control saxophone.

What did I need to listen to this time? I touched my wand and blanked out the annoying music—if you could call it music.

Not a sound. A smell. Gourmet coffee to match the quality I served in my bakery. I thought immediately of my mother and how she savored her coffee every morning.

What the heck. I'd already vowed to begin fixing the broken bridges between us. Instead of a generic card and store-bought shortbread, I'd send my folks something they'd appreciate, one of those single cup brew systems and a year's subscription for the coffee.

"Look they have it. Everyone else is sold out."

"Julie, we can't really afford it," a young man said as he stared at the shelf with the exact coffee maker I'd planned on buying. The shelves below the display were empty. This was indeed the last one.

"But, Jimmy, this will most likely be Mom's last Christmas. How can we not afford it," a girl replied. Same dark hair, same chins, same dark eyes. Brother and sister, I surmised.

They looked very young to be losing a parent. Late teens, early twenties at most.

"The doctors said she shouldn't have coffee," Jimmy said.

"What difference does it make?" Julie protested. "The doctors have given up. Chemo didn't work. Radiation didn't work. Now all she can do is wait. I say let's give her a little bit of joy while she waits."

"She does love her coffee...."

I couldn't reach around them to grab the last of the coffee makers.

That didn't stop an impatient middle-aged woman in a business suit, designer heels, and six strands of pearls. She reached both hands between the brother and sister and grabbed the candy-red machine.

The kids' faces fell. Julie looked on the edge of tears.

"We didn't have the money anyway. Maybe we should just get her freshly ground flavored coffee from the grocery store..." Jimmy's throat worked, trying to suppress his own disappointment.

"Excuse me, I may be able to help," I interrupted them with yet another of my coupon business cards. "I'm half owner of 'Magical Brews'. I couldn't help but overhear your conversation. If your mom can get out she can have coffee and a desert every day. I'll make certain she has the best cup of coffee she's ever had."

Julie accepted the card. "'Magical Brews?' I've heard about this place. Rumor has it that you are a true magician with coffee." Her mouth opened and closed twice in awe.

"Can we pick up the coffee to go when Mom gets too sick to get out?" Jimmy asked hesitantly.

"Of course."

"This is too kind. Is there anything we can do for you?" Julie wept openly.

"Make you mother's final time as easy and full of love as you can."

I had to retreat quickly before my own tears overwhelmed me.

In my flight I almost passed the popcorn boutique. But the smell stopped me short. Once more, memories took hold of me and wouldn't let go.

Dad and I having a popcorn fight in the living room. He laughed as he ducked a plain white blossom. We had a separate bowl of butter and salted treats. The unadorned ones were for stringing, or throwing. Tiny white lights blinked on the five-foot-high tree. Mom looked up at us from diligently stringing popcorn and cranberries on heavy thread. She laughed for the first time in a long time.

I rewarded her mirth with a thrown fistful of popcorn.

She'd just finished her accounting degree and received a huge promotion and raise at her work. Dad's congregation had grown by twenty new families. We could finally afford a real tree for the holidays.

The aroma of popcorn had taken me back. I wanted to linger in the warmth of happy memories. There weren't a lot of them.

Mom had her CPA now and Dad's congregation had grown into a real church building. They could afford any gift

I might send them. But there was no monetary value on memories.

After my own adventures with adolescent children stretching their wings and exploring the big bad world, I understood my folks better. Parents walk a fine line between protecting our children as long as possible from a universe we can't comprehend, and giving them just enough room to let them make mistakes so they can learn from them to cope with society when they are on their own.

Mom and Dad hadn't really spent years trying to control every breath I took. They were doing their best to protect me the only way they knew how.

Bent on gifting them with gourmet popcorn, I entered the shop burdened with gifts for my children. The big, soft bag containing Shara's party dress bumped a crowded display on my left. On the counter, beside bags and bags of colored popcorn kernels sat an upgraded and computerized version of a vintage popper that stirred the kernels to keep them from burning and making sure that the popcorn heated evenly and popped more thoroughly. It even had a "distressed" red metal shell. So very like the popper we'd used that joyful Christmas Eve when my parents and I were all happy and laughing and loving each other.

My knees nearly buckled in amazement. I had to lock them before I dropped to the ground.

The music speakers played a slow, fully orchestrated version of "Jingle Bells" that made the tired old song sound like hymn.

Holiday Leftovers

240

About the Authors

K.G. Anderson

K.G. Anderson is a late-blooming speculative fiction writer, having spent most of her career as a journalist. She writes fiction as if it were fact and believes that, somewhere, on another timeline, it is. You'll find a list of her published short stories at writerway.com/fiction.

Robert Bagnall

Robert Bagnall lives in Devon, England. He is the author of the sci-fi thriller '2084 - *The Meschera Bandwidth*', and the anthology '*24 0s & a 2*', which collects 24 of his 60-odd published stories. Both are available from Amazon. He can be contacted via his blog at meschera.blogspot.com.

Jason P. Burnham

Jason P. Burnham loves to spend time with his wife, children, and dog. He co-edits *If There's Anyone Left* (@IfTheresAnyone on Twitter) a magazine of inclusive speculative fiction with his friend C.M. Fields. Find him on Twitter at @AndGalen

Gregg Chamberlain

Gregg Chamberlain lives in the Great White North where zombies are frozen solid most of the year and pose little threat and serve as snowman substitutes for those people too lazy to go outside and build their own. He and his missus, Anne, serve the wishes of their cats, who are benevolent overlords to their humans. He writes speculative fiction for fun and his work is available in other B Cubed Press anthologies.

Scott J. Couturier

Scott J. Couturier is a Rhysling-nominated poet and prose writer of the weird, liminal, and darkly fantastic. His work has appeared in numerous venues, including *The Audient Void, Spectral Realms, Tales from the Magician's Skull, Space and Time Magazine, Cosmic Horror Monthly,* and *Weirdbook*; his collection of Weird fiction, *The Box*, is available from Hybrid Sequence Media, while his collection of autumnal & folk horror verse, *I Awaken In October*, is available from Jackanapes Press.

Holiday Leftovers

Emily Dorffer
Emily Dorffer is a technical editor with a love for baking and all things Christmas (although she's very grateful she hasn't been abducted by a rogue Santa!). Her works have appeared in *Daily Science Fiction*, *Breath & Shadow*, and various other publications. You can read more of her writing on Wattpad @sandydragon1.

Ann Gibson
Ann Gibson spent her childhood in Dublin, Ireland, and now lives in North Yorkshire, UK. She has an MA in Literature Studies from York St. John University and has published poetry in *Acumen, Prole, Obsessed with Pipework, Orbis, Ariadne's Thread, The Poets' Republic* and *Dream Catcher* magazines as well as various other anthologies.

Her poetry has also appeared online in *The High Window, Lighten Up Online, Snakeskin, Pulsar, Ofi Press Magazine* and *The Ekphrasis Review*.

Debora Godfrey
Debora Godfrey was published in several *Alternative* anthologies, and co-edited the best-selling *Alternative Apocalypse* and *Alternative War*. She recently exchanged life in a cohousing community for an existence with a husband, a dog, several grumpy hummingbirds, and a usually even-tempered lawyer, not to mention a multitude of tiny frogs and a googly-eyed vacuum cleaner named Vinny.

Maxwell I. Gold
Maxwell I. Gold is a multiple award nominated author who writes prose poetry and short stories in weird and cosmic fiction. His work has appeared in numerous anthologies and magazines including *Space and Time Magazine, Weird Tales, Startling Stories, Strange Horizons, Tales from OmniPark* Anthology, and many more. He's the author of *Oblivion in Flux: A Collection of Cyber Prose* from Crystal Lake Publishing and co-author of *Möbius Lyrics* from Independent Legions Publishing.

KC Grifant
KC Grifant is an award-winning Southern Californian author who writes internationally published horror, fantasy, science fiction and weird west stories for podcasts, anthologies and magazines. Her tales have appeared in *Andromeda Spaceways Magazine, Unnerving Magazine,* Cosmic *Horror Monthly, Dark Matter Magazine,* and many others. In addition to a Weird West

novel, *MELINDA WEST: MONSTER GUNSLINGER* (Brigids Gate Press, Feb 2023), she has also written for dozens of anthologies. For details, visit www.KCGrifant.com or @kcgrifant.

Jenna Hanchey

Jenna Hanchey has been an actress, particle physicist, Peace Corps volunteer, and afterschool-space-program teacher, and is currently a professor of critical/cultural studies at Arizona State University. Her stories appear in *Nature:Futures*, *Daily Science Fiction*, *Medusa Tales*, *Wyngraf,* and *Martian Magazine*, among other venues. Having once been called a "badass fairy," she attempts to live up to the title. Follow her adventures on Twitter (@jennahanchey) or at www.jennahanchey.com.

Michael H. Hanson

Michael H. Hanson created the ongoing SHA'DAA shared-world anthology series currently consisting of seven volumes. Michael's short story "C.H.A.D." appears in the Crystal Lake Publishing anthology *C.H.U.D. LIVES!,* his short story "Rock and Road" appears in the Roger Zelazny tribute anthology "SHADOWS AND REFLECTIONS," his short story "Born Of Dark Waters" appears in the Independent Legions Publishing anthology "THE BEAUTY OF DEATH 2: DEATH BY WATER," and his short story "Night Shopper" appears in William Morrow Paperbacks' "OTHER TERRORS: An Inclusive Anthology." Michael also has stories in the last nine of Janet Morris's Heroes-in-Hell (HIH) anthology volumes.

Elle Hartford

Elle adores cozy mysteries, fairy tales, and above all, learning new things. As a historian and educator, she believes in the value of stories as a mirror for complicated realities. She currently lives in New Jersey with a grumpy tortoise and a three-legged cat. Find more stories of Red and her friends at ellehartford.com. And while you're there, sign up for Elle's newsletter to get bonus material, behind-the-scenes sneak peeks, and terrible jokes!

Alicia Hilton

Alicia Hilton is an author, editor, arbitrator, law professor, actor, and former FBI Special Agent. She believes in angels and demons, magic, and monsters. Her work has appeared in *Akashic Books, Best Asian Speculative Fiction, Daily Science Fiction, Vastarien, Year's Best Hardcore Horror Volumes 4, 5 & 6,* and elsewhere. She is a member of the Horror Writers Association, the Science Fiction and Fantasy Poetry Association, and the Science

Fiction and Fantasy Writers Association. Her website is https://aliciahilton.com. Follow her on Twitter @aliciahilton01.

A. P. Howell

A. P. Howell lives with her spouse and their two kids. Her jobs have spanned the alphabet from archivist to webmaster and she has a master's degree in history. Her short fiction has appeared in *Daily Science Fiction*, *Little Blue Marble*, *Translunar Travelers Lounge*, *Underland Arcana*, *Community of Magic Pens (Atthis Arts)*, *Dread Space* (Shacklebound Books) and *In Somnio: A Collection of Modern Gothic Horror* (Tenebrous Press). She can be found online at aphowell.com.

Marissa James

As a fine art professional, Marissa has wielded katanas and handled Lady Gaga's shoes. As a veterinary assistant, she has cared for hairless cats, hedgehogs, and, one time, a coyote. As a writer, she can be found in *Flash Fiction Online*, *Translunar Traveler's Lounge*, *Kaleidotrope*, and many other amazing publications. She tweets @MaroftheBooks.

Tim Kane

Tim Kane loves things that creep and crawl. His first published book is non-fiction, *The Changing Vampire of Film and Television*, tracing the history of vampires in television and movies. Most recently published stories appear in *Lovecraftia*, *Navigating Ruins* and *Dark Moon Digest*. Find out more at www.timkanebooks.com.

Benjamin C. Kinney

Benjamin C. Kinney is a SFF writer, neuroscientist, and a four-time Hugo Award finalist as the assistant editor of Escape Pod. His short stories have appeared in magazines including Analog, Strange Horizons, Fantasy Magazine, and many more. You can follow him on Twitter or Instagram @BenCKinney, and find his other stories via his website benjaminckinney.com

Amanda Cecelia Lang

Amanda Cecelia Lang is a horror author and aspiring recluse from Denver, Colorado. As a die-hard scary movie nerd, her favorite things are meta-slashers, 80s nostalgia, and the rise of a fierce final girl. Her stories currently haunt the dark corners of several podcasts, ezines, and anthologies, including *NoSleep, Uncharted,* and *Mixtape: 1986.*

You can stalk her work at amandacecelialang.com—just don't be surprised if she leaps out at you from the shadows.

Wayne Lee

Wayne Lee (wayneleepoet.com) lives in Santa Fe, NM, where Christmas means mariachis, biscochitos and green chile stew. He grew up in Bellingham, Washington, though, so his childhood holiday traditions included cutting down and decorating the tree as a family, caroling around the neighborhood, extended-family gift exchanges, turkey or ham dinner and, of course, snacking on leftovers until New Year's.

Gerri Leen

Gerri Leen lives in Northern Virginia and originally hails from Seattle. In addition to being an avid reader, she's passionate about horse racing, tea, and collecting encaustic art and raku pottery. She has stories and poems in *The Magazine of Fantasy & Science Fiction, Strange Horizons, Galaxy's Edge, Dark Matter, Daily Science Fiction,* and others, and she has a poetry collection coming out from Trouble Department in 2023. She's a member of SFWA and HWA. See more at gerrileen.com.

Eric Lewis

Eric Lewis is the author of fantasy novels *The Heron Kings* and *The Heron Kings' Flight,* available from Flame Tree Press. His short fiction has been published in *Nature, Cossmass Infinities, Speculative North, Bards & Sages Quarterly,* the anthologies *Crash Code* and *Best Indie Speculative Fiction Vol. 1,* the short story collections *Tricks of the Blade* and *As It Seems* as well as other venues detailed at ericlewis.ink.

Brianna Malotke

Brianna Malotke is a writer and member of the Horror Writers Association. Her most recent work can be found in *Out of Time* from Timber Ghost Press and *Their Ghoulish Reputation* from Dark Lake Publishing LLP. She also has horror work in the anthologies *Beneath, Cosmos, The Deep, Beautiful Tragedies 2, The Dire Circle,* and *Under Her Skin.*

In 2023 her debut horror poetry collection will be released by Green Avenue Books. For more: malotkewrites.com

Kurt Newton

Kurt Newton's fiction and poetry have appeared in *More Alternative Truths, Alternative Truths III: Endgame, Space Force...and Beyond, Shout: An Anthology of Resistance Poetry and Short Fiction, Unlikely Stories Mark V, Oddball Magazine* and *Radon Journal.*

"Future Tourism Promo for Antarctica" © 2019 and 2022 by Kurt Newton, first published in *Nazi Swastika Bikini Wax Illuminati & Other Psycho-Socio-Political Commentaries.*

Marisca Pichette

Marisca Pichette hunts stories on the palest nights. More of her work has appeared in *Strange Horizons, Fireside Magazine, Fusion Fragment, Flash Fiction Online, PseudoPod,* and *PodCastle,* among others. Her speculative poetry collection, *Rivers in Your Skin, Sirens in Your Hair,* is forthcoming from Android Press in April 2023. Find her on Twitter as @MariscaPichette and Instagram as @marisca_write.

Phyllis Irene Radford

Phyllis Irene Radford, a.k.a. Irene Radford, has been writing stories ever since she figured out what a pencil was for. Editing grew out of her love of the craft of writing. B Cubed Press has helped liberate her as a writer, editor, and person swimming through the morass of modern life.

Stephen Schwei

Stephen Schwei is a Pushcart-nominated Houston poet with Wisconsin roots, published in *Wax Poetry & Art, Beneath the Rainbow, Hidden Constellation, Borfski Press,* and the *New Reader Magazine.* He has published one volume of poetry, *Bluebonnet Whispers.* A gay man with three grown children and four wonderful grandchildren, who worked in Information Technology most of his life, he can be a mass of contradictions. Poetry helps to sort all of this out. www.stephenschwei.com

Kim Sheard

Kim Sheard's short fiction has appeared in three Pocket Books *Star Trek* anthologies, the now defunct confessional magazines, and several smaller SF magazines. She is more often published in various devotional magazines and web sites. By day she owns a pet sitting company and talks to dogs and cats rather than people. She lives in Fairfax, Virginia with her husband and dog.

Holiday Leftovers

Zach Shephard

Zach Shephard lives in Enumclaw, Washington, where he's spent most of his life looking for the proper tool to catch Santa. (Butterfly net? Not enough. Commandeered military helicopter? Bit too much). When he's not busy with that project, he occasionally writes stories. Zach's fiction has appeared in places like *Fantasy & Science Fiction, Galaxy's Edge,* and the *Unidentified Funny Objects* anthology series. For a full bibliography, check out www.zachshephard.com.

David F. Shultz

David F. Shultz writes science fiction and fantasy from Toronto, Canada, where he is Lead Editor at *Speculative North* magazine and organizes the Toronto Science Fiction and Fantasy Writers. His 80+ published works have appeared through publishers such as Augur, Diabolical Plots, and Third Flatiron. Author webpage: davidfshultz.com

David Sklar

David Sklar (he/him) lives in New Jersey with 2 kids, 2 cats, and 1 spouse, in a house that's been remade repeatedly for almost a century with only its stone foundation unchanged. His published works include fiction in *Nightmare* and *Strange Horizons,* poetry in *Ladybug* and *Stone Telling,* and humor in *Knights of The Dinner Table* and *McSweeney's Internet Tendency.* For more, see davidsklar.blue, and check out the *Poetry Crisis Line* at poetrycrisis.org

Alex J. Smith

Alex J. Smith makes his home in Fort Worth Texas where he spends his time escorting women and their families to Kansas, a state where reproductive health is still allowed.

Emily Martha Sorensen

Emily Martha Sorensen writes fantasy and science fiction with realistic paths to a happy ending. She likes hope and fun and humor, and you'll find those infusing all her works. You can find out more about her at http://www.emilymarthasorensen.com.

Darren Todd

Darren is a freelance book editor for Evolved Publications, and his short fiction has appeared in more than forty publications, including Hellbound Books, *Chilling Tales for Dark Nights,* and *The*

Stoneslide Corrective. His style and reading preferences tend toward the psychological, as he enjoys stories that linger in the imagination long after he's closed the book on them. He lives in Asheville, North Carolina with his son and girlfriend. See what he's up to darrentodd.net.

Salinda Tyson

My stories have appeared in *Cricket, Abyss & Apex, Triangulation: Dark Skies,* and *Fantasia Divinity's Menagerie de Mythique.* I live in North Carolina, miss the Pacific Ocean, and since childhood have loved history, folktales and mythology, especially the Greek and Norse myths that a fifth-grade teacher read aloud to her classes.

Michael Wertenberg

Michael is a French American writer based out of Budapest, Hungary. In addition to his self-published anthology, *The Orthography of Madness and Misgivings,* his collection of modern horror fables, *Stories to Tell Your Children (assuming you are a very bad parent),* and a French-language anthology, *À l'abri de la raison,* a collection of his novellas of psychological horror, Delirium's Muse, is published by Running Wild Press.

Lynn White

Lynn White lives in north Wales. Her work is influenced by issues of social justice and events, places and people she has known or imagined. She is especially interested in exploring the boundaries of dream, fantasy and reality. She was shortlisted in the Theatre Cloud 'War Poetry for Today' competition and has been nominated for a Pushcart Prize, Best of the Net and a Rhysling Award. Find Lynn at:
https://lynnwhitepoetry.blogspot.com and
https://www.facebook.com/Lynn-White-Poetry
1603675983213077/

John Wolf

John Wolf is a librarian lurking in the Pacific Northwest. When not shelving books, he likes making things up and putting them on paper. His work has appeared in the *Fornever After* anthology, *StarShipSofa, The Wicked Library,* and forthcoming in the *Strange Aeon 2022: Hopeful Monsters* and *Superstition* anthologies. His favorite holiday leftovers are garlic mashed potatoes and cranberry sauce. You can find him on Twitter as @JohnTheEngMajor.

Jim Wright is a retired US Navy Chief Warrant Officer and freelance writer. He lives in Florida where he watches American politics in a perpetual state of amused disgust. He's been called the Tool of Satan, but he prefers the title: Satan's Designated Driver. He is the mind behind Stonekettle Station (www.stonekettle.com). You can email him at jim@stonekettle.com. You can follow him on Twitter @stonekettle or you can join the boisterous bunch he hosts on Facebook at Facebook/Stonekettle. Remember to bring brownies and mind the dogs. Death by licking is a real risk.

**It has been a great ride with some wonderful people.
I can only hope you all enjoyed snacking on *Holiday Leftovers* as much as I did.**

Bob B.

About B-Cubed Press

B Cubed Press is a small press that publishes big books about things that matter.

A percentage of EVERY book we publish is donated to Charity. Usually the ACLU.

To date we have raised over $3500 for the ACLU.

We can be reached at Kionadad@aol.com.

Our writers gather routinely on the "B Cubed Project Page" on Facebook and we can also be found at BCubedPress.com.

Made in the USA
Monee, IL
01 October 2023